Praise for Robert Schofield's *Heist*

'*Heist* is a cracker . . . a welcome addition to the shelves of Australian crime fiction.' *The Australian*

'It's a great plot. Twisty, clever, believable and with a resolution that was just right . . . exciting, fun, fast and furious . . .' *Australian Crime Fiction*

'. . . a page-turner of the highest order . . . a thoroughly enjoyable read.' *The West Australian*

'Australia's Wild West emerges again in this entertaining tale . . .' *Herald Sun*

'A fast-paced story set in the beautiful and haunting Australian outback, this is a spectacular debut.' *Get Reading!*

'. . . a polished thriller that stands up well against the best in the genre.' *Scoop*

D0169976

MARBLE BAR

ROBERT SCHOFIELD

ALLEN&UNWIN
SYDNEY • MELBOURNE • AUCKLAND • LONDON

First published in 2014

Allen & Unwin
83 Alexander Street
Crows Nest NSW 2065
Australia
Phone: (61 2) 8425 0100
Email: info@allenandunwin.com
Web: www.allenandunwin.com

Cataloguing-in-Publication details are available
from the National Library of Australia
www.trove.nla.gov.au

ISBN 978 1 74331 684 9

Set in 13/17.5 pt Bembo by Post Pre-press Group, Australia
Printed and bound in Australia by Griffin Press

10 9 8 7 6 5 4 3 2 1

MIX
Paper from
responsible sources
FSC
www.fsc.org
FSC® C009448

The paper in this book is FSC certified.
FSC promotes environmentally responsible,
socially beneficial and economically viable
management of the world's forests.

This one is for Charlie

Cedit item retro, de terra quod fuit ante, in terras.
Lucretius

ONE

'Let me ask you something, alright? You ever see a snake eat a kangaroo?'

Ford turned away and sighed. 'Can't say that I have,' he said.

He looked out of the window, through the film of red dust that caked the glass, at the train passing outside. It had been loading all night, the diesels purring low, the lights from the lead locomotive shining into the prefab office. The end of the train was out of sight, but he could see ore trucks going slowly under the bin and hear the steady rumble of ore passing through the chutes, the boom as it hit the empty truck, the noise in the hopper changing in pitch as the truck filled, then a minute of quiet while the train inched forward and the next empty wagon moved into place. A cloud of iron dust hung around the train, glowing orange in the sodium spotlights and the first weak light of dawn. He checked his watch and then the clock on the wall.

Pollard was still talking. 'That's what I'm saying,' he said. 'Nobody ever believes you, until they see the photo.'

'I'm still not picturing it,' said Ford. 'Not a full-grown kangaroo.'

'Well, maybe not that. Not a big red like you see out on the road. It was one of those rock wallabies. Much smaller, but still a big mouthful. Still an impressive thing for a snake to eat.'

'So you're telling me it was a very small wallaby, and a very big snake?'

'Big snake, yeah. Olive Python. Bastard must have been five metres long, stretched out down the rock face. Sneaking up on this kangaroo, wallaby, whatever. It's down the bottom of the gorge, head down, drinking the water. Doesn't hear the snake coming up behind it.'

Ford yawned. 'You were watching this?'

'We were up the top of the gorge, in the shadow, maybe two hundred metres away, but I'm watching this through the long lens on the camera.' Pollard held his hands up, looking at Ford through the circle he had made with them, twisting his hands to pull focus. 'I got pictures. You must be the only one on this mine hasn't seen them.'

'That's my problem in life,' said Ford. 'I'm always out of the loop.'

He sat down at the control station and watched the flickering symbols on the computer screens, toggled through several layouts and satisfied himself that the plant was running smoothly, that there were no issues worth mentioning to the day shift. He switched the screen to show his racing-form spreadsheet and picked up the newspaper, which he had folded to the horses, where he had already ringed his picks for the next meeting.

'How come you never went out to the gorges? Karijini?' said Pollard.

Ford put down the paper. 'Never found the time,' he said. 'Too hot now. Maybe if I'm still here in the winter.'

'I heard you were in Kalgoorlie. Heat shouldn't bother you.'

'It's hotter here. We're way further north.'

The temperature outside hadn't dropped below twenty-five all night. The forecast was for forty-two, and Ford was grateful he would be indoors asleep through the height of it, with the air-conditioner at home running full bore.

'Maybe you're right,' said Pollard. 'There's not much water in the gorges this time of year. Be more to see in the wet season.'

'More to see than here?' said Ford, waving at the view outside the window.

'That's what I'm telling you. You got to get out and about, explore the bush. You stay in Newman all the time, just going from the town to the mine and back again, you'll go stir crazy.'

'Maybe when Grace is a little more settled we'll go. She thinks Newman is wilderness enough after Perth.'

'You could go out there with the guys,' said Pollard. 'Leave Grace with one of the families. Some time out there can help clear your head.'

'Yeah, I know that, I know what the desert can do, but I've seen enough of it. Did years of fly-in fly-out.'

'This place is different.'

'Yes, yes it is. It's more settled here. A town rather than a camp. Schools, friends, families. We need something stable now Grace is in pre-primary.'

Pollard tried an expression that he thought would convey sympathy. 'Not the best place to bring a little girl,' he said. 'She'd be better off in Perth.'

'No work for me there.'

'Then why didn't you stay in Kalgoorlie?'

'Not welcome there. The gold industry is a closed shop for me now.'

'Why's that?' asked Pollard. He'd forgotten about showing sympathy, and now he looked bored.

'I got caught up in the Gwardar robbery. Cleared eventually, but shit sticks.' Ford watched Pollard to see his reaction. Most of the people on the mine knew his involvement, his name had been in the papers, but once he had told the story in the pub it had become just another tall tale. It was twelve months ago now, and there had been new workers moving through, fresh stories to listen to.

Pollard didn't seem to hear. 'There's boarding schools,' he said. 'Fancy places in Perth. Make a little lady of her.'

'I never saw the appeal of those places,' said Ford. 'They always look like it's just about the uniform. What is it with those hats?'

He felt his belly rumble. He usually waited to eat until he got off the night shift. He'd have a shower, eat breakfast with Grace before taking her to school, then go to bed for the day.

Pollard was contemplating the sandwich wrapped in foil on his desk. Every day he arrived on shift with a Subway bag containing three foot-long sandwiches, and he'd eat them at four-hourly intervals through his shift. He brought an apple and the same three sandwiches, with the same fillings, every day. This was his last sandwich: meatballs and tomato sauce. Pollard considered it breakfast.

'This snake, right, he opens its mouth wide, head big as your hand.' He lifted his forearm, flexed his wrist, trying to make the motions of the snake. He opened his hand and curled his fingers to show the teeth bared. 'Grabs this wallaby round the neck. Sinks its fangs right in there.'

'I didn't think they were poisonous,' said Ford. 'I've seen the poisonous ones. They're not big enough to eat a wallaby.'

'He's only getting hold of it so it can't run.'

Pollard lifted the sandwich from his desk, caught up in the theatre of his snake. 'Wraps itself around the kangaroo in three big coils. The middle of this snake is as thick as your thigh. Breaks this kangaroo's bones by squeezing it, then kinda compresses the thing into a long cylinder like this sandwich.' He held it up in front of his face, both hands around it, twisting and raising his elbows. Ford could see he was drooling.

'You want me to mail you the photos?' said Pollard.

'Don't bother. I'm enjoying the mime.'

'So this snake unhinges his jaw, and slides himself around the head of this kangaroo, then works himself down the whole body. He's like some huge green condom, sliding down over a giant hairy brown cock. By the end there's just this tail hanging out of the snake's mouth. We walked down to the water to get a closer look, and the snake's too big now to move. Just lies there in the sun looking at us like it doesn't give a shit, all his energy taken up trying to digest this fucking huge thing bulging inside his body.'

Pollard opened his mouth wide and slid the sandwich inside lengthways. When the tomato sauce started to run out of the corners of his mouth and down his chin, Ford had to turn away.

He walked across to the far side of the office, weaving through the maze of desks crammed into the space, stepping over trailing computer wires, and looked out of the opposite window down the railway.

The lead locomotive was past their office now, and Ford could see the parking lot on the other side of the compound, lit up by the train's lights. There was a long line of identical Toyota LandCruisers parked side by side at the top of the embankment overlooking the railway. They were all kitted out to the same mine specification: the company logo on the door, radio call-sign number in large letters across the side panels, a rack of flashing lights on the roof and the long pole with an orange flag that allowed them to be seen by the haul trucks. They were all reverse-parked against the chain-link fence in accordance with health and safety instructions, all except one.

A Nissan Patrol was parked at the end of the row facing the office, dark paint where all the others were white, and no lights on the roof. There was someone sitting in the driver's seat. As Ford watched, the driver's face was lit up a ghostly blue from a phone he held in his hand. Ford tried to make out the man's features. He was looking his way, maybe watching the trains, maybe watching Ford.

'How long's that guy been sitting outside in the Nissan? He waiting for someone?'

The sandwich had disappeared but Pollard was still chewing.

'Fuck knows,' he said after swallowing. 'You're the guy spends his shift staring out the window.'

Pollard had the apple now, holding it like a cricket ball in the gap between his first and second fingers. He flicked out his wrist, snapped his fingers and the apple shot upwards, spinning fiercely. Ford had seen this routine often enough, but had never seen him eat the apple. He checked the clock again but the hands hadn't moved.

'Alright, that's close enough,' he said. 'If the day shift can't be bothered showing up a few minutes early, then I can't be arsed hanging around waiting for them. You can do the handover on your own.'

Ford went to the door, picked his hard hat off the hook and plucked his safety goggles from his shirt pocket. He stuck his head outside to feel the heat. It was like opening an oven door, and the iron dust made him sneeze. He stepped back inside and felt the cool breeze from the air-conditioner.

'Where'd Grace stay last night?' asked Pollard.

'Over with Suzi Johnson. Grace is in her daughter's class. They asked her for a sleepover. It would be nice for her if that became a regular thing. Suzi and Brad have been in Newman ten years, since before their kids were born. Maybe some of that stability will rub off on Grace.'

He fished in his shirt pocket for his cigarettes and lit the last smoke of his shift.

'See you tonight,' he said, and let the pressure from the air-conditioner slam the door shut behind him.

He stood in the breezeway behind the office taking deep pulls on the cigarette and watching an ore truck pull into the maintenance yard for the shift change, the roar of its diesels drowning out the train, its headlights throwing Ford's shadow against the wall of the prefab. The driver shut it down and killed the lights, then stepped out from the cab. He saw Ford and offered a casual wave. Ford didn't recognise him. He wore the same orange work clothes as everyone else, the same hard hat and safety glasses, but without a beard or moustache as a clue, Ford couldn't identify him. He raised his cigarette in reply and gave the faintest nod of his head.

Ford walked briskly towards the security gate, swiped his card at the reader beside the gate and pushed through it into the car park. As he reached the rank of vehicles he noticed that the end bay was empty, the dark Nissan gone. He looked along the row of identical white LandCruisers and could not decide which was his. He found his key, popped the lock button and the lights on the third vehicle winked at him in recognition.

He opened the door and threw his hat and lunchbox on the passenger seat, then lifted himself into the driver's seat. The air inside was warm and stale, baked overnight and smelling of iron dust and the last trace of new-car smell: hot plastic, glue and sickly sweet air freshener. He turned over the engine, cranked the dial on the air-conditioner to full, and sat with his eyes closed, feeling the heat of the seat through his pants and the blast of warm air on his face slowly growing cooler. He jabbed the control arm on the steering wheel to start the windscreen washer jets and ran the wipers to clear the thick coating of red dust from the glass in front of him. When the air in the Cruiser was something approaching fresh, Ford took a deep breath, put it in gear, and slowly pulled away.

The gravel road ran parallel to the railway and the train was now clear of the mine and picking up speed. As he pulled alongside it he passed out of the shadow of the hills and the sun appeared behind him, reflecting off the mirror into his eyes. He squinted and pushed the mirror aside, sliding his sunglasses from the visor and putting them on.

He pulled ahead of the train as the road left the track to join the highway. As he turned south onto the bitumen, the road crossed over the railway and the train sounded its horn as it passed under the bridge. Ford adjusted the rear-view mirror so he could watch the locomotive appear on the far side of the bridge, but instead saw the dark Nissan following him. He could see now in the sunlight that it was blue, but the driver was a dark silhouette, the car too far behind for him to read the licence plate in the mirror.

Ford took his foot off the gas and let his car slow, but the Nissan matched his speed and kept two hundred metres behind him. Ford turned off the highway into Newman Drive and headed into town, the broad curve of Mount Whaleback ahead, rising from the desert. Above it hung a cloud of dust from the mine that was slowly devouring the hillside, creating a series of terraced tenements.

Ford kept an eye on the mirror and watched the Nissan make the turn behind him. He decided not to turn towards his house, but let the road take him around the town centre, passing the health centre and the football oval. The only vehicles on the road so early were a few other mining company vehicles, all white, making the Nissan in the mirror stand out.

When the curve of the road took the Nissan out of sight, screened by the gum trees in front of the hotel, Ford did a hard right into the shopping centre. He raced through the empty car park and flung a sharp left into the laneway in front of the hardware store, ignoring signs barring entry to the one-way street. He shot across the next junction and was into the network of residential streets flanked by identical nondescript weatherboard and corrugated-iron houses. He took two more quick turns, then pulled over and waited. When the Nissan failed to appear he let out a long breath.

He fumbled for his cigarettes and struggled to light one, his hands shaking. He inhaled deeply, then put his hands on the steering wheel and flexed his fingers, trying to shake the numbness. A twinge ran up his arm to the site of the bullet wound in his shoulder, and he raised a hand and massaged the scar through his shirt. The smoke calmed him and, as he stubbed out the cigarette, he wondered how long it would take him to not keep checking over his shoulder. He thought about calling the Johnson house, but it was still too early for Grace. He put the car in gear again and headed towards the rented house he was still learning to call home.

As he followed the curving streets towards the outskirts of town, the houses became newer and larger. The weather-board made way for salmon brick walls and red iron roofs, a poor imitation of a typical Perth suburb, only the thick layer of dust, the dying lawns and the relentless heat to remind him he was a thousand kilometres north of the city.

He pulled into the driveway of the house, a squat bungalow with a roof so low it sat directly on the window lintels, with no overhang that could offer shade. The windows were blanked out by yellowing blinds and shielded by torn fly-wire. There were no plants in the front yard; it was mostly red dirt with a shrinking oval of coarse lawn struggling at its centre. The only item in this spare strip was the steel mailbox, leaning at a dangerous angle on its slender post. He parked next to Harding's ute, hoping his lodger had not switched to the night shift as well. He wanted to have the house to himself once he'd got Grace off to pre-primary.

He walked around to the back of the house, into a back yard that was as sparse and parched as the front, a single Cocos palm leaning against the chain-link fence that separated the yard from the neighbour's. The screen door was standing wide open and the back door was ajar, the air-conditioner beside it sending out a steady whine as it tried to cope, a stream of condensed water snaking across the cracked concrete patio and pooling under the plastic table. Three moulded green chairs made up the full complement of furniture in the yard, their arms pitted and melted where cigarettes had been stubbed out. Ford caught the smell of cigarette smoke and looked in the can of sand near the leg of the nearest chair. There were a couple of butts of his brand in there, but they were old and dried out. He followed his nose through the back door, thinking how Harding didn't smoke and knew he didn't allow smoking indoors around Grace, angry that the door was open and the air-con was struggling.

He stepped inside and the kitchen was dark and airless. He flipped on the light and saw the cigarette on the edge of the table. It had burnt down to the filter, leaving a scorched black stripe across the Formica top. He walked through into the living room and felt something crunch under his boot. He leaned over and picked a shard of broken glass out of the rubber tread, saw the light spilling through the kitchen door reflecting off fragments of glass strewn across the floor, among scattered books and the splintered remnants of the coffee table. He peered through the gloom and saw a man slumped on the sofa, one leg propped up on the arm, his face just discernible in the weak light leaking around the edge of the window blind. Ford stepped closer and saw that it was Harding. His eyes were closed and there was the sweet smell of sweat and bourbon coming off him. Ford kicked Harding's foot off the arm of the sofa and punched him lightly on the shoulder.

'Get up, you useless bastard. I need this place cleaned up before I get back with Grace.'

He found the light switch and flipped it. The room was trashed, the bookcase tipped over, and the TV destroyed. Harding's face was bruised and blood trailed down his chin from his split and swollen lip. His skin looked pale and dull. Ford stepped across and put two fingers to Harding's neck. It was cold and there was no pulse.

TWO

Ford knelt in front of Harding and wondered how long he had been lying there. He leaned in close to check for signs of injury. The only blood was the trail from his cut lip. It occurred to him that he knew next to nothing about his lodger, and he tried to think of the number of times they had spoken in the two weeks since he had moved in. His face seemed younger in death than it had in life; there was a certain boyishness that Ford had not noticed before, maybe due to the dark fringe of hair falling loose across his forehead rather than slicked back as usual.

Harding was not in his work clothes; he wore jeans and a white short-sleeved cotton shirt, the creases still sharp along the sleeves. Several buttons were missing from the front and the seams of the right shoulder were torn. His right hand lay casually across his chest, and the knuckles were grazed and swollen. There were bruises up his forearm.

Ford was surprised that he felt no emotion. Before last

September the only deaths he had experienced had been those of his parents. He counted the number of dead people he had seen in the last year and concluded that Harding was the sixth; maybe that was the number beyond which you became immune. He had not allowed himself to feel responsible for the other five, even the one he had shot in the face, but somehow he felt he was responsible for Harding's death, and that he should be more alert to the danger this implied.

Ford stood up and listened, but the house was silent except for the whine of the air-conditioner outside. He stepped into the hallway, holding his breath. He opened the door to Harding's room. It was neat, the covers on the single bed pulled straight, the small desk tidy, with only a laptop on it. There was a set of free weights stacked neatly on a rack by the wardrobe, and a barbell resting on a frame above an inclined bench, a fresh towel stretched across it. He moved down the corridor to his own room. The bed was unmade and there were clothes strewn across the floor, but it did not look disturbed.

Grace's bedroom door was ajar. Her room was in the same state as it had been when he dressed her the previous evening, the pink floral doona pulled tight across the bed, her stuffed toys lined up along the pillow, her plastic ponies facing him in a line on the dresser, arranged in a particular order that was as important to his daughter as it was meaningless to him. He picked up her ragdoll and put it to his nose instinctively.

He found his phone and pulled a number from the memory. Suzi answered on the first ring.

'Hi, it's Gareth. How's my girl?'

'Sorry, Gareth. I've only been up, like, ten minutes.' Her voice sounded husky and sleepy.

'Everything alright?' he asked.

She hesitated, hearing the tension in his voice. 'Sure,' she said. 'Why wouldn't it be? I just looked in on the girls and they're both still sleeping. I'm going to make some coffee for me and, once I've jump-started my heart, I'll get breakfast for them.'

'How was your evening?'

'Great. She really is no trouble. You should relax. Lauren loves having her here. They were lying awake chattering even after I'd turned the lights out, but that's girls for you.'

Ford walked back through the living room and stood before Harding. 'Is Brad there?' he asked.

'You missed him. He'd have been starting his shift just as you finished yours. You didn't see him?'

'No, I snuck out early.'

She paused again, waiting for him to continue. Her patience didn't last long. 'What's wrong, Gareth? You're doing that English thing of yours, that quiet reserve. Stop being such a Pom. Spit it out.'

'Something's happened. I need another favour. Can you take Grace to school today?'

'Sure. Did they spring a double shift on you? I thought the maintenance shutdown was over.'

'It is. It's not that.'

He heard a car outside and went to the window. Parting the blinds he saw the police wagon pull up in the driveway behind Harding's ute. The lights on the cab were flashing but there was no siren. Two uniforms climbed out.

'You still there?' said Suzi.

'Yeah, sorry. I'll have to go. I'll call you later.'

'You're making me worried now.'

'It's the police. They're here. I have to go talk to them.'

The back door was still open and Ford turned off the light and moved quickly through the kitchen to close it. As he reached for the handle he saw the lock had been jimmied and the wood was split. He left the door open and was leaning against the door frame as the two cops came around the back of the house. They stopped when they saw him.

'Good morning, officers,' he said, trying to control the pitch of his voice. The policeman in front was older and shorter, heavy around the middle, short hair and a broad moustache greying at the edges. His gaze was steady, taking in the work clothes and dusty boots, then he was looking over Ford's shoulder into the kitchen. Ford noticed the three stripes on his sleeve.

'Good morning, sir,' said the sergeant. 'Can I ask you if you live at this address?'

'Yes, it's my house. Well, the company's house, but I'm the tenant.'

'Could you give me your name, sir?'

'Is there a problem?'

The younger cop yawned, then fidgeted nervously with the equipment on his belt. Ford guessed he was in his early twenties, probably in his first country posting.

'I asked you your name, sir.'

'Gareth Ford.'

'English, are you?'

Ford tried to smile. 'Is the accent still that strong?'

'And who else lives here?'

'My daughter,' said Ford, 'and there's a guy lodging with us.'

'Is he home? There are two cars in the driveway.'

'He is. What's the problem?'

'We had a report of a disturbance.'

'I just got home from my night shift.'

The cop looked at the company logo embroidered above the pocket on Ford's shirt. 'Where do you work?' he said.

'Ore Body 42. Operations.'

The sergeant nodded to his partner, who took out his notebook and started writing. 'Then we'll need to talk to the other guy.'

Ford hesitated. Both cops had taken a step closer. The young one wore an expression of bored confusion, the older one a practised look of efficient concern. Ford could read their name badges now. The sergeant was Eley, the young one Kopke. Eley rested his hand gently on the butt of the gun holstered at his hip. Ford stared at the gun, and at the taser, handcuffs and pepper spray arranged across the cop's belt. He sighed. 'You'd better come in. You'll find him on the couch.'

He stepped back and let Eley pass him into the kitchen. Kopke waved Ford in, stepping in behind him to close the door. He noticed the damage and bent over to examine the splintered wood. Eley had already turned on the living-room light and was standing in front of the couch, bent over with his hands on his knees in front of Harding.

'He's dead,' said Ford.

Eley pulled himself upright, turned to Ford and looked him in the eye. He held the stare for a few moments then glanced at his partner, braced against the kitchen doorway.

Eley returned to the corpse and checked the neck for a pulse. He pulled down one of Harding's eyelids and a glazed bloodshot eye stared back at him. He stood upright, put his hands on his hips, thinking. 'He's fucking dead alright,' he said. 'What's his name?'

'Josh Harding.'

'What a shitty start to the day.'

'For you or for him?' said Ford.

'I don't think he cares that much,' said Eley, 'but for me, it's going to be a long fucking day.'

He gave a wave to his partner and Kopke went into the hallway to check the rest of the house. The sergeant stared at Ford.

'You say you just got back from work?'

Ford nodded. 'Ten minutes ago. He was like this when I came in.'

'Have you touched him? Moved him at all?'

'Only to check his pulse, same way you did. That was all.'

'Show me your hands.'

Ford held out his hands palms upwards and Eley took hold of them, turning them over to examine the knuckles, then letting them drop.

'So what was all the noise about?'

'I didn't hear anything. The house was quiet when I got home.'

'Bit of a party, was it?'

'As I said, I wasn't here.'

'This man reeks of drink.'

Ford shrugged. Kopke came back in and shook his head. Ford looked from one to the other. 'So now what?'

Eley smiled. 'What we do now is get you out of this house so you don't fuck up the crime scene any more. Why don't you come down to the station with me and we'll have a chat.'

'Am I under arrest?'

Eley laughed now. 'Would you like to be?'

'I don't see there's any need for that.'

'I agree. Let's say you're helping us with our enquiries, making a statement.'

Eley guided Ford by the elbow through the kitchen and out the back door. Kopke stood in the doorway waiting for instructions.

'Secure the scene,' said Eley. 'I'll send someone out when we get to the station.'

'Do you want me to call it in?' asked Kopke, fidgeting with his phone.

'We're four blocks away. We'll be there by the time anyone picks up.' Eley still had a firm grip on Ford's elbow as he pushed him around the corner of the house to the police wagon. It was a four-door HiLux ute with a fibreglass Varley pod fixed to the cargo tray for prisoner transport. Eley unlocked the door to the pod and waved Ford towards the moulded plastic seat inside.

Ford shook his head. 'I didn't think I was under arrest.'

'I ride up front, you ride in the back. That's the way this works.'

'Do I look like I'm going to run?'

'Do I look like I give a shit? We can do the handcuffs if you want.'

'I need to make a phone call,' said Ford.

'You can do it at the station. You got a phone on you?' He held out his hand.

Ford took it from his pocket and slapped it in Eley's palm. Eley scrolled through the screen.

'You made a call just a few minutes ago. Who'd you ring?'

'My daughter. Well, a neighbour. My daughter was having a sleepover while I did the night shift.'

'You find a dead guy in your house, you didn't think to call us first?'

'Did I need to? I was on the phone when you arrived.'

'So who do you want to call now?'

'I thought I should ask someone's advice before I speak to you.'

'You think you need a lawyer?'

Ford shook his head.

'It's not a good look, mate,' said Eley. 'You start lawyering up, we start thinking you got something to be worried about. You worried? You look nervous.'

Ford stood with his hand out, his head tilted, waiting to see what Eley would do. The cop thought for a moment, then handed back the phone.

Ford leaned against the wagon, trying to find a patch of shade. The sun was higher now and he could feel the sweat trickling down his back. He shielded the screen with one hand while he thumbed through his contacts with the other to find the number he wanted. She answered on the third ring.

'Detective Constable Rose Kavanagh.'

Ford paused. He hadn't spoken to her since the last day of the inquest into the Gwardar robbery.

'Kavanagh. It's Gareth Ford.'

There was a moment's silence. 'Ford,' she said. He thought he heard her yawn. 'It's early. I'm still in bed.'

Ford tried not to picture her. He had never seen where she lived, and didn't want to think about whether she was alone.

'You still there?' she said. 'Tell me what's happened.'

'Why do you ask that?'

'Call me psychic. You're not one for social calls, especially before breakfast.'

'I'm in trouble. I need your help.'

'That much I guessed. Where are you?'

'Newman. I've got a police officer standing next to me.'

'Are you under arrest?'

'Not yet, but it's possible. There's a dead man in my house.'

'Do you know him?'

'Josh Harding. A young tradie billeted at our house.'

'Did you kill him?'

'How can you ask me a question like that?' said Ford.

'Reasonable question. Did you?'

'No. Looks like he was in a fight. Broken furniture, bruises.'

'Any obvious cause of death?' she asked.

'Nothing visible.'

'No gunshot or knife wounds? No head trauma?'

'Not that I can see.'

'Was he a drug user?'

'No idea.'

'So what are uniform doing with you?'

'Taking me to the station, getting a statement while they secure the scene.'

'Sounds straightforward enough. What do you need me for?'

Ford looked at Eley. 'Don't be coy,' he said.

Kavanagh yawned again. 'You said there was a fight. Could've been an accident. Wouldn't be the first one-punch death in a drunken fight in a mining town.'

'But why does this happen in my house? Why is it happening to me?'

'You're getting paranoid. Where's your daughter?'

'She's with friends.'

'So she's safe. What you need to do is let the local uniform handle this. You got a lawyer?'

'No. Wouldn't know where to dig one up in town at this hour.'

'Ford,' she said, 'listen to me. Go with the police to the station. Give a full and cooperative statement. What's the name of the attending officer?'

Ford looked at Eley, who had turned away towards the cars in the driveway. He was writing the licence numbers in his notebook, still within earshot. 'Eley,' said Ford.

'Senior Sergeant Jack Eley,' said Eley. 'Make sure your lawyer writes it down.'

'She's not my lawyer.'

'I got that,' said Kavanagh. 'I'll see what I can do.' With that she cut the connection.

Eley held out his hand and took the phone, then glanced at the screen. He nodded towards Harding's bright green ute. 'I'm assuming this garbage wagon belonged to the dead man?'

It was a Commodore SS utility, a big V8 with an air scoop on the hood and chrome wheels, the suspension sitting low on fat tyres. It had recently been polished to a showroom shine.

Eley put his hands on his hips. 'The more money these guys get, the worse their taste,' he said. 'Why would you buy a shit-hot ride like this in a putrid colour like that?'

'Harding told me it's called Atomic Green.'

'That'd be right. Drive around in something the colour of a radioactive frog. I thought he was fly-in fly-out?'

'No, he was on short-term contract, here for the maintenance shutdown. He couldn't bear to be parted from his car so he drove it up here. Nine hours' drive flat out. He showed me the speeding ticket he got outside of Meekatharra. A hundred and sixty it said. He was very proud.'

'They teach us not to judge people by their appearances,' said Eley, 'but I reckon this here Holden tells me all I need to know about young Mr Harding.'

Ford's eyes scanned the street. It was still early, and there was no sign of traffic, but the full heat of the day was on them. 'So who made the call to you guys?'

'One of the neighbours,' said Eley. 'Don't ask me which one.'

Ford turned and saw a man standing at the end of the street, maybe two hundred metres away. He was holding a black umbrella over his head, which cast such a dark shadow that the man appeared to only exist in silhouette. He wore a black suit, a pale shirt and tie, but his face was in darkness. When he saw Ford staring at him, he turned slowly and walked around the corner out of sight.

Eley put his hand on the door to the prisoner compartment and took Ford's elbow again.

'Shall we?' he said.

Ford climbed into the plastic pod, which glowed inside,

an eerie light diffusing through the plastic. It had been cleaned recently, but the smell of bleach on the smooth interior didn't cover the stench of sweat, piss and puke from the previous night's police work.

Ford tried to keep his breathing shallow as the engine started and the wagon pulled away.

THREE

Ford had waited alone in the interview room for three hours and drunk four styrofoam cups of reheated coffee and a litre of water before Eley and Kopke came in and sat down opposite him. Kopke put a manila folder on the table, opened it, and passed the first sheet to his sergeant. They had taken off their hats and their gun belts. Without his cap, Kopke's curly brown hair spilled over his forehead and he shook his head to flick it out of his eyes.

'Now then,' said Eley, stretching himself upright and pulling down his shirt where it had bunched up around his belly, 'this all took longer than I expected.'

Ford looked through the open doorway towards the corridor. The station had been empty when they arrived and Eley had run around to the rear of the front desk to boot up the computer himself.

'Isn't there a detective around to interview me?' said Ford.

Eley leaned over to shut the door, shook his head. 'There

may well be, in due course,' he said. 'You may get interviewed again later, if Karratha decides to send someone down. Right now you're talking to me.' He took the pen out of Kopke's hand and made a note on the document. 'You understand that I cautioned you when we arrived at the station?'

'Yeah,' said Ford. 'I don't know why you couldn't take my statement then. I could have been home by now.' He glanced at the dust ground into the cuffs of his shirt and caught under his fingernails and thought about how long he had been awake and the last time he had showered.

Eley snorted, then smirked at Kopke. 'You won't be going back to that house any time soon. It's a crime scene, and will be until someone in Perth decides whether they want to send up a forensics team to show us how it's done.'

'I've been here too long already,' said Ford. 'I just got off a twelve-hour night, and after drinking your piss-poor coffee all morning, my brain is heading in the opposite direction to my body.'

Eley put down the paperwork, rested his elbows on the table and stared at Ford. 'Well, excuse us for tampering with your body clock. It's taken so long because when I typed your name into our big police computer, all the bells and whistles went off. It was like hitting a jackpot on the pokies.'

Ford kept eye contact with Eley, who was smiling.

'It seems you are no stranger to police-interview rooms,' he said.

Ford shifted in his chair. 'This one is a lot nicer than the last one I was in,' he said. It was a new station, built in the half-hearted post-modern Australian style that had become common in the north, curved roofs and sloping columns at jaunty angles doing little to disguise the fact that it was a corrugated-iron shed. The interview room was white and featureless and smelled of fresh paint. On the ceiling a single air-con vent directly over the table blew a stream of cold air straight onto the top of Ford's head. They had turned up the fan before the interview began and now he felt a chill. He pulled the collar of his shirt tight around his neck and his fingers pulled his gold chain free.

Ford nodded towards the file. 'How much of my history have you got in there?'

'This?' said Eley, holding up the top sheet. 'This is just the summary, the greatest hits. We've spent the last few hours trying to work our way through all the material on the Gwardar robbery.'

'I don't see how that's relevant to Harding,' said Ford.

'Neither do we,' said Eley. 'Not yet. But this is not the first time dead people have mysteriously appeared in your home.'

Ford sighed. 'I had nothing to do with that.'

'So the coronial enquiry concluded. Two men found shot to death in your apartment in September last year.' Eley looked up. 'It says here you lived in Scarborough. Close to the ocean?'

'A partial view,' said Ford. 'Mostly blocked by that bloody hotel.'

'How very nice for you,' said Eley. 'My wife tells me non-stop that I should get a posting on the coast, somewhere with a cool breeze and a low crime rate. Anywhere but this place. She'll have to wait. I've got five years to retirement and already she's discussing coastal property prices.'

Ford leaned back in his chair and stretched. 'Maybe if you solve this business they'll bump you to the top of the waiting list for a cushy job.'

Eley shook his head and returned his attention to the file. 'These two dead blokes last year. One a known bikie with an arrest sheet that stretches to two pages, the other a former SAS officer whose service record has restricted access. This odd couple broke into your apartment and decided to shoot each other.'

Ford shrugged. 'They were accomplices to the robbery. Some sort of weird alliance that reached breaking point.'

'It isn't clear from the bits I've read why they chose to have this parting of the ways in your living room.'

'They'd taken me with them as a hostage during the robbery. I escaped.'

'And they missed you so much they wanted a reunion. Whoever tries to recapture a hostage?'

'You'd have to ask them.'

Eley laughed. 'Did you know that your record has a box where the investigating officer can make notes on an interviewee's behaviour? Normally you see warnings that a perp is violent when drunk, or depressive, or delusional. Do you know what it says here about your behaviour?'

'Tell me.'

'One word: annoying. Are you going to continue like that?'

'You're questioning me as if I were a suspect.'

'As far as the investigating detectives were concerned, you were very much a suspect in the Gwardar robbery. Initially they liked you as the inside man, they thought you'd let the robbers into the gold refinery.'

'The enquiry found I had no case to answer.'

'Still, it must have been difficult finding a job in Kalgoorlie with a Gold Squad investigation on your record.'

'That's why I'm in Newman. Iron ore, a new start.'

'And they stuck you on the night shift?'

'You make it sound like a punishment. You're wrong. I'm only on nights this week, during the maintenance shutdown. Normally I'm on days so I can fit in with my daughter. The company's good like that.'

'We don't see many single fathers up here. Doesn't suit the lifestyle.'

'Suits mine. The company looks after me pretty well, and there's a network of families that help out.'

'Harding ever help out, do a bit of babysitting?'

'You're fishing now.'

'You were found in the house with the victim, and you were evasive when we asked you to come in. You have a history of adorning your furniture with dead people. That makes you our only person of interest at this time.'

'Now you've read my record, you'll understand why I was nervous. You arrived only a few minutes after I found him. I was still shaken.'

'What time did you leave work?'

'I expect you'll have checked with the company by now. You know what time I swiped out.'

'We've spoken to the company alright. There's one of them sitting outside right now. Very concerned she is.'

'Can I talk to her? I might need help getting a lawyer.'

'She's not here for your sake, mate. Don't make the mistake of thinking they give a shit about you. Their first concern was that Harding's death might be work related. The woman out there is some community-relations bullshit artist looking after the company's image, but she's not half as big a pain in the arse as the Health and Safety Nazi who's been bending my ear on the phone.'

'This has nothing to do with the company.'

'You'd think that, wouldn't you? But these bastards still think this is a company town. You'd think I had the company logo on my shirt, not the crown, the way they talk to me.'

'Harding had been in a fight. It's hardly a safety issue.'

'Every death in a mining town is a safety issue. It gets them shit-scared it will reflect badly on the company. Tell me what you know about Harding.'

'I don't. The company billeted him in our house for the shutdown. No room at the inn, or anywhere else. He was only here for two weeks. Severe accommodation shortage, booked solid, so they stuck him with us. He's an electrician. Only just got his ticket and straight away he's up here on the mines making the big money.'

'The house is registered as being owned by the company, so you and Harding were sharing. Why did you call him the lodger?'

'I used to call him that to piss him off. He hated living with us. He had no idea how to behave around a kid.'

'How old's your daughter?'

'She's six,' said Ford. 'Harding was trying hard to find another room. He wanted to get a place in a single men's house, so he could stand around the yard with a bunch of blokes like him, burning meat and scratching his balls, building a pyramid out of empty beer cans.'

'Harding had been drinking last night. Did he smoke?'

'No, he was a fitness freak.'

'What about you?'

'Yes, I smoke,' said Ford. He took his cigarettes out of his shirt pocket and slapped them on the table and placed his lighter on top of them. 'I don't smoke indoors. I don't smoke inside my house and I haven't had a cigarette at home since before my shift.' He stared at the packet and fought the craving. 'If you're leading up to asking about that cigarette butt that burnt its way across the kitchen table, it's not mine. Test the filter for DNA and I reckon you'll have your man.'

'As I said, forensics haven't yet been dispatched.' Eley was looking tense now.

'You haven't taken my clothes for testing,' said Ford, sensing that the advantage was passing to him.

'All in due course,' said Eley, fidgeting with the paper-work. 'Let's talk about the gym equipment in the bedroom. Was that Harding's?'

Ford sighed. 'Do I look like the kind of bloke who stands in front of a mirror each morning with my shirt off?' He picked up his lighter and flicked it open and closed. 'Did you take a look at Harding's body? He spent hours every day pumping iron so he could leave a beautiful corpse. He'll have the best developed pecs in the morgue.'

'We've only just transferred him to the cool room at the Health Centre. The duty doctor is going to take a look.'

'Do you know what killed him yet?' asked Ford.

Eley cast his eyes down onto the paper, took another couple of sheets from the file. 'Would you say that Harding would be able to take care of himself?'

'Sure,' said Ford. 'He was into all sorts of martial arts and kung fu shit. Used to sit there late at night watching Jackie Chan movies and criticising the guy's moves. Wanted me to go halves with him to get a satellite dish so he could watch Ultimate Extreme Fight Club stuff. He thought it was a proper sport.'

'Not your style?'

'Two shaved men in tight shorts wrestling in a cage? I tried to explain the homoerotic subtext to Harding, but it only upset him.'

'So you didn't get along?'

'His habits irritated me,' said Ford. 'I'd asked him a few times to turn the TV down, not to watch violence when Grace was around, and not to exercise when I was trying to get her to sleep. There was always a lot of grunting and crashing of metal.'

'Did you argue?'

'Yes, but we didn't fight. I'm confused why you're still keeping on like this when it's clear I was at work.'

'I'm trying to get an idea of Harding's character and habits.'

'He was exactly as he appears,' said Ford. 'He was a young, arrogant, vain, cashed-up bogan. He liked to boast that he worked hard and played hard. The sort of guy whose police sheet would say: violent when drunk.'

The door opened and a female officer came in. She was slim and pretty, her uniform hanging loose on her as if it had been made for a man. Strands of red hair strayed from under her cap and her freckles made her look even younger than Kopke. Ford smiled at her and she dropped her eyes. She knelt down between Eley and Kopke and whispered in her sergeant's ear. Eley scowled, then threw a glance at Ford. He leaned towards Kopke and spoke in a low murmur. Ford strained to listen, but could not make out what was said. Eley jerked his thumb towards the door, and Kopke nodded. The two young officers left and Eley slid the file across in front of him and pretended to rearrange the papers while he regained his composure.

'We get a lot of young men like Harding in town these days,' he said. 'Cocky little shits who think the Pilbara is one big theme park for their own enrichment and amusement. Big wages, meals and accommodation laid on, flights in and out, short rosters and long breaks. Worse than fucking teachers. They flash their money around as if they somehow deserve it. They are easy people to dislike. Did Harding have any enemies?'

'I don't think he'd been here long enough to upset anyone, but it's not like we had long girly chats. When he did talk to me it was mostly about how much money he was making, and how he was going to spend it.'

'What about friends?'

'Nobody I ever met.'

'So you can see how this looks to us? He knows nobody in town. No friends, no enemies. You're the only link we have, and you're the bloke who likes to collect corpses in his living room.'

'Except, of course, I have a solid alibi.' Ford wondered how many suspicious deaths Eley had dealt with. He seemed to be enjoying it. 'Look, Harding had been drinking. I'm off the booze. Teetotal. There's no alcohol in the house, another thing we used to disagree about, so he must've been drinking somewhere else. There's only a handful of bars in this town, and a few bottle shops. Go ask some questions.'

'We will do, but just now we're trying to understand you.' Eley shuffled his papers and started reading from his notes. 'You were working in the gold room at the Gwardar mine when it was robbed at gunpoint. You left the scene in an armoured van full of gold and then handed yourself in to the police the following day at the Kalgoorlie racetrack after enjoying a day of drinking and punting. There's no record of any police interview, nor why you were released, but you show up two days later at a shooting at Perth Airport, where two officers gun down a man, Henk Roth, who was later charged with the robbery. Somehow this Roth guy manages to get bail, then skips the country.'

Ford felt his fingers go numb, and his shoulder throbbed at the memory. He tried to massage life back into his knuckles as Eley continued.

'That same night those two men are found shot at your apartment in Scarborough. Nobody ever stands trial for the robbery or the shootings. The officer in charge, Detective Inspector Bill Chadwick, does not oppose bail for Roth and then gives testimony backing your evidence to a coronial enquiry. Then promptly retires from the police force and gets a cosy job in the public service.'

'That's in my file?'

Eley put the file aside. 'No. That's not in your file. Chadwick is mysteriously absent from your record, but he's well known in the force. Quite a reputation, old Bill, the last of a dying breed. There was a lot of gossip when he retired. A lot of us were wondering what he was covering up. I was hoping you might be able to tell me. You seem to be at the centre of things.'

'I wasn't anywhere near the middle. I'd be interested to know if anyone found out who was behind the robbery,' said Ford.

'There's that journo at the *Gazette*, Alannah Doyle,' said Eley, warming up now. 'She keeps digging. The inquest concluded that the guys found in your apartment were behind it, but Doyle's been writing articles smearing Alan McCann, trying to connect the robbery to the bankruptcy of his mining company.'

'Because I'd been on McCann's payroll at the Gwardar mine, his lawyer represented me at the inquest.'

'I see that. I'm just making a stab in the dark here, but I'd say there's a lot you know that you're not telling.'

'I've been questioned a dozen times. I don't think you'll discover anything that the coroner and Serious Crime don't already know.'

'I'll tell you what I know,' said Eley, leaning across the table and jutting his chin towards Ford. 'I know that you're here in Newman, and there's a smell coming off you, a stench of death that seems to follow you around. I don't want you stinking up my town.'

The door opened and Kopke stepped in. He knelt down behind Eley and spoke softly in his ear. Ford watched the sergeant's face fall into a scowl, which then compressed into a grimace. 'Fuck!' he grunted and stood up from his chair so quickly that it pitched backwards and would have fallen if Kopke hadn't caught it. Eley scooped up the file from the table and stormed out without a backward glance at Ford. Kopke gave him a sheepish grin before following Eley into the corridor. The door locked behind them.

Ford sat motionless in the chair, staring at the door. After ten minutes they still hadn't returned. He looked at the cigarettes on the table and then at the security camera in the ceiling and decided to see what would happen. He lit a cigarette and had enjoyed half of it before Eley returned, his face still dark with anger. He stood in the doorway, rubbing a hand through the grey stubble on his head. 'Put that out,' he said. 'Now.'

Ford dropped it in the styrofoam cup on the table. He swilled it around in the dregs of coffee and listened to it hiss.

'You really do lead some sort of charmed fucking life,' said Eley. 'There's two women in the front office now, arguing about who you belong to. Lookers, both of them. Both telling me I've got no business questioning you any further. You'd better come out here before they start scratching each other.'

FOUR

As Ford walked down the bright corridor towards the door to the main office, he could hear voices through the toughened glass of the security door. Women's voices: one angry and harsh, the other one calm, almost inaudible. He stopped at the door and peered through the wire glass, and Eley reached around him to punch the keypad. When the door opened the voices fell silent.

He noticed Kavanagh first, standing almost within touching distance of him. He smiled at her, but her face was locked in an expression of frustration that hadn't changed with his arrival.

She had let her hair grow a little longer in the six months since he had last seen her. He could remember that day, standing in the corridor outside the courtroom after the inquiry. She had perjured herself to protect him, and kept quiet while the police whitewashed the enquiry, then she had simply left. He had watched her all the way to the exit, hoping she would turn around and look at him, but she hadn't.

Her hair was still bleached a stark white, as pale as her skin. She wore a plain white T-shirt under a short red leather jacket, plus faded jeans and crimson cowboy boots. Ford looked at the Cuban heels on her boots and wondered if she was on duty. He was trying to calculate the travelling time for Kavanagh's trip from Perth to Newman when the other woman stepped between them and thrust a hand towards him.

'Mr Ford?' she said, her voice loud and confident, as if pitched to be heard through closed doors. 'My name is Lisa Romano. I work with Legal Affairs. The company asked me to come down and offer whatever help I can.'

He shook her hand; her grip was firm and practised. 'I'm just fine,' he said. 'I'm not sure I need the company's assistance just now.'

She was a handsome woman, easily Ford's age, but with the sort of strong face that looked better with age. Her dark hair was coiled and pinned in a bun, strands hanging loose in curls around her face. Her cheekbones were as sharp as her nose, and her brown eyes sat behind frameless spectacles calculated to lend her gravitas. She wore dark blue jeans that looked as if they had been ironed that morning, and a plain white blouse with the company logo sewn above the breast pocket. Ford studied the embroidery until it became apparent to him that he was staring at her chest. A change in the tone of her voice made him concentrate on her eyes.

'I must say I'm rather disappointed,' she said. 'You shouldn't have agreed to be questioned without legal representation.'

'I didn't know I had a lawyer.'

She gave him a smile devoid of any warmth. 'I've been asking Constable Kopke here to allow me into the interview room and he's been making some rather pathetic excuses in an attempt to prevent me.'

The young constable, who was standing at the duty desk, seemed bewildered. Romano was still talking. 'This drama could have been avoided if you had called the company as soon as you were arrested.'

'I wasn't arrested,' said Ford, looking past Romano and hoping for eye contact with Kavanagh, but she had walked towards the exit and was staring out of the window, her attention fixed on something distant. Ford turned to Romano. 'I came in here voluntarily. I haven't any reason to hide behind a lawyer. I found the body, that's all.'

Romano scowled. She put her hand on Ford's elbow, steering him away from the duty desk until their backs were turned on Eley and Kavanagh. She leaned in close and spoke quietly in his ear. Her perfume was cloying and smelled expensive.

'The company is very concerned about the death of Mr Harding,' she said. 'I'm sure you have done everything to help with their enquiries, but the detective constable over there wants you to go with her.'

Ford glanced towards Kavanagh, but she was still looking out of the window.

'I know DC Kavanagh,' he said. 'If I have to leave with her, that's not a problem.'

Romano was whispering now, her head so close that a lock of her hair brushed against his face. 'She says that she wants to question you about other matters. She won't discuss them with me.'

'Her and me, we have history.'

'She says she's from the Gold Stealing Detection Unit. Why would the Gold Squad have an interest in Mr Harding's death?'

Ford studied her closely, trying to gauge how much she knew about the Gwardar robbery, wondering whether she'd had the opportunity to read up about him before she came out to the station. Her dark eyes gave nothing away, and he worried that might be a skill she'd honed as a lawyer. 'I have no idea,' he said, and waited to see if the expression in her eyes changed.

There wasn't a flicker so he let the silence hang for a few moments before he spoke.

'I think Sergeant Eley has asked me all the questions he needs to. I've agreed to be interviewed again by detectives when they arrive, so I'm happy to help DC Kavanagh however I can. I'm grateful for your time, but perhaps it would be put to better use helping Harding's family.'

Eley stepped forward and cleared his throat theatrically. They turned to him, and he pulled himself upright. 'I'd prefer to keep Ford at the station until we have eliminated him from our enquiries. We need to complete our canvass of the neighbours and have some indication from the doctor as to the cause of death.'

Romano put her face close to his and started telling him that if he wanted to keep Ford, he'd need to arrest him. Ford let the voices drift away and, as he looked at Kavanagh, she turned towards him and he lost his bearings in the room. The other people shrank away to a distant murmur and all that was left was her face. He searched her pale blue eyes for a sign from her, a hint of a smile or a twitch of an eyebrow that might acknowledge that she too felt trapped in the tedium and irrelevance of the conversation. Her mouth slowly pursed and twisted sideways into the smallest of smirks, but he didn't know if it was for his benefit, since her eyes were on Eley. She could have been flirting or she could have been enjoying a private thought.

She swung her eyes in his direction and her smile widened for a second, then she put two fingers to her mouth and whistled, a long piercing shriek that echoed off the bare walls and made Kopke wince.

'If I could have your attention for a minute,' she said, her voice low and measured. Everyone in the room was facing her now. She made them wait as she rubbed the dust off the toe of her right boot down the back of her left leg.

'Thank you,' she said. 'Until detectives arrive from the coast to take charge of the investigation and interview Mr Ford, I think it best to let him go and get some sleep while uniform finish their door-to-door.'

'I need to pick up my daughter,' Ford said.

She looked at him and her eyes softened. She nodded. 'You got somewhere to sleep?'

He shook his head.

'I'll take you to find somewhere.'

She spoke to Eley quietly and he put his hand in his pocket and handed her Ford's phone. 'Don't leave town,' he said to Ford.

Kavanagh went to the door and opened it, tilting her head towards Ford as an invitation for him to leave. Romano opened her mouth to speak but Kavanagh held up the palm of her hand and the lawyer closed her mouth, her shoulders slumping. Kavanagh waved Ford out the door, stepping out behind him into the heat of the afternoon sun.

Ford took three steps off the kerb then stopped and reached into his pocket for his cigarettes. He lit one and pulled hard on it, then continued. He was halfway across the car park before it occurred to him that he didn't know where he was going. Kavanagh was several paces behind him. She stopped and put her sunglasses on, mirrored aviators. Ford could see two of himself, distorted in her lenses. He bent his knees a little so he could see himself better. He looked thinner than usual, sickly and pale. His thick greying hair was sticking up, matted with sweat, and his hollow cheeks were hidden behind a few days' growth. There was red dust ground into the wrinkles on his face, a contrast against his green eyes. He made a habit of avoiding his reflection in harsh sunlight; he didn't like being reminded how old he was getting, how his life was slipping away. It was like looking at someone else.

Kavanagh popped the locks on a white Toyota hatchback and Ford headed towards it. He pulled open the passenger door and folded himself down into the seat. The plastic sleeve containing the rental contract hung loosely from the dashboard and brushed against his knees, so he opened the glove box and stuffed it inside. He fumbled under the seat until he found the lever and pushed the seat back, but he still didn't have enough leg room.

When he reached over his shoulder for the seat belt, he looked behind him and saw the blue Nissan Patrol parked down the street. It was a hundred metres away, facing towards them, under the shade of a jacaranda tree on the opposite side of the street.

Kavanagh took her seat but he didn't look at her. He leaned forward a little until he could see the Nissan in the side mirror.

He could clearly make out two dark shadows in the front seats. The driver's outline was big, his body a solid black rectangle; his head sat on his torso with no sign of a neck, reaching almost to the roof. The passenger was smaller, narrow, with a round head that made Ford think it was the man with the umbrella he'd seen on his street earlier. His heart raced and he took a deep breath.

Kavanagh started the engine and cranked up the air-conditioner. The cold air swirled up his arms and goosebumps erupted on his skin. They sat there and didn't say anything for a while, waiting for the car to cool down and getting used to each other's presence once again. She leaned forward to adjust the air-con controls and he caught her perfume, recognising the scent, a mixture of citrus with a warm rush of sandalwood.

She pulled out of the cark park, turning right, away from the Nissan. Her eyes kept straying to the rear-view mirror. Ford checked the side mirror and saw the blue car pull out and follow them, keeping a hundred metres behind, no other traffic on the road. Ford waited for her to mention it. When she stayed silent and the tension became palpable, he decided to speak first.

'Eley didn't put up much of a fight.'

She turned to look at him, then quickly returned her eyes to the mirror. 'He had nothing on you,' she said. 'They checked what time you left the mine and spoke with your work colleagues. You have a solid alibi.'

'So why was Eley trying to keep me at the station?'

She pursed her lips. 'He was just fishing,' she said. 'He looked at your file and thought he had stumbled into something. Typical country copper wanting to play detective.'

'But then a real detective shows up and pulls rank.'

He caught a small smile flash across her face. 'Something like that. It doesn't take much to put them back in their box.'

She reached the end of the street and took a left, then kept checking to see if the Nissan would turn behind them.

'So what else do you know about how much the guys in uniform know?'

'Just that the doctor made a stab at the time of death. Nothing fixed, just a guess based on rigor mortis, lividity, body temperature and all the simple stuff. He reckons Harding was several hours dead before you got home.'

'Any idea of what killed him?'

'The doc is stumped. The only injury he found, apart from the bruising, was a broken hand. Fourth metatarsal in the right hand. The doc called it a boxer's fracture, probably sustained by punching an immovable object. That was the only x-ray that showed anything. Skull was intact. The doctor's pushing for us to send the body to Perth, to get a more thorough post-mortem. Don't expect anything to happen in a hurry round here.'

'Where did you get all this?'

'From that young kid behind the desk, the tall one with the curly hair.'

'Kopke?'

'That's the one. Constable Cupcake. He was a sweetheart. Very cute but very dumb.'

'And he just told you all this?'

'I leaned over the desk and smiled at him. Teeth and tits. Works every time.'

'I didn't think you'd work it like that.'

'What would you know? I never met a man so impervious to flirting.'

'I flirt,' said Ford.

'No, you don't. That woman back there was pushing that chest of hers in your face and you just stood there with your mouth opening and closing like a goldfish.'

'But you've never flirted with me.'

'Haven't I? You wouldn't have noticed if I had.'

'But it worked on that cop.'

'It helped that I outrank him. Guys like him don't know what to do with a woman who's their superior. They don't know whether to be afraid or excited. It doesn't take much to make them spill.'

'So what else did he tell you?'

'They finished their door-to-door. Didn't take long. Everyone was either still asleep or already at work. The only witness who saw anything was the guy who made the call. He'd been woken by a car revving its engine and chirping its tyres. He looked out his window and saw Harding pull into his driveway in that puke-green car of his. Ten minutes later there was crashing from the house and the neighbour called it in at four. Apparently he'd had words to Harding before about him doing burnouts in the street.'

'What was Harding doing out until four?'

'He'd been seen at the pub, the Red Sands, drinking until closing, and then he fell off the radar. Not seen again until the neighbour saw him.'

'If the neighbour called it in when Harding arrived home, why did it take Eley and Kopke several hours to respond?'

Kavanagh smiled. 'That's why they're being so defensive, messing you around. They don't want to admit that they waited until Eley started his morning shift before they responded. Kopke had been on the night desk, but assumed it was just a domestic, so didn't think there was any hurry.'

'But now Eley thinks it's part of something bigger. What does he reckon that might be?'

'He just saw your history with the gold robbery, your links to McCann and Chadwick. He was only trying to join the dots, see if he could connect you to Harding.'

'And what connections are you trying to make?'

'Me? I'm just here to point out to these rednecks that they've got no reason to hold you.'

'Much as I'd like to believe you came here for my sake, I'm not as gormless as that young cop. You jumped on a plane as soon as you got off the phone to me. I've been sitting here waiting for you to tell me what's going on.'

She took a deep breath and took another left turn into a back street full of identical brick houses, then waited for the Nissan to come around the corner. 'What's happening,' she said, 'is that these guys are still following us.'

'I was wondering how long you were going to keep playing it cool,' said Ford.

'They were outside the station when I arrived,' she said. 'They were watching the front door. Sat there in a car in this weather. I hope they had the engine running and some cool air circulating.'

'If you let them get closer we could read the licence plate,' said Ford.

'Got it when I arrived,' said Kavanagh. 'I asked Cupcake to run the plates. The car was bought two days ago in Hedland with cash. Registered to a company called Dugite in Fremantle.'

She reached the junction and looked both ways, took a right, then cursed when she saw that the street only ran fifty metres to another junction. She shook her head and took a left.

'Do you know where you're going?' said Ford.

She shrugged. 'Haven't a clue, never been here before. You could tell me where to go or I could just keep winging it.'

'Are you trying to lose the guys behind us or catch them?'

'I've got no reason to stop them.'

'Haven't you got enough cause to take them in for questioning?'

'That's not something I'd risk my neck over without back-up.'

'You've got a gun, handcuffs. I've seen you take on longer odds.'

'That's just the point. I haven't got a gun. They'd never let me on a plane with a gun without all the paperwork, and I just didn't have the time.'

They reached a junction and Kavanagh slowed the car. 'Now would be a good time for directions,' she said.

'It's a small town. Difficult to lose a tail around here.'

'Then I guess we just keep driving until someone runs out of fuel.'

'Go left. Let me think,' said Ford. She kept her eyes on

the mirror, waiting for the Nissan to appear behind them. They came up to the shopping centre and Ford pointed to the next turn.

'I know of one little shimmy through a one-way street near the hardware shop,' he said, 'but I used that when I lost him this morning. I don't think he'll fall for it twice.'

'How long were you going to wait before you told me this?'

'I only saw him once, on the way home from work. I thought I was over-reacting. I've been looking over my shoulder continually for the last twelve months. I think every car in my mirror is following me. It was becoming boring.'

'But this isn't boring. This shit is real.'

'Yeah, I figured. Dead guy and all that. I think the bloke in the passenger seat was watching my house this morning. Just standing there.'

'Did he have an umbrella?'

'Yeah,' said Ford, surprised.

'One of the neighbours saw him hanging around on the corner when she took her garbage bins out. She said the guy gave her the creeps with that umbrella. She thought he might be Asian.'

'He's small, skinny. Got a very round head.'

The road curved left around the hotel and playing fields. 'I recognise this,' said Kavanagh. 'Are we heading out of town now? I don't want to get stuck on the open road with these guys up my arse.'

'Take the next left,' said Ford. 'That'll take us back past the police station. Let's see if these guys are embarrassed at following us on a complete lap of the town.'

Once they had passed the police station, Ford gave Kavanagh a series of directions through residential streets.

'Where are you taking me?' she said.

'To my house. If you want to lose them, you won't do it in this little hatchback.'

'I'm not swapping cars just so you've got more leg room.'

'Trust me. I need to pick up Grace so we need to lose these guys. I need my car.'

She turned the corner into his street. His LandCruiser was still in the driveway next to Harding's ute. He looked for a police car but the street was clear. As Kavanagh swung into the drive, they both turned their heads up the street. The Nissan rounded the corner and as soon as the driver saw them park, he gunned the engine and accelerated past them. Both driver and passenger made a vain attempt not to show their faces but they were too late; Ford had caught a glimpse of them. The passenger was Asian, his features flat and his skin pock-marked, his straight black hair in a bowl cut that accentuated the roundness of his head. The driver was big, his skin dark, his hair cropped short. Ford looked at Kavanagh and she nodded.

'Chinese,' she said. 'Don't know about the driver.'

'Black maybe, all muscle. That's all I got. We'd better get moving before they come around again.'

Ford was around the back of the house by the time Kavanagh had the keys out of the ignition. She grabbed her backpack and followed him, checking up and down the street, and found him staring at the new hasp and padlock that had been fixed to the back door. There was black and yellow hazard tape across the frame and a sign indicating it was a police line.

'Well,' said Kavanagh, 'what did you expect? They've sealed the place until they can get forensics up from Perth.'

Ford twisted the padlock to test the strength of the hasp and the new screws driven into the door frame. 'My spare keys are in there,' he said.

'Anything else you need from the house?' asked Kavanagh.

'Everything,' said Ford. 'At the moment all I've got is the clothes I'm standing in. Eley took my phone, my wallet, my keys.'

Kavanagh dug into the side pocket of her leather jacket, then tossed a bunch of keys to him. She took his phone and wallet out of her inside pocket and held them in her outstretched palm. Ford raised an eyebrow.

'I persuaded Cupcake to release them to me,' she said.

'How?'

'I called him a good boy and gave him a biscuit.'

Ford back-tracked towards the driveway and flipped the locks on the LandCruiser, then hauled himself into the driver's seat and started the engine. Kavanagh strolled up behind him, and swung open the passenger door. She threw her backpack in the footwell, took off her red leather jacket, folded it carefully and laid it on the bench seat between them. She then took her place, plucking at the sleeves of her shirt where wet patches had spread from under her arms. Ford leaned across her and opened the glove box. He took out a roll of oiled canvas bound in a leather strap and laid it on the seat on top of her jacket. He undid it and put the pistol on the dashboard in front of Kavanagh. 'You'd better take this,' he said.

She thought for a few moments before picking it up. It

was a heavy black automatic with a short barrel and a star embossed on the grip.

'Wow,' she said. 'You really are paranoid.'

She pulled back the slide and peered into the chamber, then released the clip and counted the rounds.

'There's another clip in the glove box and some sort of webbing shoulder holster that I could never quite work out how to wear,' said Ford.

'This is a Makarov,' she said. 'Do I want to know where you got it?'

'You know where I got it.'

'If I can't get a gun on a plane, how did you?'

'I had it delivered,' said Ford, 'by special motorcycle courier. One of our old friends from Kalgoorlie.'

'Anyone else know you've got this?'

'No.'

'You're lucky Eley was too dumb to search your car or impound it,' she said, 'or nothing I could've done would've got you out of that station.'

She banged the clip back in the pistol, examined the safety, and put it under the seat between her feet. 'Alright,' she said, 'let's see where those two clowns have got to.'

Ford reversed out of the driveway. The Nissan was parked a hundred metres away, facing them. Kavanagh smiled. 'You were telling me you had a way to lose them,' she said. 'Why don't you show me?'

FIVE

By the time they reached the end of the street the Nissan had turned around to follow them, keeping a hundred metres back but staying in plain sight.

'They don't seem to worry about being seen,' Ford said. 'You think they had something to do with Harding?'

She thought for a moment. 'I think whoever killed him wasn't too fussed about leaving evidence.'

'You mean that cigarette?'

'I didn't know about that. Constable Cupcake said there was physical evidence all over your house. I thought he meant fingerprints. He said the forensics would have plenty to work with.'

'There was a cigarette butt left burning on the kitchen table.'

'Does Harding smoke?' she said. 'I mean, did he used to?'

'No. I do, but it wasn't my brand. It was a Marlboro. I saw the writing around the filter.'

'I didn't think anyone smoked those lung-busters anymore.'

'It's more than that. Australian smokes don't have branding on them now. New plain-packaging laws. Whoever left that cigarette bought the packet overseas.'

'And left his DNA all over it.'

'Do we need forensic evidence to point us to the culprit? Surely you've got enough to stop the guys behind us?'

'You think I should apprehend them using an illegal handgun previously used in an armed robbery? I think I'll wait for forensics and armed back-up.'

Ford turned on to Newman Drive and the houses petered out as the road started climbing uphill.

'Where are we headed?' asked Kavanagh.

'We're going to lose these guys, then go pick up my daughter.'

'Where is she?'

'With neighbours. A sleepover with one of her little mates.'

'Does she do that every time you're on the night shift?'

'Just this week. I normally work the day shift and she's at pre-primary, then afterschool care.'

'Seems a bit hard on her.'

Ford shook his head. 'It's easier here than you'd think. You ever tried to find decent out-of-school care in Perth?' Kavanagh looked at him and raised an eyebrow. 'We're both better off up here, at least in the short term,' he said. 'The company looks after us, there's a decent school and out-of-school care, and a network of families that shuttle one another's kids around.'

'Surely you'd be better off in your own home?'

Ford sighed. 'Grace and I lived in her mother's house in Shenton Park for six months, until the end of the enquiry and the police told me I was no longer a person of interest. It didn't feel like a home to either of us. It was difficult for Grace, her mother leaving both of us. Took her a while to get used to only having me, thinking her mother didn't love her, and I felt like a trespasser among all Diane's things. The place felt spooky, if it's possible to be haunted by the absence of a living person. When this job in Newman came up, it didn't feel like we were leaving much behind.'

'I didn't think you needed to work. I thought you had that trust fund.'

'We did, but some lawyers showed up. They'd been appointed by the receivers chasing McCann's money. They claimed there were some bullshit irregularities with the trust fund that Diane had made him set up for Grace. I don't know if Diane had done it out of guilt for Grace, or if it was part of the plan to take her away from me. Anyway, they're contesting it. Until it's sorted out I have to work, and this is the best offer I had.'

'How many offers did you get?'

'Let's not talk about that.'

'So this is your life now?'

'Only until the legal dispute is settled, and while Grace is at pre-primary. Another eighteen months maybe. I want to be back in Perth when she's ready for primary school.'

'And you're happy with that?'

'Happy with what? A life that's flat and stale, like an old glass of beer?'

'I thought you chose this?'

'It was my decision. I wouldn't say it was my choice. Just making the most of what was left to Grace and me when Diane left with McCann. It's not the life that Grace deserves, up here on the mines.'

Kavanagh's eyes softened. 'You seem to be coping alright.'

'I try. I never thought life as a single parent would be so hard. The company helps, the other families are great, but it's still tough.'

'Plenty of kids are raised without their mother, who's dead or crazy or a junkie. I see enough of it on the job.'

'Grace's mother is none of those things.'

They were beyond the town now, the road rising steadily to meet the great red curve of Mount Whaleback. The mountain was barely recognisable as natural landscape, stripped of trees, carved into a series of flattened steps, dressed with spoil from the mine, a vast fortress of red dirt shrouded in dust.

'My mother died when I was young,' said Kavanagh, the slightest tremor in her voice. She cleared her throat, regaining control of her voice. 'My dad did his best to raise me on his own and be a good cop at the same time. The whole town expected so much of him.'

Ford sighed. 'Maybe I'm not as good a man as he is.'

'You're not wrong,' she said, gazing out the window.

Ford waited for an opportunity to change the subject. He saw the boom gate that barred the entrance to the mine and checked his mirror. The Nissan was keeping its distance, as if unsure where they might be going.

'This is it,' he said. He reached under his seat and pulled out a baseball cap with the company logo stitched on the front. 'Put this on and act like you belong here.' He opened his window as he stopped the car in front of the guardhouse, a low brick building in the centre of the road, with boom gates each side. He leaned out the window and ran a pair of swipe cards over the scanner, smiling at the guard sitting behind the glass in his air-conditioned booth, then looking at the camera mounted on the roof. As the boom gate went up the guard lifted a finger to the peak of his cap in mock salute. Ford accelerated away from the gate then pulled over, watching to see what the Nissan would do.

'They following?' asked Kavanagh, trying to see in the side mirror.

'They're not even trying. They've pulled in way back down the road. Looks like they're going to sit there and wait.'

'Is this the only entrance to the mine?'

'Would I have trapped us in here if it was?'

'And so you know a way out of here that those muppets don't?'

'Natch,' he said, allowing himself a smirk. He waited for a semitrailer to come through the boom gate behind them and block the line of sight from the Nissan, then he pulled out ahead of it, switching on the flashing orange light on the roof. As the road curved around towards the mountain they crossed the railway, over a long train of ore cars snaking its way beneath the bridge. Ford turned on the two-way radio hanging under the dash, and the car filled with static and chatter from across the mine.

'Are those guards back there armed?' said Kavanagh.

'No, why would they be?'

'So what's the point?'

'They are more concerned about health and safety than anything else. They don't want any outsiders wandering around the mine causing accidents. You think those guys are armed?'

'If they were, they'd have made a move by now, rather than just trying to spook us.'

The road ran parallel to the base of a vast slope of shattered rock, and Kavanagh leaned forward to watch the huge haul trucks crawl along the sky line. Ford stopped the LandCruiser at an outsized set of traffic lights showing red. The other road was twice as wide, coming off the hill in a broad curve, and down it came an empty haul truck, throwing up a plume of orange dust behind it. Without slowing, it raced across the junction in front of them.

'I didn't think those things could go so fast,' said Kavanagh as she watched it drive into the service yard and park at the end of a long line of similar trucks in front of a maintenance workshop the size of an aircraft hangar.

'They don't travel so fast when they're laden. They only go that fast when it's the end of the shift.'

'I take it they always have right of way?'

'You don't want to get in front of one. They show you a safety video of what happens when one of those things runs over a light vehicle like this. Flat. Splat. Like *Tom and Jerry*.'

He reached across for the radio handset and put it to his mouth. 'LV four-two. Pulling on to haul road above workshop. Over.' He waited a moment for a reply, and when none came he swung the Cruiser right and started up the slope the truck had just come down. As the road climbed the view opened up to show the line of hills marching eastwards from Mount Whaleback, the railway weaving its way along its base and the vast featureless plain spread out to the south. Ford saw where Kavanagh was looking.

'Those hills are the tail end of the Ophthalmia Range,' he said.

'What a romantic name,' she said, her voice flat. 'Those pioneers certainly had an imagination.'

'When Ernest Giles came through this country in 1876 he was temporarily blinded. He'd travelled for weeks from the coast by camel, and had sandy blight, couldn't even see those hills, had to be led over them by his men. He named them after his condition.'

'Makes a change from naming the landscape after royalty, kissing arse for a knighthood.'

'Giles stayed around here until his sight returned,' said Ford, 'then decided there wasn't much to see and moved on.'

'I know the feeling.'

The road reached the top of the hill and veered left as the ground fell away into the vast open pit that stretched five kilometres along the length of the ridge, carving out the inside of the mountain into a series of steep terraces. Excavators and ore trucks were operating at the far end of the pit, hundreds of metres below them.

'Impressive, huh?' said Ford.

Kavanagh shrugged. 'I've seen the Kalgoorlie Super Pit. It's bigger. Once you've seen one enormous hole in the ground, it kinda spoils you for the next one.'

They crested the top of the hill and a man in a hard hat stepped out of a small hut and waved a pair of orange flags at them, holding them out wide to block the road. Ford checked his watch and waved at the man in acknowledgement. Kavanagh glanced at her own watch. 'Now what?'

She had opened her mouth to speak again when the ground shook and the Toyota rocked on its suspension. As Kavanagh turned to look into the pit the deep rolling boom of the explosion engulfed them. Jets of dust spat upwards from the edge of the pit and a long wedge of rock slid slowly down the wall and crashed onto the terrace beneath it, breaking like a great wave as the dust boiled into the air.

Ford smiled. 'Twice a day, every day.' He was shouting over the crashing echo of the blast. 'It will be a while before they give the all-clear.'

'And what do we do until then?'

'We talk.'

Kavanagh waited for the rumbling to subside before she spoke.

'I thought we had exhausted all the niceties,' she said. 'We've done family, jobs, all that crap. I'm all out of chit-chat.'

'You shouldn't bother with small talk. You're not good at it,' said Ford. 'Maybe just skip that and tell me why you came up here so fast.'

Kavanagh tilted her head backwards against the headrest and closed her eyes. She took a deep breath and let the air escape in a slow hiss, then turned her head to gaze out the window at the cloud of dust floating across the pit. The air outside was so hot the dust seemed to give off its own light.

'That why you brought me up here?' she said. 'Keep me here until we talk it out?'

'I came up here to lose those guys. Maybe you could tell me what you know about them.'

She didn't answer. She looked through the windscreen at the man with the flags. Ford, deciding to give her all the silence she might need, listened to the last rumbling of the rock rolling down the wall of the pit, felt the heat radiating off the windows.

'Henk Roth came back into the country last week,' she said. She let it hang in the air for a moment, let the cold air from the dashboard vents blow it around the cab. Ford was gripping the steering wheel, flexing the fingers of his left hand. She carried on.

'He jumped off a bulk ore carrier in Port Hedland using a false passport that we had on record. There was no passport scanner at the port, and by the time customs logged his entry and the computer flagged him, he was gone.'

'You think these guys work for Roth?'

'Maybe. I don't know. I found out three days ago that Roth was in the country and then today you call me, bleating that there's a corpse in your living room. I haven't had any kind of lead on this for months, then two things happen within days of each other. That's why I'm here.'

'You're still chasing the Gwardar gold?'

'My hunch is that it's still in the country.'

'You thought it had gone on McCann's boat, or on his plane.'

'So why has Roth come back? If he's got the gold, he'd be long gone.'

'Maybe he's come back for me. Unfinished business.'

'Don't flatter yourself. Roth is a professional, not the sort to bear a grudge.'

'Not even for the man who shot him?'

Now she was smiling. 'You're letting your paranoia get the better of you.'

'So those guys behind us, you don't think Roth sent them to kill me?'

'Not those muppets. They're not the sort that Roth would hire. He gets mercenaries, soldiers, trained killers. If he'd wanted to hit you, you'd be on a slab, not Harding. And they wouldn't leave a burning cigarette on the table.'

'So where was Roth before this week?'

'We always assumed he was still with McCann in Macau.'

'You assumed?'

'We don't have any intelligence. We made some enquiries with the Macau police but they blanked us. All we got was that McCann is living at the Penglai Island Casino as the personal guest of the owners.'

'So why don't you go get him?'

'Because we still don't have a warrant for him, even if we could get through all the Chinese red tape to get him extradited. Currently he's only wanted for bankruptcy hearings and for questioning about trading irregularities. The receivers are still chasing assets they reckon he's squir-relled away offshore. If they find them, they might be able to persuade the prosecutors to charge him with fraud, but they keep getting stalled at every turn by McCann's lawyers.'

'Can't the Macau police take him in for questioning?'

'They are too cowed by the casino owners, the Lau family. Rich, powerful, connected. The police walked into the casino and requested an interview with McCann and the next day the Chief of Police was hauled before the Secretary of Justice and given a spanking. That's the kind of reach the Laus have.'

'Is Diane still there with McCann?'

She turned and looked at him now. He was massaging his knuckles, then his hand went to his shoulder and rubbed it.

'I thought you were all healed?' she said.

'Yeah, the wounds are fine. They just twinge sometimes when I think about these things. Is Diane in Macau?'

'As far as I know. We have no interest in your wife.'

'No interest?'

She saw the pain in his eyes; the memory of his wife leaving him for McCann was etched into his face. She put out a hand towards the steering wheel, as if to lay it on his, but pulled it back.

'They found Diane's business partner, Matthew Walsh,' she said. 'He's dead.'

He looked at her, his eyes wide.

'His jeep went into a ravine, some place in Indonesia, up in the jungle somewhere. One of those islands, I forget which. When they found him he was still strapped in his seat.'

'An accident?'

'Yeah. Maybe. There wasn't much of him left to be able to tell. He'd been there for weeks. Animals had been at him. They identified him from his wallet.'

'So what does that mean for Diane?'

'McCann's lawyers are still claiming that the geologist's report on the Gwardar mine was prepared by Walsh, and that McCann thought it was genuine. Until they've done independent drilling to show that the claims of a new gold discovery there were bogus, and that McCann profited by speculating on his own company, then there's nothing for the police to do.'

'But he made a shitload of money.'

'He's claiming it bankrupted him. Until they can track down the offshore companies he used to trade his own shares, there's no proof.'

'And they can't prove Diane wrote that report?'

'Ford, you're the only one who still thinks that. Everyone else is losing interest.'

The man with the flags spun them around his head to get their attention, then waved them through with a flourish and disappeared into his hut. Ford drove slowly away from the edge of the pit and onto a track that weaved between spoil heaps. They were into rolling scrubland before Ford spoke again.

'So this Chinese guy watching us, leaving his foreign fag-ends to burn a hole in my Formica, you reckon he's from Macau?'

'It's a reasonable assumption.'

'So if he's not working for Roth, who?'

'I have no idea.'

'So please tell me you have some sort of plan.'

Kavanagh sighed. 'I got nothing, except to keep you out of trouble and wait for Roth to show himself.'

'Are you dangling me out on a piece of string, hoping he'll take a bite at me?'

'That's your paranoia talking. You still drinking?'

'I have to blow zero at the mine. I'm not drinking. Is that what you mean by keeping me out of trouble?'

'I meant that I'll protect you from whatever enemies present themselves and, since you're your own worst enemy, that includes protecting you from your own self-destructive tendencies.'

'You sound like my wife.'

She didn't answer that.

The road straightened out and they could see where it joined the Great Northern Highway, their progress blocked by a high chain-link fence and gate. Ford jumped out, swung the gate open then climbed back to drive through. Once he had closed the gate, he had his phone in his hand.

'Hi Suzi, it's Gareth. Yeah, I know that. I got delayed. I owe you. Look, I'm driving past in exactly five minutes, and I'm in a real hurry. Could you have Grace waiting on the driveway so we can make a quick getaway? Yeah, it sounds weird, but it's been that kind of a day. Yeah, five minutes.'

He put down his phone and, turning south onto the highway, accelerated towards town.

SIX

Ford saw his daughter as soon as he turned the corner, standing in the sun at the end of the cracked concrete driveway, as tall as the faded steel mailbox and leaning at the same angle, pulled over by the pink overnight bag slung on her shoulder. He could read her defiance in the way her arms were crossed in front of her chest, her elbows jutting out. She held her head high towards the oncoming car, squinting into the sunlight, her wayward blonde hair scattering the harsh light like a dazzling halo. She was dressed in a faded blue pinafore dress, bare legs scabbed at the knees and dotted with bruises and mosquito bites, her feet stuck into canvas sneakers that were scuffed and torn. Her neck was bare and the sun had turned it a dark honey colour, almost as golden as the chain that hung around it, carrying the small gold nugget. Her folded arms bore temporary tattoos of flowers and ponies that she always begged Suzi to stick on. Ford had asked Suzi not to give her any more but, once Ford was out of sight, his daughter was not to be denied.

He stopped the Toyota at the end of the drive and jumped out. Grace's brows were knitted into a frown. When he thought she had finished punishing him for being late, he went down on one knee and spread his arms open wide. She held the frown for a few seconds, showing him how stubborn she could be, then her face broke into a smile and she ran to him. She threw her arms around his neck and buried her face in the collar of his shirt. She smelled of fresh soap, something floral and slightly medicinal.

'Daddy, why didn't you pick me up this morning?' she said.

'Sorry, sweetheart. I got busy with something. Did Suzi look after you?'

'She said you phoned. She was worried about you.'

Ford held her tight, stood up and swung her around just to hear her laugh.

'Upside down!' she squealed, but Ford scooped her up and carried her to the car. He strapped her in the back seat and when she looked into his face, her eyes clear and without fear, he took strength from that. He kissed the top of her head and inhaled her scent.

When Ford stood back to close the door, Grace saw Kavanagh for the first time. They stared at each other for a few moments, neither sure what to make of the other. Eventually Grace recognised something of herself in Kavanagh's pale blue eyes and blonde hair and smiled. Kavanagh smiled back and they left it at that. They sat in silence, watching Ford walk up the driveway to talk to Suzi, a shapeless woman in a sagging tracksuit, her face tired and washed out.

She spoke quietly to Ford, a voice of hushed conspiracy. 'You don't need to explain. Word has already gone around town. Police at your house, then an ambulance.' The spark of curiosity and excitement in her eyes was obvious to Ford.

'Thanks,' he said. He could think of nothing. He waited to see if she had anything else to say, but all she could offer him was a weak smile, so he turned and walked back to the car.

He sat behind the wheel. 'Grace, this is a friend of mine,' he said. 'Her name is Rose.'

Kavanagh snapped her head around at the sound of her first name, scowling at him, and Ford noticed the similarity with his daughter: the blonde hair, the knitted forehead, the narrowed eyelids, the fierceness. It wasn't something he'd ever noticed in his wife, so he wondered if these were traits that Grace had inherited from him, and that he had responded to in Kavanagh. She caught him staring and wiped the scowl from her face, replacing it with an approximation of a smile.

'I have roses on my arm,' said Grace, stretching her hand towards Kavanagh to show her the tattoos.

'So you do,' said Kavanagh. 'I'm very pleased to meet you, Grace. How old are you?'

'I'm six,' she said, and smiled with pride.

'Then you've had a birthday since I last saw you. Do you remember me?'

'We met one time before,' said Grace, her gaze steady.

'Yes,' said Kavanagh. 'Yes, we did.'

Ford noticed the look that passed between them. He remembered the fear on his daughter's face as she had hung on to him in the aircraft hangar, surrounded by men and guns, and wondered how a girl could have such strength and calm inside her to be able to watch her mother board a plane and leave without her.

He drove off down the street, checking his mirrors again, and didn't start to relax until he had turned the corner, away from Suzi's stare. He swung into Newman Drive then took a sharp left into the Seasons Hotel. He parked in the driveway under the shade of a tree and left the engine running as he undid his seat belt and opened the door.

'Where are you going?' asked Kavanagh.

'See if I can find us some rooms. I've been in these work clothes for nearly twenty-four hours and I'm starting to hum. The pool looks good.'

She grabbed his arm and dug her fingers into his bicep. Leaning towards him, she spoke quietly and firmly. 'How long do you think it will take those guys to find us here? We're right in the centre of town.'

'All the hotels are in the centre of town. This town only has a centre.'

'Then we need to stay out of town.'

Ford sat back down and closed the door. He looked at his daughter and smiled, and through his gritted teeth tried to mimic Kavanagh's calm tone.

'The next town with a hotel is Hedland, and that's four hours north. Or we could head south to Meekatharra, which would take just as long. What exactly is your plan?'

'Those places are too far away. We need to stay close to Newman, wait to see how this plays out.'

'That doesn't sound like much of a strategy.'

'Where else can we go?'

'The Capricorn Roadhouse is ten kilometres south of town on the highway.'

'Do they have rooms?'

'Yeah, but it's pretty basic. It's a truck stop. We occasionally put guys in there when the rest of town is booked up and they whinge like crazy. There are a few brick units out the back and a camp site. Communal bathrooms. Not what I feel like just at this moment.'

'Let's go,' she said.

Ford thought about it for a minute, then saw Kavanagh's expression.

'Let's not sit around in plain view,' she said. 'It's only a matter of time before they start searching for us.'

Ford took the highway south across the plain, the road passing through red sandy country dotted with sparse trees. They passed the airport and on a long straight stretch, as they passed a road train pulling three fuel tankers, he pointed out the sign that said they were crossing the Tropic of Capricorn.

They pulled into the roadhouse a few minutes later; nobody had said anything. Ford stopped on a broad gravel hardstand beside the highway, crowded with semitrailers and road trains, low-loaders carrying mining equipment north, and a handful of tourist caravans. He parked the Toyota in the shadow of an ore truck that was trussed onto the back of a low-loader, facing backwards and stripped of wheels and tray. He glanced over his shoulder at Grace, who was rummaging in her bag and pulling out her toy ponies. Kavanagh was watching her, a distant expression of fascination on her face.

'I'll see what accommodation I can find. Anyone hungry?'

Kavanagh shook her head. Grace watched her and then copied the gesture, shaking her head wildly, her hair flying from side to side.

Ford crossed the forecourt, pushing through the glass doors into the roadhouse. It was busy for late afternoon, truckers buying fuel and eating at the diner. He looked down the crowded counter and caught the attention of a middle-aged woman with a face flushed pink from the heat of the kitchen.

'Who do I see about accommodation?' he asked.

She offered him a thin smile and waved him down to the till at the end of the counter, where she took out a battered leather folder and started running a finger down the names and dates.

'You're in luck,' she said. 'Late cancellation. It's been busy. All these blokes coming through for the shutdown. Like getting a bed in Bethlehem.'

'How many beds?'

'Just a single.'

'En suite?'

She looked at him and rolled her eyes. 'You want it or not?'

He nodded and gave her his credit card. She swiped it, then handed him a worn brass key on a heavy wooden fob, the room number burnt into it. He was opening his mouth to ask directions to the units when she jerked her thumb to the right then turned her attention to a trucker waving at her from the other end of the counter.

Ford stepped out from the smell of fried food and stewed coffee into the hot air saturated with petrol fumes and diesel smoke, and felt his phone vibrate in his pocket. He took it out and looked at the screen, but didn't recognise the number. He walked away from the fuel pumps and found a bench under the shade of the verandah before he hit the answer button. 'Hello,' he said.

There was silence on the other end. He looked at the screen to check he had a connection. 'Hello?'

'Gareth?' It was a woman's voice, distant, the signal breaking up.

'Yes, it is.' His voice was hesitant, his mind making connections, trying to place the familiar voice.

As soon as he recognised it, she said, 'Gareth, it's Diane.'

SEVEN

He looked across the forecourt to where the LandCruiser was parked. The windows were too high for him to see anything of Grace except a swirl of blonde hair, but Kavanagh was watching him.

'Gareth? Are you still there?' Her voice was clearer now; she seemed much closer.

'Yes, I'm here,' he said. 'Where are you?'

'I'm in Australia, in Broome.'

Kavanagh was waving to him now, trying to get his attention, beckoning him towards the car. He shook his head.

'Who are you with?' he said.

She paused. 'I'm on my own,' she said hesitantly.

'So where is McCann?' He heard the tone in his voice and didn't like it. He took a deep breath and closed his eyes.

'Alan's not here,' said Diane, her voice faltering now. 'That's why I'm here. I've left him.'

'Left him in Macau?'

'Left him for good. Things have changed.'

'You're not fucking wrong,' he said, then caught himself and took a moment. 'Why are you calling me?' He was keeping his voice steady, concentrating on making it sound neutral. There was silence, but he decided to wait for her to think about her answer.

'I guess you have a right to be angry,' she said. 'But right now I need you to drop the tone and listen. I need your help.'

'You might want to begin that sentence again. Next time maybe you could start it with an apology.'

'I don't have time for that now.'

'Ten years together, you never say sorry once. Now would be a good time to start. Start with an apology for leaving us, and work backwards from there.'

'Please, Gareth, there's a lot I have to explain,' she said. He could hear her breathing down the phone, quick and shallow. 'It needs more than a phone call to explain it. I want to tell it to your face.'

'You don't need to explain it to me, you need to tell Grace. You should worry about whether she is going to forgive you. I doubt you care whether I will.'

'Is Grace with you?' Her voice was urgent.

He looked across to the car. Kavanagh had turned in her seat, talking to Grace in the back, her head bobbing up and down like she might be laughing.

'She's right here with me now,' said Ford.

'I want to see her,' said Diane. 'Can you bring her to me?'

'Back up a little here. This doesn't get solved in a phone call. You don't get to carry on as if nothing's happened. You don't get her back just because you ask.'

'I'm not asking for her back, Gareth. I'm just asking to see her.'

'And why would I let you do that?'

She paused again. He could hear background noise down the line: voices, a radio maybe. He waited.

'What happened was not what I wanted,' she said. 'I need the opportunity to explain that to you.'

'I'm listening.'

'Not on the phone. You, who never wants to talk on the phone. Now you want chapter and verse?'

He looked at his reflection in the window of the road-house. 'You need to explain it to the police, too,' he said.

'I'll do that. I want to do that. I want to hand myself in.'

'There's a police station in Broome. Just walk right in.'

'If I do that, I might never get out again. I want to see Grace first. You must understand that. Are you still in contact with that detective, the one from the Gold Squad?'

Ford stopped pacing. Kavanagh was staring at him again. She opened the car door and made to get out but he shook his head.

'Which detective?' he said, wondering whether he was starting to enjoy this.

'Don't be obtuse, Gareth. The blonde from the airport.'

'I can contact her. Why?'

'Tell her I know where the gold is.' She sounded pleased now. Pleased with herself for the way she'd dropped it in, trying to make it casual.

Ford didn't want to give her the satisfaction. 'You can tell me where it is,' he said.

'No, I'll only tell her. To her face.'

'What's your game?'

He knew she was getting to the point at last. 'I need a deal,' she said. 'I'll tell her where to find the gold. I'll tell her where Alan has hidden his assets, but I need immunity. I can give the police a whole lot of dirt on Alan.'

'He's not going to like that.'

'Yes, why do you think I'm in Broome?'

'I figure you're getting around to telling me.'

'I told him I wanted to see Grace. He didn't understand.'

'If you're going to talk to the police, I'd guess that things are a little more serious than that. I'd say that would pretty much end things.'

'Alan is not the sort of man who would let me go as easily as that.'

'You think he's sent someone after you?'

'I know he has.'

'Chinese guys?'

'I don't know what they look like. Probably some of the goons from the casino.'

'What about Roth?'

'I haven't seen him for weeks. Alan is surrounded by the casino staff now.'

'How did you get to Broome?'

'The long way. A lot of small plane rides, cars and ferries through Indonesia. I came into Broome on a private boat.'

'Did you see Matthew Walsh in Indonesia?'

There was a pause on the line. 'I haven't seen him since I left Australia.'

'Anyone know where you are?'

'Only the skipper of the boat, and he only knows me by the name on my passport.'

'Where are you staying?'

'At the Cable Beach Club.'

'I thought you were hiding? Five-star incognito. I guess you brought money.'

'Alan's money. He gave me the fake passport too. Irish. I guess he never imagined I'd use it to leave him.'

'Anyone else got this number?'

'Just you. It's prepaid. Bought it today.'

He thought about that for a minute, wondered why this felt easier than it should. 'I'll come and get you,' he said. 'It's a ten-hour drive from here to Broome, and it will take me a while to set things up with the police. I'll need to ring you back.'

'You think she'll go for a deal?'

Kavanagh was out of the car now, leaning against the bull bar, waving for him to come over.

'Maybe. Sure, why not? Remind me why I'm doing this.'

'I'd hoped that would be obvious. Maybe there's a little bit of feeling left between us. If not for me, then at least for Grace.' She let that hang, wanting to see if he'd bite.

'That's your kind of olive branch, Diane. More wood than fruit.' He hung up.

EIGHT

Kavanagh's arms were folded across her chest, her chin down, looking at Ford through a fringe of loose hair as she leaned on the car. She patted the bull bar and he joined her, facing away from Grace. She shuffled sideways until her shoulder brushed his, and leaned her head towards his ear.

'Why the fuck did you leave us sitting out here in full view of the highway?'

Ford still had his phone in his hand. He waved it gingerly as explanation.

'I could see what you were doing,' she said. 'So you leave me alone with your kid? What do I have to talk about with a six-year-old?'

'Ponies,' said Ford. 'She likes ponies. Do you have any good stories about horses?'

'I had my own horse and a shelf full of trophies. Who was on the phone?'

'My wife.'

'Diane?'

'That's the one.'

Kavanagh's eyes widened.

'She's in Broome,' he said, and waited to see if her eyes got any bigger.

A smile broke across her face. 'Is McCann with her?'

'No, she's on her own. She says she's left him.'

Kavanagh walked off across the forecourt, her head down. As she stepped from the shadow of the low-loader, a car cut across in front of her, sounding its horn and snapping her out of her reverie. She jogged back to Ford.

'Why's she calling you?'

'Why wouldn't she? She's in trouble. Who else would she turn to?'

'Does she know where Roth is?'

'No, but McCann's still in Macau.'

'So why's she in Broome?'

'Hiding from McCann. False passport, cash only, came into the country all cloak and dagger.'

'So what's she want from you?'

Ford looked down at his hands, noticing how dirty they were. 'She wasn't calling for me. She wants to speak to you. And she wants to see Grace.'

Kavanagh stepped closer to him. He could smell her sweat and the last stale remnants of her perfume, burned off by the day's sun. She was almost whispering. 'Why me?'

'She wants to cut a deal. She has information. She wants amnesty, immunity, whatever.'

Kavanagh stepped back, thinking. 'That's not easy,' she said. 'Needs the Crown Prosecutor. That's a big problem.'

'I can see a whole conga line of problems,' said Ford.

'Chadwick,' said Kavanagh. 'If her name shows up any-where in the system, Chadwick will hear about it.'

'He's retired. Why are we still worried about him?'

'He's still got plenty of mates inside the detectives. They'll tell him, and he'll tell McCann and she'll be a sitting duck.'

'Then we'll just go get her.'

'I need to talk to her. What's she trading?'

Ford hesitated a fraction too long. 'She wouldn't say,' he said, but Kavanagh was already on to him. She took a step closer, her eyes narrowing. He noticed the way she pushed her chin forward, a slight underbite when she was focused.

'Don't lie to me, Ford. You're shit at it. No wonder you never cheated on your wife. She'd sniff it on you in a minute.'

Ford felt the dust in his mouth. He tried swallowing. 'She said she could tell you where McCann has hidden his assets. Those offshore accounts.'

'Bullshit,' she said, spitting out the word, a fleck of saliva landing on Ford's cheek. He was leaning back against the car, his back arching away from her, feeling the heat of her breath.

'If it was about his assets, she'd have gone to the receivers, the Fraud Squad, or direct to the prosecutors. She rang you looking for the Gold Squad. So come on, I'm going to make you say it.'

Ford tried a smile. 'Is this police technique or are you always so aggressive?'

'Spill it.'

'Diane says she knows where the gold is.'

Kavanagh smiled now, her eyes creasing, her teeth showing. Her fist was clenched and she was nodding to herself.

'I know how much this means to you,' said Ford. 'But I thought if I told you, you'd go off thinking about the gold. I'm thinking about Diane.'

'Well if you're worried that I don't care about her, then you're right.' Ford opened his mouth to speak but she cut him off. 'Conspiracy to steal the gold from Gwardar, conspiracy to fraud for falsifying the geological report on the Gwardar mine. Conspiracy to attempted murder. Of you.'

Ford's hand crept to his shoulder and rubbed the scar. He hunched his shoulders and rolled the joints. Kavanagh saw his expression and took a step back, her eyes softening.

'Is it all connected? Is your daughter part of the deal?'

'I don't know,' he said. 'I guess so. She said McCann had stopped her from trying to see Grace, from coming back. That's why she left. Maybe this is the only way she can do it, see Grace and avoid going down.'

'And what are you thinking about this?'

'I only just got off the phone and you were in my face.'

Kavanagh looked him in the eyes. He saw how small her pupils were in the sun, the tiny flecks of brown in the irises. She turned away and made to get back in the car. 'Did you get us accommodation?'

Ford showed her the wooden key fob. 'Last room. Single bed.'

She took the key. 'Don't worry yourself,' she said. 'I'm not banking on getting any sleep tonight, not with those two bastards floating around. At least we know why they're shadowing us. I don't want to find out what they'd do if Diane showed her face.'

She stepped around Ford and opened the driver's door,

slipping behind the wheel and waving Ford to the other side. Ford smiled at his daughter, nodding off to sleep on the back seat.

Kavanagh drove the LandCruiser around the back of the roadhouse and parked it behind the motel units under the thin shade of a crippled acacia, the last few strands of yellow blossom clinging to its bare branches. A winding concrete path crossed in front of the car, linking the rooms to the toilet block. Behind that Ford could see caravans parked among the sparse trees.

The motel rooms were split into two rows, facing each other across a patch of bare red gravel. Six rooms made up each plain brick block, their doors opening on to a thin strip of concrete under a corrugated-iron verandah. Each room had a single window, most of it filled with a boxed air-conditioner, and the remaining glass blocked out with aluminium foil. A plastic chair sat next to every door, and the rooms that were occupied had a pair of dusty site boots under the chair and a rattling air-con dripping water onto the concrete.

Kavanagh had her backpack and Grace's pink bag over her shoulder as she jammed the key into the lock of the last door and leaned into it. Ford followed her inside, holding Grace by the hand. The room was dark and stuffy, clogged with hot, damp air. Grace hesitated in the doorway and wrinkled her nose.

'It's only for tonight, sweetheart,' said Ford, as Kavanagh found the light switch. The single light bulb in the ceiling flickered as the air-conditioner wheezed into life.

'Suzi said I can't go home today,' said Grace, peering into

the room without daring to cross the threshold. 'She said the police were there.'

Ford looked at her to see how much she understood, but her face showed no sign of knowing what he had found at the house. 'Someone broke into our house,' he offered. 'Smashed some things. Stole some stuff. Nothing we can't replace.'

Kavanagh dropped the bags on the bed, a plain steel frame with a foam mattress and a thin floral coverlet. The bed filled most of the room, the walls lined on all sides by fake wood panelling, big sheets nailed directly to the concrete walls. The only other furniture in the room was a side table next to the bed, and a small TV on a bracket high on the wall opposite the bed, secured by a chain. Ford reached up to turn it on and caught a blast of his own sweat and stopped. Kavanagh smelled it too and wrinkled her nose.

She picked up the small towel laid out next to the pillow and threw it at him. 'Why don't you take a shower,' she said, passing him a small square of soap. 'Leave us girls to make this place more cosy, eh?' She smiled at Grace, who stared at her blankly before turning up the corners of her mouth in a forced smile.

Ford sat on the chair outside and pulled off his work boots, peeled off his damp socks and wiggled his toes. He picked up the towel, coarse and threadbare and scarcely big enough to go around his middle, and shuffled off down the path to the communal showers. He thought he heard giggling behind him.

When he came back down the path he was still wet under his dirty clothes, the towel saturated before he was halfway dry from the shower. He enjoyed the brief feeling of cool relief as the water evaporated from his skin, but it was soon replaced by a film of fresh sweat as he came out into the sunshine. The sun was touching the horizon on the far side of the highway, catching the dust and diesel fumes trailing behind the trucks and scattering orange light, the trunks of the gum trees glowing pink, the heat of the afternoon still trapped in the air.

The bedside table had been moved outside the room and Kavanagh's cowboy boots sat on it, wiped clean of dust.

When he stepped into the room the cool air hit his face and with it a burst of Kavanagh's perfume, which was so strong he thought she had used it to fumigate the room.

Grace sat on the end of the bed beneath the TV, her overnight bag open, her clothes and toys strewn across the bed. She held one of her plastic ponies in her lap, patiently teasing out the bright pink mane with a tiny plastic brush. The hair stretched out across her thigh, longer than the pony's body. Kavanagh sat behind her, brushing Grace's hair with a broadbacked brush, holding the stream of yellow hair in her hand, tugging at the tangled mess. With each knot Grace's head was pulled back, a grimace passing across her face, but not strong enough to displace the smile. Kavanagh looked up when she heard the door.

'Don't you ever brush this poor girl's hair?' she said. 'It's like a bird's nest.'

Grace giggled.

'She never sits still for me like that,' said Ford.

'You should cut it short,' said Kavanagh, 'if you're not going to look after it.'

Grace turned, her hair pulled taut. 'I don't want short hair,' she said. 'I don't want to look like a boy.'

'I have short hair,' said Kavanagh. 'Do I look like a boy?'

Grace thought about that and went back to combing her pony's mane. 'You have tattoos,' she said, in a small voice. 'I want tattoos like yours.' She picked idly at a peeling transfer on her arm.

Kavanagh laughed. 'Real tattoos hurt,' she said. 'You need to be brave. Are you brave?'

Grace nodded, her lips pursed, her eyes narrow.

'This is how much it hurts,' said Kavanagh, and pinched the skin on the back of Grace's arm. Grace winced and then laughed.

Kavanagh pulled Grace's hair back into a ponytail and secured it with a loop of elastic, then stood up. She picked up her backpack and pulled out a towel, then swung both over her shoulder and moved to the door. She put a hand on Ford's arm. 'Tag, you're it,' she said. 'My turn in the shower.'

Once she was out the door, Ford turned on the TV and flicked through several channels of static before finding a grainy kids' channel. He put Grace in her pyjamas and tucked her up in bed under the thin covers. He lay beside her watching cartoons until her steady breathing told him she was asleep.

He left the TV playing and tiptoed outside. Kavanagh was sitting on the plastic chair on the verandah, her wet towel draped over the back. She wore a fresh white singlet and a pair of shiny running shorts, her wet hair slicked behind her ears, her skin pink and glowing. Her legs were stretched out in front of her and Ford's eyes moved along the length of them until they reached the Celtic bands tattooed around her ankles.

It was dark now, just the remnants of an orange glow in the west where headlights moved along the highway. Kavanagh had moved the table into the pool of light thrown by a bulb hanging from the verandah ceiling, the light filtering through a cloud of mosquitos swarming around it. There was the buzz and intermittent pop of a bright blue bug zapper fitted to the wall at the end of the block.

Kavanagh's boots still sat on the table, now polished to a shine, and beside them were the components of the pistol, dismantled and arranged in rows. She held the barrel in her hand, wiping it with a red bandana.

'This looked like it hadn't been cleaned since you got it.'

Ford looked around at the other rooms. All had their air-cons running, their occupants shut inside out of the heat. 'Isn't it a bit public out here?' he said.

'I could do this in front of your daughter if you prefer.'

'I thought we'd be safe here,' said Ford.

'For tonight, maybe. Those guys will show up sooner or later.'

'They're looking for Diane. I don't think they'd hurt us.'

'They killed Harding,' she said. 'I can't find any logic in that. I don't want to think about what they might do if they find Diane. You should ring her.'

Ford took out his phone and found the last call received and thumbed it. He watched the bug zapper spark as he let it ring for a whole minute before hanging up.

He shrugged at Kavanagh. 'No answer.'

'Try the resort.'

'She didn't tell me the name she was using.'

Kavanagh reassembled the gun, her fingers moving quickly and precisely, her eyes focused directly ahead. She slammed the magazine into the grip, racked the slide and only then looked down to check that a round was in the chamber. She put the pistol back on the table and laid the bandana over it.

'You told Grace about her mother?' she said.

'No, that would be cruel,' said Ford. 'She'd want to see her now. Right now. You don't know much about kids, do you?'

'No, but I know a bit about fathers.'

'It's the five-minute rule. Only tell them what's about to happen five minutes before it happens. When you're going to leave, when a friend is arriving. Otherwise they pester the shit out of you, "Are we there yet?"'

He picked up the chair from the next room and put it beside the table so he could sit with her. Kavanagh turned to him, her hands flat on the table. 'Your wife tried to have you killed,' she said.

'That's your interpretation,' said Ford, watching the headlights moving along the road. 'Roth was going to kill me during the robbery. I have no idea if Diane knew that was going to happen. Her showing up here puts a different light on it. Maybe McCann hadn't told her what would happen.'

'You keep telling yourself that, and you might eventually start believing it.'

Ford took out his phone and found the number again. When he got no reply he stared at the screen as if waiting for it to provide an answer.

'I have no right to keep my daughter from her mother,' he said.

'She seemed to have no problem keeping your daughter from you. If we hadn't stopped her at the airport, Grace would be in Macau now.'

'I have to move past that,' said Ford. 'When Diane and I separated, I shut down, and Grace bore the brunt of that. I had to learn how to open up again, and now that I've learnt to do that I need to keep myself open to every possibility.'

'She'll hurt you again.'

'When I look at Grace I see her mother's face. The eyes, the smile. It's not something that you can deny.'

'She didn't get your wife's red hair, lucky girl.'

'Sure she did. If you catch her in the right light, you'll see the strawberry. Mostly she got my colouring though. My hair, my skin, my love of the sun.'

'What about that toughness, that stubborn streak? That yours or your wife's?'

'Kids are resilient, what she's been through.'

'But I saw it in that hangar, when you shot Roth. It didn't faze her. No kid should have to see that.'

'Maybe she gets that from her mother.'

'Stone cold she was.'

'That's not fair on either of them.'

'There won't be any happy families with her.'

'It's way beyond that. You can work at a relationship but, if the underlying love has gone, then it will finally break and you have to admit to yourself that it was always going to go that way.'

'So you don't love her?' Kavanagh asked.

'Grace does. I can't decide who Diane loves.'

'But you're picturing some kind of future for her?'

'Something better for Grace? Sure. Anything is better than this. The only constant for her is change.'

'You sound like you're trying to convince yourself.'

'All children scare their parents. You're forever expecting to meet yourself. However you imagine your kid will turn out, they turn into something different. Something that is you, but not you. Maybe the bits of you that could've been better.'

'You go looking for redemption like that again, you're going to get shot. You were not to blame for anything that happened at the mine, or afterwards. McCann set up the fraud, Diane wrote the fake geo report. Roth arranged the robbery and set you up as the fall guy. You did what you had to do. Get over yourself.'

His eyes flared. 'That job of yours, did you ever worry it might twist you? Leave you with no sense of what's normal? Do you only see the world in polar opposites? Black and white, victim and perp?'

Kavanagh put her hand under the bandana and rested it on the pistol, then stared at him. He could see her pale blue eyes flashing under the shadow cast by her brows. 'You should go indoors and curl up next to your daughter. Get some sleep,' she said. 'Let the girl with the gun stay awake all night out here in the world of good and evil.'

NINE

Ford was woken by his phone ringing, a persistent trill that had entered his dreams before it woke him. He sat upright, thinking it was some strange bird trapped in the room, and was disoriented by the overhead light bulb shining in his eyes. He caught a flicker of movement through his squinting eyes, tried to focus them on the light, and when his vision cleared he saw that there was no bird, just a fat blowfly circling the bulb, its wings buzzing in harmony with the phone.

When he shook off the last of his dream and recognised where he was, he saw that Grace was sitting at the end of the bed, dressed in clean clothes: blue dungarees and a candy-striped red and white T-shirt. Kavanagh stood behind her, pulling back Grace's hair and weaving the strands together in a French plait. Her fingers moved with the same graceful movement she'd used on the pistol.

Ford rubbed his eyes, trying to remember where he'd left his phone. He looked for the bedside table but it had gone, leaving only a tide mark on the wall where the light had faded the wood panelling. He rolled across the bed and hung over the edge, searching for his pants on the floor. He felt the cold blast of the air-conditioner on his bare legs and became aware that he was dressed only in his boxers. He glanced at Kavanagh and pulled the sheet around himself. He found his pants and rummaged through the pockets until he found the phone. He looked at the screen but his eyes still stung from the bright light and the numbers were a blur. He pressed to answer and put it to his ear.

'Hello?' he said. There was silence on the other end. He looked at the screen again and could now read the number.

'Diane?' he said. 'I tried calling you last night. I was worried.'

There was a long pause before she spoke. 'Where are you now?' she said.

'I'm still in Newman.'

'Then I'm glad I caught you before you left.' Her voice was still hesitant. Kavanagh continued to plait Grace's hair, her back to Ford, but he could tell by the angle of her head that she was straining to hear the voice on the phone. Ford stood up and went to the door, pulling the sheet with him. He opened it and felt the warm air outside hit his face. He meant to step outside, but it was still dark.

'What time is it?' he said, shutting the door. 'You woke me.'

'Nearly six,' said Diane. 'Have you found that detective?'

'Yes,' said Ford. At this Kavanagh raised her head and looked at him and he knew she could hear it all. He moved the phone away from his ear so she could hear more clearly.

'DC Kavanagh will be travelling with me to Broome.'

'You can't come here,' said Diane, her voice urgent. He started to speak but she cut him off. 'Someone's here in Broome. Looking for me. I've seen them. Chinese guys.'

'Have they seen you?'

'No. I changed my hair. I wear hats, dark glasses. I walked right past them and they didn't see me.'

'But you recognised them?'

'Maybe. At the casino.' She sounded short of breath.

'We can be there in ten hours, mid-afternoon. Can you keep out of sight until then?'

'I've left Broome already. I'm scared. I hired a car yesterday. I left last night. My phone wouldn't have got a signal out on the road.'

'Where are you now?'

'Sandfire Roadhouse. Three hours south of Broome. Is Grace with you?'

'She's right here.'

'I want to see her.'

'That's what we're trying to sort out here,' he said. 'You can come to us.'

Kavanagh shook her head, her eyes wide. She leaned in close and he put his hand over the phone. 'We need to stay away from those two in town,' she whispered. Ford nodded.

'Meet me halfway,' said Diane. 'That would be quickest. Marble Bar. That's about the same distance from you as it is from me.'

'I know the road,' said Ford. 'It's unsealed all the way from here. Four hours maybe. We can be there by lunchtime.'

'Is that detective with you now?'

He looked at Kavanagh and she shrugged.

'You want to talk to her?'

'No. I'll tell her everything in Marble Bar. Please hurry.' With that she hung up.

Kavanagh checked her watch then nodded at Ford. 'We'd better get on the road before the sun comes up,' she said.

Grace was looking up at him, her eyes wide. 'Was that Mummy?'

He was so used to the tone and pitch of her voice that sometimes she caught him unawares, her voice as small as her body, reminding him how young she was. He wondered how much she had understood. He tried a limp smile. 'Yes, that was Mummy.'

'I want to speak to her,' said Grace.

'We'll see her soon,' Ford said.

Grace's face fell. 'Doesn't she want to talk to me?'

'Of course she does. She wants to see you.' Grace started pulling at her hair. 'Don't mess it,' said Ford. 'I like your hair like that.'

She ran a hand over the neat plait, from where it started on the crown of her head down to the elastic tied around its tip. She tilted her head and gave him the broad smile she had learned from some princess movie on TV. 'Rose did my hair,' she said.

'I watched her do it,' said Ford.

'It's pony hair,' said Grace. 'Rose has a pony.'

Kavanagh looked from Ford to his daughter and hesitated before she said, 'I used to have a pony. Years ago now. In the country. I would wear my hair like this when I competed at country shows. Point to point mostly, show jumping sometimes. My mother would plait it for me.'

'I can't imagine you with long hair,' said Ford.

'I don't believe that for a minute.'

'Then maybe I can't picture you as a child.' Ford picked up his shirt and thrust his arms into the sleeves.

'I wore it long until my mum died,' said Kavanagh. 'After that I got it cut by the same barber as my father. This old bloke in town with one of those hydraulic swivel chairs that he'd pump with his foot. Then I'd sit on the bench reading old fishing magazines while my dad got his hair cut in the same style, giving the barber all the gossip from the police station. I was fifteen before I plucked up the courage to ask him to drive me to the next town. There was a ladies' hairdresser there.'

'But you still wear it short,' said Ford.

'Makes it easier on the job.'

'Still the tomboy,' he said.

'Because my dad didn't know how to dress me,' she said, pulling at the straps of Grace's dungarees and adjusting the length. 'This is how a man dresses a little girl.'

'I've tried girly clothes but she won't touch them,' he said. 'I put her in a pink tutu and fairy wings for a party once. She came back with it ripped and covered in dirt. These clothes last a little longer.' He knelt down next to Grace and put her shoes on, then tickled her as he stood up, listening to her laugh.

Kavanagh had the door open, looking out at the sky for the approaching dawn, and Ford felt the warm air flood into the room. She pulled on her leather jacket, then picked up her backpack and Grace's bag and stepped through the door.

Grace padded behind her and when Kavanagh let her hand drop to her side, Grace took it in her own and they stood together on the verandah under the flickering bulb, waiting for Ford. He pulled on his pants and stumbled barefoot on to the verandah, shutting the door behind him and leaving the key in the lock. He sat on the chair, pulled on his boots, then marched off towards the car, his boot laces trailing behind him.

He was in the driver's seat with the engine running before Kavanagh caught up. She buckled Grace into her seat, then climbed in the back next to her. Kavanagh slammed the door and jammed her backpack against the window and laid her head on it. Ford looked over his shoulder at her and without opening her eyes, she said, 'Get moving. I've got some sleep to catch up on.'

He closed his own door and the internal light went out. He listened to them trying to get comfortable in the back seat, the car rocking gently on its springs as they settled. The light in the east was visible through the trees, the sky turning pink, and Ford leaned forward in his seat to look up through the windscreen to catch the last stars. He turned on the headlights and they disappeared.

He reset the trip mileage counter to zero, then looked at his watch. Just after six, and two hundred kilometres of dirt road to Nullagine. They could be there for breakfast and Marble Bar was only an hour beyond that.

He drove slowly between the trees and out on to the forecourt, studying all the vehicles lined up in front of the roadhouse. They were all trucks, most with lights showing behind the curtains pulled across their windows, their drivers awake and readying themselves for the journey ahead. A road train passed on the highway, ranks of coloured bulbs along its flanks, its headlights flooding the road. Ford waited until the highway was empty and dark as far as he could see before he pulled out and turned north.

After passing the airport he checked his mirrors to make certain his were the only lights on the road before he took the right turn signposted to Marble Bar. The road went east into the rising sun, hovering just above the horizon and forcing him to reach for his sunglasses. The road then swung north to pass through the gap in the Ophthalmia Range, the sun now hitting the front of the ridge, painting it orange and lighting the sky behind it a deep blue.

As he passed through the gap he adjusted his mirror to look at the girls in the back seat. Kavanagh had found his picnic blanket and spread it over them both, so he could only make out their hair spilling over the edge of it.

As the road levelled out on to the broad rocky plain, the tarmac stopped and the road became a broad strip of red gravel, corrugated and dotted with potholes. He felt the car snaking on the loose surface, so he dropped his speed. The road stretched straight to the horizon ahead of him and, in his mirror, through the cloud of dust boiling behind him, he could see it stretching out to the shadow of the ridge. On all that stretch of road, maybe thirty kilometres, he was the only thing moving. He allowed himself to relax. He turned the radio on and hit the scan button, but could only find scraps of music fading into static. He turned it off and let the rhythm of the road take him, the rumble of the wheels on the corrugations, the vibration passing through the steering wheel into his fingertips, the quiet whirr of the air-con. He let his thoughts drift and his mind wander as the rocks and spinifex drifted past.

He thought about the last time he had seen his wife, watching her walk out of the hangar to the plane, leaving her daughter behind. He pictured the expression on her face, and not for the first time he tried to decipher it. For the first few days after she had gone, those nights alone with Grace in his bare apartment, clinging to each other in his bed, he had thought that Diane's tears had been brought about by despair. He decided she had boarded the plane under duress, McCann with a firm grip on her arm, guiding her up the steps to the plane, whispering threats in her ear.

After that first week he changed his mind. He decided her tears had been remorse for what she had done to him, leaving him at the mercy of Roth and his men. He had expected to hear from her soon after she left. He knew she was in Macau with McCann, and thought about trying to contact her there, for Grace's sake, but as the weeks stretched into months he changed his mind again. He had heard the evidence at the inquest, learnt how meticulously she had presented the fraudulent geological report at the Gwardar mine, had seen how complicit she had been with McCann in using the report to boost the share price, and came to know how thoroughly she had covered her tracks and pointed the finger of blame at her business partner, Matthew Walsh.

Now that Walsh was dead he had reinterpreted her actions in the hangar, and he knew he could not allow himself to be blinded again. He remembered this, along with all the other mistakes he had made, and promised never to make again.

Promises were easier now. He had made a lot of them when he'd been drinking and none of them had been worth much.

As the sun rose higher the temperature climbed and he could feel it radiating off the windows. The sky was now a pale bleached blue. The flat mesas of the Chichester Ranges were visible ahead and signs showing the distance to Nullagine had appeared. From habit his eyes went to the instrument panel and he checked the fuel, the engine temperature and the distance travelled since he had reset the trip counter. It would be wise to refuel at Nullagine when they stopped for breakfast and a toilet break.

The road wove through the ranges, lonely flat-topped hills rising from the plain. He could see the bare hills ahead, scarred by shallow strip mining of iron ore, a column of dust rising almost vertically, no breath of wind to disturb it. The readout on the dashboard told him the temperature outside was thirty-five degrees.

The trees clustered in a hollow between the hills showed him where the town was, and soon he saw the first tidy weatherboard houses. The road crossed the dry river bed and he came to a stop at the junction that marked the centre of town. On the corner stood the group of squat buildings that made up the Conglomerate Hotel, its roof a harlequin patchwork of mismatched corrugated-iron sheets of different colours, its low verandah strewn with antique mining equipment assembled for display. He followed the sign to Marble Bar and as the road started rising to the ridge out of town, he saw the petrol station, a featureless concrete block with the word 'ROADHOUSE' painted on the end wall in metre-high block letters. A single eucalypt clung to life next to a telegraph pole in the broad expanse of the bitumen forecourt, and a simple steel roof stretched out from the building to cast a small rectangle of shade over the fuel bowsers.

He stopped the Toyota in the shade beside the diesel pump and left the engine running while he got out to stretch his legs. A wave of oppressive heat and humidity hit him, bearing down on him and squeezing a long yawn from his chest. He opened the back door and found Grace peeking at him from over the top of the blanket.

'We've stopped for breakfast,' he said.

She caught his yawn as if it were infectious, stretching her jaw before she said, 'I want pancakes.'

'I doubt they'll have them here,' he said. 'It's only a roadhouse.'

'I want you to make me pancakes.'

He sighed. 'I make pancakes on a Sunday. What day is it today?'

When Grace didn't answer, Kavanagh said, 'It's Saturday.' Her eyes were still closed.

Ford had to think carefully, count back to when he had been at work. It felt like days but it had only been one night. Time seemed to have slowed.

TEN

Ford stood by the fuel tank, pumping diesel into the LandCruiser. Kavanagh opened the rear door yawning, squinting against the bright light. She stepped down and looked around through narrowed eyes until she saw the door to the roadhouse and then shuffled off in that direction, putting her hands behind her head and stretching as she went.

Grace threw off the blanket and watched Kavanagh walk away, then put her hands behind her head and repeated the stretch. Her hands found her plait and pulled it forward in front of her eyes to study it.

By the time the big tank on the Toyota was full, Kavanagh had come back out of the roadhouse wearing a cheap straw hat, broad-brimmed cowboy style, to shade her eyes.

'You find anything good for breakfast in there, pardner, or just the hat?' said Ford, hanging up the fuel hose.

She didn't speak, just lifted her hands to show him a fistful of muesli bars in one, and a pair of water bottles dangling from between the fingers of the other.

'I need something more substantial,' he said.

'Roadhouse food,' she said. 'It'll clog your arteries.'

Ford felt his mouth water and checked his pocket for his wallet before wandering inside. Two women watched him from behind the counter as he swung open the door and the bell rang. The young woman behind the till gave him half a smile, swept the lank blonde hair from in front of her face and waited while he studied the menu on the wall. It was all fried food, and there was a pie warmer full of pre-cooked burgers and rolls. Ford ordered a bacon sandwich and a coffee from the second woman, whose face was red and damp from standing over the grill. She wiped her brow with her apron and gave him a look that made him wish he had taken something from the pie warmer.

He paid for the fuel and the food and the woman handed him a paper bag. He looked inside to find two flat, limp slices of white bread with a thin stripe of barbecue sauce between, the bacon only evident by its smell. He heard the car horn sounding outside, and saw Kavanagh waving to him, her face a picture of frustration. He tucked the sandwich under his arm, picked up the ribbed cardboard cup of coffee and with his free hand opened the door.

When he stepped out into the heat the big man was standing in the middle of the driveway facing him, between him and the Toyota. It was a moment before Ford took in the black suit and tie, the broad brown face, and recognised the driver of the blue Nissan. He looked around and saw it parked in front of the Toyota, nose-to-nose, their bull bars touching. Beyond both vehicles the Chinese man was standing out on the forecourt in the blaring sun under the shade of his umbrella. His black hair was cut short and thick in a mop-top bowl cut, and he wore the same black suit and tie. A cigarette dangled from the corner of his mouth, smoke curling up around his face, and he was watching Kavanagh. She was looking at him through the windscreen from the driver's seat of the Toyota, her eyes wide with concentration. She turned to Ford and pointed to the door to let him know she had locked herself in the car. Ford couldn't see Grace, and he hoped that Kavanagh had made her duck down in the footwell out of sight.

He turned back to face the man in front of him, who had not moved. He'd been letting Ford take his time assessing the situation, allowing him to work out how much trouble he was in. He was huge, easily six inches taller than Ford, with broad shoulders that only a tailor-made suit could cover. His crisp white shirt and black tie fitted snugly around a bull neck and the top button was done up despite the heat. The only sign that he was aware of the temperature was a few beads of sweat on the dark skin of his shaved head. Tattoos twisted up his neck and looped around his right ear in a series of spirals, spreading into delicate swirls that cut across his forehead and cheek. His arms were folded across his chest, his back straight.

'How are you today?' he said, the faintest smile curling his lips. The vowels were short and the consonants clipped, and if the size and colour of the man had not told Ford he was Maori, then the tattoos and the accent did.

'I'm doing fine,' said Ford. He grinned to show the Maori he was easy-going, keeping it together, but the man just kept staring, widening his eyes slightly. Ford took the sandwich from under his arm and lifted the coffee to take a sip. 'You were following us all of yesterday,' he said. 'Maybe now you'll introduce yourself.'

'Are you asking me my name?'

Ford nodded. 'And I'd like to know why you're following me.'

'Oh, I think you've got a fair idea, mate.'

'You're looking for my wife,' said Ford. That provoked a smile from the Maori, so he tried again. 'You work for Roth.' This time the smile vanished.

'Look at the colour of my skin, man,' he said, holding his hand up in front of his face and looking at the brown skin across the back of it, flexing the scarred knuckles. 'Why would someone like me take orders from an Afrikaner bastard like him?'

'So you know him?' said Ford.

'Of course I know him. That guy thinks everyone works for him, even when he's a hired hand himself. Thinks everyone's just waiting around for him to give the order.'

'You know where he is?'

'Oh, he'll be around here somewhere. That fucker always shows up when there's trouble. Don't know if he causes it or if the smell attracts him. When you run into him, be sure to let me know where he is.'

'You met him in Macau?'

'The man called me a *kaffir* to my face. The first man I ever met who, when he looked at me, didn't think twice about making trouble.'

'I heard he left Macau. You looking for him here?' said Ford.

'I'll tell you what I heard. I heard you were the man that

shot him.' The Maori held out his hand and took a couple of steps towards Ford. 'My name is Bronson. I'd like to shake your hand, brother.'

Ford looked at his hand, then showed him his own, the coffee in one, the sandwich in the other, and shrugged.

'I hope you're not going to start fucking with me,' said Bronson, leaving his hand outstretched.

'What kind of thing would I do that you'd think of as fucking with you?' said Ford.

'You're fucking with me right now.' Bronson let his hand drop, his arm swinging loose at his side; he seemed to be finding his balance on the balls of his feet. Ford saw his right hand starting to move and watched it rise. He moved to duck out of the way of the uppercut, shifting his head swiftly into the path of Bronson's left jab. It caught him on the nose and the eye socket, a jet of blood shooting down across his chin.

'Fuck!' said Ford, dropping the coffee and staggering three steps backwards, his eyes streaming tears. He sat down hard on an oil drum beside the door and put a hand to his nose to stem the bleeding.

Bronson bent over, his hands on his knees, and looked Ford in the face. 'Oh, come on, man,' he said. 'That was just a little love tap. Make sure you were paying attention. You listening to me now?'

Ford nodded.

'I need you to tell your girlfriend to unlock the car and get out, or else I'll have to fetch a tyre iron from my car and break the windows, and that might mess up her face a little.'

'Don't bother,' said Kavanagh from behind him. 'I'm out

of the car.'

Bronson straightened up slowly and turned around. Kavanagh was leaning against the side of the LandCruiser, her arm stretched out along the bonnet and the pistol pointed at Bronson. His Chinese partner took three steps forward before Kavanagh swung the gun on to him and he stood still, his face as impassive as before.

'So you're the cop,' said Bronson.

'You're a smart guy,' said Kavanagh, turning the gun towards him.

'Nobody pulls a gun just to threaten someone. You draw, you shoot. You don't stand there talking, unless you're police.'

Ford could see that Kavanagh was afraid of him, and afraid of showing it. Her expression was vague, lost, then came back into character with an expression of determination.

'Take five steps backwards away from him,' she said. Bronson held his hands out to his side, palms towards her, and stepped back. Kavanagh looked over her shoulder at his partner.

'You need to walk around here behind our car where I can see you,' she said.

The Chinese man didn't flinch; he just finished his cigarette and dropped it on the ground.

'He doesn't speak much English,' said Bronson.

'Then you tell him to move,' said Kavanagh. 'He got a name?'

'We call him Wu.'

'Is there a surname to go with that?'

'That is his last name. At least, I think it is,' said Bronson.

'You never know with these Chinese names. One day it's forwards, the next they turn it around the other way, last name first.' Bronson was still relaxed, his arms hanging loose, showing her that he was cool, still in control despite the gun. 'We call him Wu Song,' he said, 'but that's just some nickname he was given by the boys.'

'Well, you tell him to move or things are going to get loud around here.'

Bronson jerked his thumb at his partner and said something short and harsh in Cantonese. Wu carefully folded his umbrella and stepped under the shade of the canopy. He walked slowly past the Toyota, Kavanagh tracking him as he went, until he was standing several metres away from Bronson, so that Kavanagh still had to swing the gun from one to the other.

'What's with the umbrella?' said Kavanagh.

'He's just staying out of the sun,' said Bronson. 'These Chinese, they're obsessed with white skin. Wu gets the piss taken out of him by the brothers in Macau for being so yellow. They tell him he's a peasant. He should see what life's like with skin like mine.'

'I need you to drop your guns,' said Kavanagh, moving to the back of the Toyota so she had a clearer line of fire.

'If we had guns, would we still be talking like this? We're unarmed, darling.'

'I'm not,' she said.

'We don't need guns.'

'You're going to need one soon.'

'It's not my style,' said Bronson. 'I never needed a gun in my life.' He tensed his arms, opening and closing his fists.

'I thought Macau was crawling with gangsters?'

'On the street, sure, but I'm in the casino. The creeps on the street know better than to step inside carrying. They do that and they end up at the bottom of the Pearl River.'

'That your job?'

'No, that's Wu's business. He deals with the brother-hoods. Don't let that Moe Howard bowl cut fool you. He's stone cold.'

'If he's Moe, you must be Curly with that shaved head,' said Ford. He was standing now, blood splashed down his shirt, still pinching the bridge of his nose. 'It looks like you're one Stooge short.'

'How you doing now?' said Bronson, turning to him and smiling. 'Let me see it,' he said. Ford took his hand away from his nose. 'You're alright, man. It's not busted.'

'If Wu is the muscle, what's your job?' asked Kavanagh.

'I'm more of what you might call middle management.'

'And who's at the top of the tree? McCann?' asked Ford.

Bronson laughed out loud at that, but didn't answer. Kavanagh nodded at Ford to join her at the car. He shuffled across the forecourt, unsteady on his legs, and turned to look through the window of the roadhouse. The two women behind the counter were staring back at him wide-eyed. He put a finger to his lips, then went and stood behind Kavanagh.

'Which one of you killed Harding?' she said.

Bronson shrugged. 'Who's that?' he said, his face as blank as Wu's.

'The guy in my house,' said Ford. 'His name was Harding.'
Bronson shook his head.

'You didn't make much effort at being inconspicuous,'

said Kavanagh. 'We saw you following us all day.'

'Yeah, well,' said Bronson. 'Macau's the most crowded city on the planet. Easy to get lost in a crowd. Out here, seriously, where the fuck is everybody? We drove three hours through this wasteland, and never saw another car. All we saw were flies. The only other creature we saw was a dead kangaroo on the road, and all that fucker was doing was breeding more flies.'

'You were seen outside my house,' said Ford. 'You're quite the odd couple.'

'We don't exactly blend into the environment,' said Bronson. 'You know what you get if you cross a Maori with a Chinaman?'

'Tell me.'

'A car thief that can't drive.'

Kavanagh's face stayed determined, the gun resting on the roof of the car. She opened the driver's door and waved Ford inside. 'Get in, you're driving,' she said.

'You should do as your girlfriend says,' said Bronson, grinning, still enjoying it.

'She's not my girlfriend,' said Ford.

'You sure about that?'

'I would've noticed.'

'You're right,' said Bronson. 'You don't have what it takes to handle a woman like her.'

Kavanagh stepped forward to let Ford sit behind the wheel. He looked over his shoulder for Grace in the backseat. There was movement under the blanket in the footwell, but no sound. He unwrapped the bacon sandwich and took a bite.

'Start the engine,' said Kavanagh, trying to keep her voice

steady. She circled around the back of the Toyota, the gun staying levelled at the men in black. She opened the passenger door, and turning swiftly brought the gun to bear on the blue Nissan. She fired three times, putting a bullet in each front tyre and the third in the radiator. She sat down, slammed the door and slapped the dashboard. 'Get us out of here,' she barked.

Ford slammed the LandCruiser into reverse and, as it lurched backwards with the wheels spinning, the two men calmly watched them pass.

When clear of the bowsers, Ford put it in drive and gunned the engine, roaring off down the highway, the silhouettes of the two men receding in his mirror.

ELEVEN

The road north from Nullagine passed through a series of stony valleys, the ridges bare and blackened from a recent bushfire, the rocks painted from a simple palette of red and black under a bleached blue sky. The gravel road looked no different from the landscape either side of it, a barren strip swept clean of boulders, bearing the imprints of vehicles that had snaked between the potholes.

Ford and Kavanagh made no attempt to talk to each other. Even if they had felt the need for conversation, the noise inside the Toyota prevented it. The rumble of tyres over the corrugated road provided the bass line, the roar of the engine filled out the middle range and the rattle of the air-conditioner played over the top of it all.

Kavanagh was sitting up front, the cowboy hat pulled low over her eyes, her Cuban heels resting on the dash, cradling the pistol in her lap. She was pretending to sleep but Ford saw her hat twitch to one side every few moments to check the side mirror, which she had adjusted to let her see the road behind. Ford checked his own mirror regularly, but the view behind was the same as the road ahead, the only difference being the cloud of dust thrown up by the Toyota.

The road emerged from the hills and the horizon opened out to the east, falling away to a featureless plain of rocks and spinifex, and Ford had the sense of the continent stretching away from him, a thousand kilometres of flat desert reaching to the state border and carrying on beyond it. Ford watched as a willy-willy moved across the country, a dark column of dust swirling across the plain, a spinning vortex of hot air pulling red dirt upwards, swaying as it danced towards the horizon.

In the back seat, Grace had drifted off to sleep again, her plastic ponies arranged on the seat beside her, her head lolling against the window, her bare arms raised in goose bumps from the air-con. He reached around and tucked the blanket over her.

'You two don't talk much,' said Kavanagh from under the hat.

Ford turned his eyes back to the road, his hands resting lightly on the steering wheel, letting the four-wheel drive find what grip it could on the loose gravel so it could weave between the ridges of sand.

'I'm not much of a talker,' he said, 'and she takes after me. Self-contained.' He glanced at Kavanagh. 'I thought you'd understand that.'

'Does she miss Perth?'

Ford shook his head. 'She knows she'll be back there

soon. I'm just doing a year in Newman to tide us over, until the legal dispute over the trust fund is settled. Diane can help with that. Tell the receivers it's her money, not McCann's. Tell them to leave it alone.'

Kavanagh tilted the hat back on her head and opened her mouth to speak, but as she did the Toyota bucked and there was a solid thump in the suspension. The rear end swung sideways and Ford gripped the steering wheel harder as he fought the slide, gritting his teeth as the car bounced between potholes, the rear end fishtailing. As the car straightened, Ford stamped on the brake pedal and the Toyota skidded to a stop, spitting gravel from under the tyres and kicking up dust. Kavanagh was holding the handle on the dashboard, her hat fallen in her lap. Ford took a deep breath and let it out slowly. 'Puncture,' he said, trying to keep his voice level. 'In this heat, when they let go, they do it suddenly.'

He turned to Grace and smiled at her as she rubbed her eyes. 'Don't worry,' he said. 'I'll have it fixed in a few minutes.'

He stepped out of the cab into the furnace of the desert, the hot air hitting him in the face. He could feel the moisture in his eyes drying instantly and he blinked against it and squinted in the searing sunlight. He walked around to the back of the LandCruiser and surveyed the damage. The rear left tyre was flat but intact. He looked back down the road at the snaking skid mark in the gravel, and at the pothole they had hit. He waited for the cloud of dust to clear so he could see further down the road. There were no other cars in sight, the road empty to the horizon.

He could tell where the sun was without looking, he

could feel it on his body through his clothes, feel it burning through his hair onto his scalp. Heat shimmered off the road like fumes from fuel. There was nothing moving besides the willy-willy, still lazily waltzing eastwards. It looked black now, and following the column of air downwards he saw a smudge of smoke close to the ground, strands of it being pulled upwards into the spiral, and he stared at it until he could see the flames among the spinifex. The bushfire was at least a kilometre away, not moving fast enough to threaten the road. Something caught his eye among the flames, a dark shape moving swiftly, looping in the smoke above the fire. It turned and he saw its outline, a bird with broad wings and a forked triangular tail. It dived suddenly and disappeared into the long grass.

Kavanagh stepped down and blew out her cheeks in disgust at the heat, adjusting the hat on her head. She watched Ford as he opened the rear of the car and took out the spare and the jack, setting them down beside the rear wheel. 'Need a hand?' she asked.

'See if you can find me a flat rock,' said Ford, 'something to spread the load from the jack.'

She took the gun off the seat and tucked it into the back of her jeans, all the while staring back down the road. She walked around the front of the car and gazed out across the plain. Beside the road was a stack of boulders, rising above the spinifex where they had been cast aside when the road was cleared. Daubed across the flat face of the largest boulder in large white letters were the words 'Welcome to Hell'.

She stepped off the road and found a flat stone twice the span of her hand. She bent her knees and got her fingers under it to test it for weight. By the time she had shuffled back to the car Ford had the nuts off the wheel and was kneeling beside the car, waiting. She dropped the stone next to him, raising a plume of dust in his face. He coughed and nodded his thanks, scooting the rock under the car and lining up the jack on top of it.

While Ford lifted the car and swapped the wheel she stood with her back to him, her hands on her hips, squinting from under the hat, watching the road. There was no sound but the slight hiss of wind through the spinifex, and the occasional clash of metal against metal from the tyre iron, the ringing muffled by the heat in the air.

Ford dropped the jack and tightened the nuts on the new wheel, then stood the flat tyre on its rim. He rolled it slowly forward until he found the puncture. It was a small, neat hole in the middle of the tread. He felt the hole with his finger. 'Not so bad. The last blowout I had up here shredded the whole thing. Scattered ribbons of rubber across the road and left me riding on my rim.'

He lifted the tyre into the back of the Toyota, opened the esky and picked out a water bottle. He took a long drag and tugged at his shirt where the sweat was sticking to his skin. He passed the bottle to Kavanagh and followed her gaze down the road.

'How far behind us are they?' he said.

She took a drink and thought about it. 'It doesn't really matter,' she said. 'They knew we'd be on this road. They were in Nullagine ahead of us. That means they know where we're going as well. Our only chance is to keep moving and get what we want from Marble Bar before they catch up.'

'And what is it exactly you want from there?'

She handed him the bottle. 'Gold,' she said.

He slammed the back doors and walked around to the driver's door. 'Gold is not the only reason we're going there.'

She looked at him over the roof of the car and swatted away the flies from her face. 'You're right,' she said. 'Roth is going to be there.'

TWELVE

A series of rusted iron signs announced their arrival in Marble Bar, proudly declaring it the hottest town in Australia. It nestled between low yellow hills, the highest topped with a water tank offering another welcome to the town, painted in large black letters across the concrete. The buildings either side of the road seemed deserted, the houses shuttered against the midday heat. There were no cars on the street, nobody outdoors at all. The wide main street swept gently downhill, a row of slender gum trees casting almost no shadow, and on their right Ford spotted the Ironclad Hotel, a low accretion of squat buildings with gables of varying heights, tied together by a sagging verandah. The walls and roof were clad in corrugated iron, and all the windows were dark and lifeless. There were two cars parked outside, the only ones in the street, and the front door was open, a dark rectangle with no light showing inside.

The broad median strip in the road stopped them from

pulling in to the pub, so they continued on. Opposite the hotel was a petrol station with two old bowsers, the building behind it declaring itself a post office and general store, but it was closed up and looked as deserted as every other building in the town.

As the road crossed over a dry stony creek bed an illuminated sign reminded Ford again that he was in the hottest town in Australia. To illustrate this the sign displayed the current temperature in large red digital numbers. As they passed it, the sign flicked over from thirty-nine to forty degrees Celsius.

Overlooking the creek bed was an imposing stone building, the only two-storey structure in the town, a series of steep roofs and high gables laced with elegant windows. Topped by tall chimneys and a tower, it stood proudly, a colonial relic from the time of the first gold rush, deposited in the bush in an optimistic gesture of civic pride as the foundation stone of a town that never grew to achieve the ambition of its first public building.

A sign pointing down the street identified it as the Government Buildings, and directed them to the police station. Ford swung the Toyota down the side street that led in front of the façade, and as they drove past he saw that it was a terrace broken into several departments, each with its own front door, and he read the signs over each. A large arched porch in the centre was marked as the Mining Registrar. The door next to it had a sign with the blue and white checkerboard of the police, but there were no vehicles outside. Under the shade of a small verandah, wedged between two gables, was a large white door. It was closed and there were no vehicles outside. Ford stopped the car beside the blue sign.

'You want to check in?' he asked.

Kavanagh shifted in her seat and plucked at the sleeves of her shirt. She looked past Ford at the white door to the station and then sucked her teeth. 'Nobody home,' she said. 'These small country stations are never open twenty-four seven. If the duty copper gets called away, they lock up.'

'I thought they'd have more than one guy to each station,' said Ford.

'Three, most likely,' she said. 'But they might not all be on shift.' She stared out the other window, across the creek to the town. 'Turn around and we'll check out the rest of the place. There must be life somewhere.'

Ford swung the car around at the end of the street and back on to the main street, away from the hotel. After a few hundred metres the old weatherboard houses petered out, the bitumen stopped and they were back out on a gravel road, a line of barren rocky hills running along the horizon in front of them. Ford stopped the car and turned it slowly in the road.

A white horse stood in the parched yellow grassland that bordered the road, sheltering under the sparse shade of a bloodwood tree. It was old, its mane grown long, its back concave. It leaned against the tree, one hind leg lifted off the ground, its tail flicking at the swarm of flies that surrounded it. It gazed at them forlornly, blinking its eyelashes to fend off the flies crawling around its eyes, seeking out the moisture. Kavanagh laughed. 'That's the first inhabitant we've seen,' she said. 'It really is a one-horse town.'

Ford drove back up the main street and pulled up in front of the Ironclad Hotel, beside the two other cars. One was a battered Land Rover with a vast bull bar on the front, most of its panels replaced with plain aluminium that looked as if it had been hand-beaten. The other was a new HiLux ute, fitted with lights on the roof to the same mining spec as Ford's vehicle, a red, black and yellow logo he didn't recognise on the door.

Ford got out and opened the back door for Grace, her eyes squinting against the bright light, yawning as she got down. 'Where are we?' she said, as Ford led her under the shade of the verandah. Ford looked into the shadows beyond the open door, a trickle of cool air leaking from the darkness out into the bright sunshine. Kavanagh joined them, her hand fidgeting with the hem of her shirt, pulling it down over the waistband of her jeans where she had tucked the pistol. Grace stood between them, looking from one to the other, waiting for them to speak. One hand found Kavanagh's and took hold of it, the other grasped her father's hand, then she stepped forward, pulling both of them through the door of the hotel.

They stood together just inside, waiting for their eyes to adjust to the gloom, enjoying the cool. The front door opened directly on to a large room with a vaulted ceiling, clad in the same corrugated iron as the exterior, decorated with road signs and old enamel advertisements. A wooden bar ran along one wall, and the woman behind it turned to them and smiled. Ford returned her smile and stepped forwards, pulling Grace and Kavanagh with him. The wall opposite the bar was lined with furniture: a pair of battered couches covered with threadbare patchwork blankets, and a single armchair with great curved arms.

The only customer was sitting in it, a small dark man, wiry

arms poking out of a black American football shirt, Pittsburgh Steelers, yellow stripes on the sleeves and a large number 69 across the chest. The shirt had been made for a bigger man, and it hung off him like he was a coat-hanger. He wore a pair of loose black athletic shorts and his skinny legs were stuck out in front of him, thongs dangling from his broad toes. He was slurping noodles loudly from a bowl in his lap, poking them into his mouth with a pair of chopsticks. Brown eyes stared at Ford from under a new baseball cap, the brim ironed dead flat, twisted slightly to one side. Ford smiled at him and guessed his age as mid-twenties. The man's expression did not change, he kept staring, and Ford realised he was not looking at him, but over his head at the TV screen mounted high on the wall opposite, which was showing football with the sound down.

Ford turned back to the woman behind the bar. She was big and pretty and pale-skinned, broad across the shoulders and hips, heavy breasts pushing against the front of her black singlet, the neck of it straining to contain her cleavage. She pushed back the lank brown hair that hung past her shoulders. 'Hi there,' she said, her voice deep and husky. She spread her arms wide in welcome and put her hands flat on the bar, leaning forward so that her chest rested on the counter. Her small brown eyes creased as she smiled. 'What can I get you?'

'Hi,' said Ford, trying to maintain his smile. He looked past her along the bar and through the archway that led to a back room. It was unoccupied, bare except for a pool table and a jukebox, which was playing soft rock at low volume. 'We were supposed to be meeting someone here. Has anybody been in?' he said.

'We only just opened for lunch,' she said. Ford saw her smile slide as she noticed the cut across his nose and the bruising on his eye, before she recovered and pumped it back up into a wide grin. 'Were you looking for one of the regulars?'

'No, someone from out of town. Any strangers been through?'

'Only youse three,' said the man from the chair. He was watching them carefully now. He stood up and carried his drink and empty bowl over to the bar. He put the bowl on the counter and took a last swig from the beer before pulling the empty can from the foam stubby-holder and crushing it. 'Same again, Stacey, darling,' he said.

The barmaid opened the galvanised steel door on the large icebox that filled the wall behind the bar and reached for a can of beer. 'Not that one,' he said. 'Get me a frosty one from the back.'

She gave it to him and he popped the top, watched it foam, then took a long pull.

'You're going to have to settle that tab soon, Muddy,' said Stacey, 'or the man will cut you off.'

'He'd never do that,' said Muddy. 'End of the month, I always settle.' He smacked his lips and winked at the barmaid, taking off his cap and running a hand through his long curly black hair, pushing it back and tucking it under the cap, adjusting it so the peak pointed backwards. He then looked over Ford's head at the TV screen, occasionally dropping his eyes to glance at Kavanagh.

'Can I get you a drink while you wait?' said Stacey to Ford, wiping the bar and trying to look busy. 'How about some lunch?'

Ford sat down on the stool at the end of the bar. He noticed there were no beer pumps; all the beer was in cans and bottles in the icebox. 'I'll have whatever this fella's having,' he said. He then turned to Kavanagh. She stood behind his daughter, a hand on either shoulder, looking warily around the room.

Grace was wide-eyed, and Ford realised it was the first time he had taken her inside a bar. 'Hungry?' he asked her. Grace nodded and Kavanagh shrugged.

He turned to the man called Muddy and nodded towards the empty bowl. 'Those noodles good, mate?'

Muddy grinned. 'They're deadly, bro,' he said. 'The cook's Chinese. He does cracking noodles, stir-fry, all that stuff. Good curry too. He hasn't quite mastered the parma yet, so best give that a miss.'

Stacey put Ford's beer on the counter and he picked it up and pressed the cold can against his forehead, rolling it down his temples, then held it against the bruise on his eye. He pulled the tab and drank deeply, feeling the icy beer burn his throat, the bubbles bursting up his nose. When he lowered the can he saw Kavanagh glowering at him. 'I thought you were on the wagon?' she said through her teeth.

'Did I say that?'

'I haven't seen you take a drink since I came up north,' she said.

'I've hardly had the chance,' said Ford. 'It's my day off today. I don't drink when I'm rostered on, because the testing is stricter up here, big multinational and all. The gold industry was all about security, but here it's all health and safety. Bigger trucks, more explosives, a lot more mess to clean up if someone fucks up.'

'Your old lady nagging you, man?' said Muddy.

Ford turned to him. 'She's not my wife.'

'Sure sounds like one.'

Kavanagh scowled at both of them. 'Why don't you ring your wife?' she said. 'See when she's going to get here.'

Ford finished the beer, took his phone out of his pocket, and hit redial. As he listened to it ring, Kavanagh stepped up to the bar with Grace and waved to Stacey to bring two beers. When the barmaid laid the two cans on the counter, Ford noticed a mark on the inside of her forearm. At first he thought it was a scar, but looking closer he saw it was a tattoo in blue ink: a long straight line running from her wrist to the inside of her elbow, the line interrupted at regular intervals by a zigzag.

The phone rang out and he killed the connection and put the phone in his pocket, shaking his head at Kavanagh. He picked up the beer and drank it. 'That first beer disappeared into me like water into the parched earth,' he said.

He picked up Grace and sat her on his knee. 'Would you like some noodles?' She nodded, and so he ordered two bowls from Stacey. As she wrote it out on her pad, he said to her, 'That petrol station over the road, will it open today?'

She shook her head. 'They're Seventh-day Adventists,' she said. 'They open Sunday. Don't ask me how that works. You need fuel?'

'No, we had a flat tyre out on the road. I thought someone over there might be able to fix it. I don't like driving out here without a spare.'

'I can fix that for you,' said Muddy, turning his attention away from the TV. 'Bring it round the back into the yard and I'll sort you out.'

Ford looked unsure. 'You know what you're doing?'

Muddy folded his arms across his chest, cuddling his beer. He tilted his head and looked sideways at Ford. 'I'm a fully trained diesel fitter,' he said. 'I can fix a fucking puncture. I heard you pull up outside. Without looking I can tell you're driving a LandCruiser with the big VD eight cylinder. Your timing's a bit off and you're running a little rich. I can fix that for you too, if you're not going to be a condescending bastard about it.'

'Muddy will fix you up,' said a voice from the back room. Ford looked around to see an old man walking through the archway. 'He can fix anything. Muddy's the guy they can't root, shoot or electrocute,' he said.

The old man was small, skinny, and he walked with a stooped back. He wore a faded khaki shirt and matching shorts, frayed at the hem with red dust ground into the seams. His legs and arms were thin and gnarled, dappled brown and white with liver spots and sun scars. He peered at them from under the wide brim of a battered grey Akubra, its crown stained black with a ring of sweat.

He stopped at the bar and looked hard at Ford, his eyes sparkling behind his wire-rimmed glasses. He tugged at the long grey beard that hung from his chin and spilled over the collar of his shirt, cut square at the end in the colonial style.

'Jeez,' he said, 'you step out of the bar for ten minutes for a shit and a smoke and some bastard steals your place at the bar.'

Ford and Grace both looked at him and then at all the empty stools along the bar. The old man leaned across in front of them and tapped a calloused finger on a small brass plaque screwed into the counter. Ford leaned over and squinted to read the words engraved into it: 'This seat is reserved for Bobby Dazzler, revered patron of this establishment.'

'I take it this is you?' said Ford.

The old man smiled and showed two large gold teeth. 'Would you jump in my grave as quick?'

Ford gave him a small bow from the shoulder, and stood up, carrying Grace. He walked to the other side of the bar.

Bobby Dazzler took his place of honour at the end of the bar. He nodded to Stacey and she put a cold beer in front of him. He smiled at her. 'Shame on you,' he said. 'You just can't get the staff these days.'

'I thought you'd gone home,' she said.

'Thirty years I've been smoking and drinking in this hotel,' said Bobby Dazzler. 'Half those nicotine stains on the ceiling must be mine. Now you make me go outside to smoke in the yard with the dogs.'

'We didn't change the law,' said Stacey.

'I don't mind,' he said. 'Them dogs can hold a better conversation than half the dumb bastards that hang around this bar.'

Ford looked at the yellow stains on the man's fingers, the dirt caked under his nails and the dust coating his scuffed boots.

'You been working today?' he asked.

The old man stared at the can of beer in his hands. 'I have,' he said. 'Not working now.'

'Knocked off early?'

The old man sighed and didn't answer. Muddy said, 'Bobby Dazzler works like the meat ants. Gets up early and gets his work done before the heat gets unbearable.'

'And if you'll all leave me in peace, I might let that bloke in the kitchen ruin a steak for me,' said Bobby.

Kavanagh tapped Ford on the shoulder and spoke quietly in his ear. 'If we're going to be waiting here for her, it would be good to get the car out of sight. You should take him up on his offer. Take it around the back.'

Ford nodded and set Grace down on a stool at the bar. The cook came through from the back. He was young and fresh-faced, his hair gelled up in spikes, his cheeks glowing from the heat in the kitchen and from the steam coming off the two bowls of noodles he was carrying. Stacey nodded towards Ford and the cook put them down on the counter. 'Chopsticks or cutlery?' he asked, no trace of an accent.

'Chopsticks for me,' said Ford, 'and a fork for the little lady.'

'And I'll have the steak,' said Bobby Dazzler, his voice too loud, echoing off the iron walls. 'But only if you promise me you'll only turn the bastard once. I don't know how they cook it where you come from, but I don't want you to cremate the bloody thing.'

The cook rolled his eyes and winked at Grace, who smiled.

'Where do you come from?' asked Ford.

'Broome,' said the cook, disappearing back towards the kitchen.

Kavanagh sat down next to Grace and dug the chopsticks into the second bowl, scooping a strand of noodles into her mouth. Ford was about to speak when she jabbed the air in front of him with the chopsticks. 'I couldn't resist, they smelled good,' she said. She turned to the old man. 'So,

Bobby Dazzler, you must know everything that goes on in this town.'

He fixed her with a stare. His eyes moved up and down as he took her in, then he leaned back away from the bar and stared at her legs. He leaned in towards her and spoke quietly.

If we can score a beer or gin,
in payment for the tales we spin,
to strangers who have wandered in
to Marble Bar.

Kavanagh paused while she swallowed a mouthful of noodles and then leaned even closer towards Bobby Dazzler. 'Don't recite that bullshit bush poetry to me ever again. Got it, Bobby?'

The old man smiled, giving her a full flash of the gold teeth. 'Only the mongrels in this hotel call me by that name. You can call me by my proper name. Henry, Henry Dussell.'

'Well then, Henry, what's been happening around here?'

'Why don't you buy me a drink?' Dussell said. 'Nothing would make an old prospector happier than a fine sheila buying him a drink.'

'You want another beer?'

'Nah,' he said. 'I'm trying this new whisky diet. I lost three days already.' He laughed, a low rumbling growl that broke into a cough. Kavanagh nodded to Stacey and she fished a whisky bottle from under the counter and put a glass in front of Dussell.

Kavanagh smiled at her. 'We might be staying here a while,' she said. 'I'm not sure the front bar is the best place for a little girl. Do you have somewhere else we could go? Maybe somewhere where Grace can watch TV?'

Stacey nodded. 'We got rooms out the back. I'll find the boss.' She pressed a button mounted on the wall over the till, and a distant door chime sounded.

A man Ford assumed was the owner appeared from the back room. He was younger than he'd expected, mid-thirties, thin and athletic, his dark hair cropped short and three days' growth on a chiselled chin. Sharp eyes looked towards Stacey with an eyebrow raised and she nodded at Ford.

The man stepped forward, forced a smile and extended a hand. 'I'm Tom Reynard. I own the place. Can I help you?'

Ford shook his hand and tried to return the firm pressure. 'Gareth Ford,' he said. 'We're in town for the day and wondered if there's somewhere we can freshen up. Stacey said you might be able to rent us a room.'

'In the middle of the day?' Reynard looked past Ford, his eyes moving up and down Kavanagh.

'We're waiting for somebody,' said Ford. 'I'd rather not have my daughter hanging around the bar.'

'Sure. We don't like kids in the front bar,' said Reynard, shifting his gaze to Grace, who was leaning over the counter with noodles hanging from her chin.

'Muddy here has agreed to fix our car while we're here.'

Muddy had his back to them, engrossed in the football, but raised a thumb in acknowledgement.

'What's wrong with it?' asked Reynard.

'A puncture in the spare, and Muddy reckons the timing's off.'

'Well, he'd know,' said Reynard. 'That little guy is as

good with diesels as he says. He has high self-esteem and a low centre of gravity.'

Muddy didn't turn around, but raised his middle finger in salute.

'The rooms are out the back,' said Reynard. 'Bring your car around and I'll show you.'

Ford stepped out of the front door and stood in the shade of the verandah. He lit a cigarette and looked up the main street, but the town was as deserted as when they had arrived.

'You won't see anything moving out here in this heat,' said Reynard, standing in the doorway. He studied Ford's car, taking in the company logo on the door. 'You're up from Newman,' he said. 'Just a day trip?'

'That was the plan,' said Ford. He glanced down the street at the digital sign, which now said the temperature was forty-two degrees. 'They tell me that Marble Bar has the highest mean temperature of any town in Australia.'

Reynard stepped up beside him and looked at the sign. 'And when they say it's mean, it's mean as a bastard,' he said. 'Every town has to have something to be proud of. Ours is a run of one hundred and sixty consecutive days when the temperature climbed above one hundred degrees Fahrenheit. That was back in 1924.'

'Is that the only thing this town has going for it?'

'It has a fucking awesome hotel.'

'Why so hot? We're only an hour from the coast. I'd have thought there would be places out in the interior that would be way hotter.'

'They reckon it's something to do with the hills,' said Reynard, waving a hand towards the range that crowded the horizon to the west. 'They hem us in, and it's like being at the bottom of a cauldron. The sun belts down on these rocks and the reflected heat belts back like a blast furnace.'

Ford took a deep drag on his cigarette and the smoke didn't seem any hotter than the air he was breathing.

'You one of those fucking gypsy miners from Newman?' said Reynard. 'The sort that can only stand to travel north of the twenty-sixth for two weeks at a time and then have to go running back to your accountant?'

Ford shook his head. 'I live in Newman. Permanent. What about you? You don't look like a local.'

'No. I was a driller. In Kalgoorlie first, then chasing around these hills looking for copper and molybdenum.'

'And you never got around to leaving?'

'I like this place. Marble Bar is the only town left up here untouched by the mining boom. These other towns, Newman, Hedland, Karratha, they make them look like Perth suburbs. All those suburban brick houses and double garages, fucking mini-malls and drive-through fast-food joints.' His eyes sparkled with something like pride. 'Marble Bar still looks like a frontier town, a place for pioneers and prospectors. Men of independent mind and spirit. Not these ranks of fly-in fly-out pussies that expect the world to be given to them on a fucking plate.'

Muddy poked his head out the door. 'I wondered what youse were doing out here,' he said, 'but since you're taking the air, you can crash me a smoke.'

Ford handed him the packet and his lighter.

'I was just telling our guest about Marble Bar,' said Reynard. 'How the rugged individualism of the Pilbara has gone, for the most part. That this town might just be the last stronghold of it.'

Muddy lit his cigarette and inhaled. 'You're talking to the wrong blackfella. Plenty of rugged individualism among my mob.'

'I can't stand Newman,' said Reynard. 'Company town, completely fucking corporate. Armies of you FIFO fuckers buzzing around the desert in matching hi-viz shirts, like little yellow worker bees.'

'They're not bees,' said Muddy. 'Bees give you honey, pollinate the trees. Those miners are parasites, eh? They're like *wajapi*, like locusts. Strip the country bare then move on.'

Ford nodded towards the Toyota HiLux with the red, black and yellow logo on the door. 'That your ute, Muddy? You work in mining too?'

Muddy laughed, blowing out smoke. 'Don't you try lumping me in with your mob. I work for a blackfella company. Independent contractors, working for all them multinationals. Difference is, the work and the money stays in our country, goes back into community, for the kids and that.'

Ford dropped the butt of his cigarette on the ground and stomped on it, then popped the locks of his car. He sat behind the wheel and Reynard pointed down the street and around to the right to show him the way. He pulled out, followed the directions, and looked for the back way into the hotel. Reynard appeared and opened a chain-link gate, a pair of big brown dogs at his heel, jumping up at him, tails wagging. Ford drove through into a wide gravel yard; there was a small square of grass under the shade of a sturdy eucalypt, surrounded by a collection of scattered outbuildings. Most were corrugated iron, like the hotel, but some were prefab dongas salvaged from mine sites.

Reynard waved him towards a low cinder-block building along the east side, a single row of rooms opening on to a verandah, identical to the room they had stayed in the previous night at the roadhouse. Kavanagh and Stacey were standing under the shade of the roof, and Grace waved to him from one of the plastic chairs that stood outside each room.

By the time he had parked Reynard had opened the door to the end room and ushered everyone inside. The air in the room was hot and stale. 'What are you going to do with yourselves?' he said.

'I'm going to have one more beer in the bar, and then take a long, cold shower,' said Ford.

'You do that, but you'll soon be thirsty and dirty all over again,' said the landlord. 'And besides, the cold water here is the same temperature as the hot.' He gave Ford the key and shooed Stacey out the door as he left.

Kavanagh stood between the two double beds, trying to work the remote control to the air-conditioner. She slapped it against her thigh and the fan rattled into life, throwing a blast of damp air across the room. A counter ran down one side of the room, with a small fridge beneath it and a TV and kettle sitting on top. Ford turned on the TV and waited for a grainy picture to appear. Grace jumped onto the bed, arranged the pillows, and lined up her ponies to watch the television with her.

'If we're going to be hanging around here waiting for

your wife, then I'm going to take a shower,' said Kavanagh, 'so maybe you could go back to the bar and give us some space.'

Ford went to the door. 'Maybe I'll see if they have any more noodles. I never got the chance to eat mine.'

He stepped through the door and looked out across the yard. The main part of the hotel stretched along the far side towards the gate, and a low iron building ran along the side of the yard adjoining the road. A sign on its door announced that it was private, and Ford decided it must be where Reynard lived. In the angle between the two buildings was a paved area with a barbecue and a collection of mismatched chairs, a small lemon tree breaking through the concrete. A rusted swing set was standing on the square of lawn.

He crossed this patio and walked through a door into the hotel, finding himself in the pool room. He stepped through the archway into the bar and was met by a row of terrified faces.

Reynard and Stacey stood behind the bar, Muddy and Dussell were leaning on the stools in front of it, and all four of them looked at him with expressions of fear and bewilderment. Ford caught Muddy's eyes darting to his right; following them, he saw the silhouette of a man in the doorway, framed in bright white light from outside. He recognised the furled umbrella in the man's hand, and the outline of his bowl haircut.

'Here he is!' said a voice behind him, and Ford turned to see Bronson leaning casually against the wall beside the archway.

THIRTEEN

Bronson stepped out behind Ford, his broad shoulders fill-ing the archway. He leaned forward and stared at Ford's face, at the cut on his nose and the blackening ring around his eye. 'Jeez, that came up quick,' he said. 'You must bruise easy.'

Wu took a step inside the front door and lit a cigarette, the umbrella hooked over his elbow to leave both hands free.

Reynard was the only other person in the room who seemed relaxed; Stacey, Muddy and Dussell fidgeted, waiting to see what Bronson would do.

'Are these the people you were waiting for?' said Reynard, throwing Ford a little smile to let him know he was cool with the situation.

Ford turned around in the centre of the room, looking first at Wu and then at Bronson, blocking both his exits. There was a doorway behind the bar that led to the kitchen, but he had no route to it. Bronson was enjoying working the room.

Ford sighed and perched on the end of the sofa, his

elbows on his knees. 'These are a couple of guys I thought I'd left behind.'

Stacey took a couple of steps towards the kitchen door but Bronson raised a finger and with the slightest shake of his head she stopped.

'I'd hoped it might have taken you longer to fix your car,' said Ford.

Bronson turned to him and smiled. 'Normally it would take me about three minutes to jack another car,' he said. 'We waited an hour in that roadhouse and no other cars came through. Still, those ladies kept us going with coffee, no trouble at all, although Wu had never seen anything quite like those deep-fried spring-roll things they serve round here. What do you call them?'

'Chiko rolls,' said Ford.

'That's the beast,' said Bronson. 'Wu took one bite out of it and spat the thing onto the counter. No table manners, the Chinese.'

If Wu understood what was being said, there was no change in his expression to signal it.

Reynard walked lazily to the end of the bar and stood next to Dussell, put his hands flat on the counter, his head held high, letting them know they weren't yet in complete control. Bronson turned to him next, staring at him for a long while, making him wait for it. 'Would I be right if I said you were the manager of this place?' he said, folding his arms across his chest, leaning one shoulder against the frame of the arch.

'My name is above the door,' said Reynard. 'I'm the owner.' He straightened his back, pushed out his chest a little more.

'You make a living in this town?' asked Bronson,

keeping it casual. 'The streets are deserted. Where the fuck is everybody?'

Dussell took a small sip of his beer, watching them both out of the side of his right eye. 'There are more citizens of Marble Bar in the cemetery than there are walking the streets,' he said.

Bronson laughed, a deep rumble from his chest. The jukebox had gone quiet. 'I reckon there might be a few more underground before the weekend's over.'

Muddy sniggered, swivelling on his bar stool to face Bronson, his legs dangling, his thongs waving up and down, slapping against the soles of his feet. 'Is that why you two are dressed like undertakers?'

Bronson looked down at his black suit, brushed some specks of dust off the lapels, grabbed hold of the hem of his jacket and pulled it straight. 'You ever see an undertaker wearing tailoring as fine as this?'

'Must be difficult getting off-the-peg suits to fit, big bloke like you,' said Reynard.

'I get my suits hand-made in Savile Row,' said Bronson, holding his arms out wide to show the cut. 'Get measured up every time I pass through London.'

Muddy took off his baseball cap, swept his hair back under it and screwed it down onto his head, the peak still backwards. 'You dress like that, you look like you never been round here before, but you just walk in here like you own the place, brother.'

Bronson pushed off from the wall and took two quick steps towards Muddy, towering over him. 'Don't call me your brother,' he said. 'You're insulting my mother.' He licked the beads of sweat off his top lip, ran a hand across his damp forehead. He looked Muddy up and down, taking in his clothes. 'Just because my skin is a shade darker than these *pakeha*, you think I'm your brother? I got no connection to you. You're just some bush blackfella dressed up like he's straight outta Compton.'

The tension was broken by the cook appearing behind the bar, holding a plate laden with an oversize steak crowded by vegetables. His eyes swept the room, taking in Bronson and Wu and the apprehension on everyone's face, and a similar expression crept across his own. He put the steak in front of Dussell, then turned back towards the kitchen.

He was stopped by Wu shouting from the doorway, something sharp and unintelligible, abrupt and high-pitched. They all turned to face him in surprise, Ford thinking that it was the first time he had heard him speak. Wu's mouth barely moved as it let out three more bursts, which sounded to Ford like a small dog barking. Bronson didn't flinch but turned calmly to the cook. 'What's your name, buddy?'

The cook looked at his feet. 'Charlie,' he said.

'Well, Charlie, why don't you do as my friend asks and stay right where you are until we've sorted all this out.'

Charlie's eyes were wide, still trying to work out what was going on. 'I didn't understand what he was shouting about,' he said, wiping his hands on his apron, then brushing his hair from in front of his eyes. 'Where's he from?'

'We've come here from Macau. You ever been there?' asked Bronson.

Charlie shook his head. 'Never left Australia.' He looked at Reynard, and the landlord nodded his head slowly, trying to show the cook that everything was alright.

'My grandparents are from Hong Kong,' said Charlie, his face apologetic. 'My Cantonese is a bit old-fashioned. I only got bits of that.'

Bronson smiled, stepping forward into the room. 'My friend here is from the hills of Wenzhou,' he said, with a sweep of his hand towards Wu. 'He speaks some thick mountain dialect of Wu Chinese. He worked his way down the coast to Hong Kong and hopped on a ferry to Macau. Nobody could understand a word he said, so he had to learn Cantonese, but he's still got that thick hillbilly accent.' He was in the middle of the room now, enjoying the audience. 'The boys take the piss out of him, call him a peasant, so my brother here has learnt to keep his mouth shut. That's a lesson we could all use, eh?'

Muddy took a swig of his beer, watching Bronson. 'How come you call him your brother? You're not my bro but you're brother to this guy?'

'You think brotherhood is about skin?' Bronson said. 'I'm a brother to Wu because of an oath I took.'

Muddy's eyes were wide. 'That some sort of triad thing?'

Bronson laughed at this. 'You think you know something about that? You think they'd let me into something like that? You know fuck-all about Wu or me.'

'I know something,' Dussell said. He'd been sitting quietly staring at the steak, and now he was licking his lips. 'I know that if you'd stop grandstanding for a moment, perhaps Charlie could bring me a knife and fork and I could eat my fucking steak.'

Charlie nodded a quick apology and grabbed cutlery

from a pot beside the till. He laid them beside Dussell's plate and took a step back. Dussell looked at Bronson. 'You're welcome to watch,' he said, 'but I warn you, I chew with my mouth open.' He cut the steak and loaded his fork, then pushed it into his mouth. He looked at Stacey and winked.

Bronson walked up to the bar in front of Stacey, between Muddy and Dussell, and put an elbow on the counter. 'I reckon the old fella could do with another beer to wash down his lunch,' he said. He took a wallet from his inside pocket and placed two crisp fifties on the bar. 'Why don't you get everyone another drink, darling?'

Stacey looked across at Reynard, who nodded calmly. He was leaning against the icebox, his arms folded casually across his chest, his eyes swinging from Bronson to Wu and back again, until he caught Ford's eye. Ford felt that whatever Bronson had planned would be coming soon.

Stacey opened the icebox door beside Reynard and took out a six-pack of beer, handing one to her boss and putting one in front of Muddy and then Dussell. She clutched the remaining beers to her chest. 'You want one?' she asked Bronson.

He shook his head. 'I'll have a bourbon, neat,' he said. Stacey put down the cans, found a glass and a bottle from the shelf, and poured him a shot. He left it sitting on the bar.

'What about him?' said Stacey, nodding towards Wu.

Bronson raised an eyebrow. 'Wu doesn't touch alcohol,' he said. 'His body is a temple. All that Taoist shit.'

Bronson picked up the glass and downed the shot. His fingers passed back and forth across his forehead, tracing the swirls and spirals of his tattoo, his eyes fixed on the barmaid. 'I bet you hear everything, standing behind this bar,' he said. 'I bet you know all the dirty secrets of this town.'

She took a step back away from him, leaned against the cooler beside Reynard until her arm touched his. Bronson held out his hand to her. 'You don't need to be afraid of me, sweetheart. Come talk to me.'

She took a hesitant step forward. Reynard's eyes didn't move from the big Maori. Bronson reached out and took her hand in his, gently lifting it forward to rest on the polished wood of the counter, turning her wrist so that the tattoo along her forearm faced upwards. He lowered his head to examine it.

'I thought I'd seen all sorts of ink,' he said, 'but this line has got me.'

'It's my pulse,' Stacey said, trying to keep her voice steady.

Bronson ran his thumb down the line, stopping at each little zigzag. 'I don't get it,' he said.

'I got this fear of dying,' said Stacey, her voice breaking. 'Dying sudden, spontaneous like, in my sleep. I look at this tattoo and it reminds me I'm still alive.'

Bronson looked into her face, something like concern in his eyes. 'Why would a beautiful young woman like you worry about dying?' he said. 'Prime of life, you are.'

'Beautiful?' she said, a small smile creasing her mouth, her hair falling over her eyes. 'I'm not that. I'm kinda big.'

'You're not big, you're magnificent,' Bronson said. 'I've been in Macau so long, I forgot what a beautiful *gwailo* woman looks like. Haven't seen a big heavy pair of milky-white titties for years.'

Stacey looked up now, uncertain. Bronson's eyes were

fixed on her chest.

'I mean, you gotta love those little Chinese chicks,' Bronson said, 'but they're so small you have to have a few before you feel satisfied. They got no curves on them, just straight up and down.'

He looked up at Stacey and narrowed his eyes and she tried to take a step back but he had a firm grip on her wrist. 'So tell me why you're afraid of dying,' he said, his voice quiet, his eyes on her, ignoring everyone else in the room.

'My parents,' said Stacey in a small voice. 'They died when I was a kid. One of them dodgy old gas heaters on the wall. Carbon monoxide leaked out when we were asleep. They died, I didn't. They got me in an ambulance and revived me. I remember the machine by the stretcher, the little pulsing line right by my head. Twelve years old I was.'

Bronson pressed his thumb into her wrist where the tattooed line ended. 'I can feel your pulse here,' he said. 'Good and strong. You feel you're alive now, eh, girl? Fear and excitement, so similar, don't you think?'

Ford watched this from the sofa, looking at Bronson then at Reynard, wondering how long the landlord could watch it. Ford had the feeling that Bronson had finished, had had his fun. He was getting to the point now.

'Now, Stacey, I'm going to ask you a question,' Bronson said softly. 'And I'm asking you because I reckon I can trust you more than anyone else in this bar to give me an honest answer.' Stacey looked over her shoulder at Reynard, but Bronson tugged on her arm. 'Don't look at your boss,' he said, 'he's had plenty of opportunity to get involved with this conversation, but he's just stood there watching.'

Bronson surveyed the room, making sure all eyes were on him. Dussell was chewing slowly on his steak, but was watching Bronson closely. Bronson turned back to Stacey. 'There are two people travelling with Ford here,' he said. 'A woman and a girl. I want you to tell me where they are.' She glanced at Ford, and he gave a small shake of his head. She bit her lip, avoiding Bronson's eyes, not knowing what to do.

Bronson waited, enjoying himself, giving Ford a little smirk. As his eyes moved back to the barmaid they caught the row of hooks fixed to the wall above the telephone. Five hooks, all numbered, each holding a single key on a wooden fob, but the first hook was empty. He let go of Stacey's hand and she snatched it off the counter, rubbing her wrist, leaning close to Reynard. Bronson smiled at Wu, said something in Cantonese, and Wu nodded.

Bronson turned and took a few paces towards the archway and the back of the hotel, but Reynard stopped him with a shout. Pushing Stacey and Charlie through the door to the kitchen, Reynard turned to face Bronson, reaching under the counter and pulling out a baseball bat. It was old, wooden, with most of the paint chipped off it. He held it a hand's breadth above the counter and let it drop, the wood clattering as it landed, getting everyone's attention.

Bronson turned to him and gave him a taut smile, rolled his shoulders, and pulled down the cuffs on his jacket. He waited, letting Reynard think about what he was going to say.

'I've let you shoot your mouth off, bail up my regulars, manhandle my staff, but the guest rooms are private. This stops here.'

'This is good,' said Bronson. 'Good that you're looking after your pub. I was beginning to wonder if you were ever going to step forward, stop me having the run of the place.'

'You never had the run of anything. You're just another big bloke, full of himself, telling tall stories in the front bar. You think we don't get that every Saturday night in here?'

'You seem relaxed about this,' said Bronson, moving his head from side to side, skewing his jaw, and stretching the muscles in his neck.

'We get trouble enough in here,' said Reynard. He was looking at Bronson, but every few seconds his eyes darted sideways to check the man by the front door. Wu was leaning against the doorframe, a cigarette hanging from his lip, showing little interest in the conversation.

'You ever seen trouble like me before?' Bronson asked.

'Not so well dressed,' said Reynard, 'but take away the suit and you're just another bloke with too much muscle. You shouldn't do the steroids, mate, they shrivel your balls. We've had Maoris bigger than you before, blokes that worked the mines. They were roaring drunk and we still threw them out on the street.' Reynard's hands rested lightly on the bat, his fingers tapping the wood.

'What about Wu?' said Bronson. 'I'm pretty sure you never saw anything like him before.'

'The guy looks like he's in a coma,' Reynard said.

'Nah, he's sharp, don't you worry,' said Bronson. 'He is a master of *wu-wei*, the action of no action. He has the profound conviction that no harm can come to him, because he doesn't really exist. But when he wants to, he's going to take that bat off you. He'll move so fast you won't have time to piss your pants.'

Reynard turned to check where Wu was standing and Bronson took two long strides to the bar, slapped a hand down on the middle of the bat and snatched it from under Reynard's hands. Before the landlord could react, Bronson put his free hand on the knob at the end of the handle, swivelled the bat until the base pointed towards Reynard, and jabbed it forward into his gut just below his rib cage.

Reynard let out a grunt as the air escaped his lungs and he stepped back against the cooler before doubling over, sucking hard to get air.

Bronson took three quick steps backwards, neat movements, light on his feet for such a big man. The bat was still held out steady and level in front of him. He paused a moment, finding his balance, then spun the bat around in neat vertical strokes, first past his left shoulder, then his right, before spinning the bat in front of himself, working his hands one over the other in a blur, the bat coming to a stop upright in front of him. He then repeated the sequence, this time spinning his whole body, his feet dancing, and the arc of the bat filling the room, Ford feeling the rush of air as it passed over his head. Bronson brought the bat up high and then down in a great axe-swing onto the bar, smashing the bourbon glass and scattering beer cans. Then he returned the bat to the upright position beside his head, his face contorted into a grimace, his eyes wide, the whites showing all around, his tongue hanging out of his mouth in a hideous curve.

Silence fell over the bar, the only movement the flicker

of the television in the corner. After a moment the quiet was broken by a beer can that rolled off the counter and clattered to the floor. Henry Dussell tipped his lunch plate to empty it of spilled beer, and picked a shard of broken glass from his half-eaten steak. 'Well,' he said, 'if Charlie hadn't already ruined that steak, you've well and truly fucked it.'

Bronson still held the bat poised ready, looking at Reynard slumped against the cooler. 'This little thing isn't as long as a *taiaha*,' he said, 'or as properly balanced, but I could still clean you all up with it. I'd hoped to come in here and have a quiet word with Ford here, just the two of us. Discuss the situation. You understand? Not get emotional about anything, right? Tell him what I thought, the two of us laying it out, looking over what we have, not letting that blonde break things up. I never figured I'd have to deal with the whole fucking pub. So I'll say this once, and make it clear. Me and Wu have some business to conclude in this town, and I suggest you all stay out of our way.'

Muddy had backed up to the end of the bar, huddled in the corner where it met the wall by the till. He uncurled himself and sat upright on his stool. 'That's some seriously deadly kung fu moves you got there, bro.'

'This is my culture, you little fuck,' hissed Bronson. 'Wu over there knows the Chinese styles, he knows the Wu Tang sword, all that, but none of his stuff is anywhere near as good as *mau rakau*.'

'The man is Wu Tang?' said Muddy, his eyes wide in excitement. 'Respect, bro! Bring the motherfuckin' ruckus!'

Bronson swung the bat one more time, then let it drop, hanging loose from his hand. He put the end on the floor and leaned on it like a walking stick.

'Did you guys bring guns?' asked Reynard, who had recovered his breath. 'Or do you just use sticks and umbrellas to threaten a bloke?'

Bronson grinned. 'I'm big enough not to need a gun,' he said. 'Shit, I'm big enough that most of the time I don't even need to fight. Fuckers take one look at me and turn away.'

'The last of the knucklemen, that you?' said Reynard. 'That could be a problem for you.'

Reynard reached under the bar again, and when his hands appeared above the counter they held a shotgun. It was a handsome sporting gun, an over-and-under Beretta, the wood of the stock polished to a deep shine.

The smile didn't flicker on Bronson's face. 'That's not the problem,' he said. 'That's the juice. One reason I don't carry a gun, it makes it all the more fun taking one off someone else.'

Reynard swung it up to his shoulder in a practised movement, tucking his cheek against the stock, sighting along the barrel at Bronson. 'Drop the bat,' he said, cool about it.

Bronson let the bat go and it bounced twice on the hard tiled floor, coming to rest at his feet. 'You've only got two shells in that thing,' he said. 'Can you move that fast?'

Now Reynard let himself smile. 'If you look above my head, top shelf, next to the bottle of good whisky, that silver trophy there. It's for skeet shooting. Two targets, two shots.'

'Shooting at crockery isn't the same as shooting a man,' Bronson said, holding his hands out wide.

'You're right,' said Reynard. 'Men are bigger and they don't move so fast.'

'You ever shot a man?'

'Never had to. I used to shoot bush melons off the fence post out the back. I always imagined a man's head would come apart the same way. Still waiting to see how that might look.'

'A hell of a mess is how it looks.'

'First rule of running an outback pub,' Reynard said, 'is that you don't put anything in the front bar that can't be hosed down. Now back up towards your mate by the door.'

Bronson stayed calm and took two steps backward. Ford scooted along the sofa, trying to stay out of the line of fire. He thought that Bronson was the most in-control person he had ever met in his life.

'Are you sure this is the direction you want to take?' Bronson said, as Reynard swung the shotgun, tracking him towards the door. 'Remember this moment. This is the point at which it will start to go wrong for you, at which you'll wish you'd taken a different route. When Maori warriors travel to battle, we are careful to look out for the first enemy that crosses our path. *He maroro kokati ihu waka*, the first flying fish crossing the bows of the canoe. We make sure this first enemy is slain, to bring good luck in battle. Are you making yourself my enemy?'

Reynard kept his cheek hard against the butt of his gun. He was swivelling from his hips, his whole upper body, arms and gun moving as one unit, pointed at Bronson as he backed towards the entrance. When Bronson reached the door he turned, said something quietly to Wu, and the two of them slipped out into the white light beyond.

Reynard waited a few moments until he heard a car start, then relaxed his grip on the shotgun. 'Go close the front door, Muddy,' his voice casual, trying to disguise his shallow breathing. Muddy tiptoed across the room, closed the door and threw the large bolts top and bottom.

Henry Dussell picked another shard of glass from his steak. 'At least the bastard didn't make us sit through a *haka*,' he said. 'Any of those noodles left?'

'Sorry, mate,' said Reynard. 'Lunch is over. We're closed.'

FOURTEEN

Ford ran out of the back door of the bar into the yard, dodging the chairs scattered across the patio as he hurried towards the room. He slowed when he saw Kavanagh on the verandah in front of their door, hanging wet clothes on a makeshift line she had strung between two of the roof posts. She looked up as Ford walked the last few yards to her. She had washed her jeans and shirt, and now wore running shorts and a singlet. She turned away to pick up the wet jeans lying on the plastic chair and Ford saw the tattoo that stretched down her left shoulder blade. At first he thought it was a scratch, something made by a large cat, five parallel lines running jagged down her back. He was about to take a step towards her for a closer look when she turned around, the jeans dripping in her hands, her eyes uncertain.

'Every day is a perfect drying day up here,' she said, as she pegged the pants to the line.

Ford took a second to catch his breath before he said, 'Bronson and Wu, they just walked into the front bar.'

Kavanagh glanced quickly at the door to the room, which was ajar, the sound of the television and the air-conditioner drifting out. She then looked at Ford and her eyes narrowed. 'Where are they now?' she asked.

'Reynard pulled a shotgun from under the bar, shooed them out the door.'

She raised an eyebrow. 'Where did they go?'

Ford shrugged. 'I don't know. They left in a car. I guess they won't have gone far.'

Kavanagh's eyes tracked beyond Ford and along the fence, gauging its height, taking in the barbed wire on the top, the gate and the padlock.

'How's Grace?' Ford asked.

'She's inside, watching cartoons,' said Kavanagh. 'Poor kid doesn't know what's going on. You need to spend some time with her. Tell her about her mother.'

Ford looked down at the ground, noticing Kavanagh's bare feet, the toenails painted red, the varnish chipped. 'I've been putting it off,' he said.

'You've spoken with Diane?'

Ford raised his eyes again, looked into Kavanagh's, taken aback by how blue they appeared in the bright sunlight. 'Her number is still ringing out.'

Kavanagh thought about that, put a hand to her forehead to shade her eyes. 'We'll just have to wait here until she shows. She's got further to travel from Broome. Maybe her phone is out of range.'

'And if Bronson comes back?'

She didn't answer. She reached into the pocket of her shorts and pulled out her phone. 'Let's see what uniform are doing,' she said, as her fingers danced over the screen. 'Fucking lousy internet coverage here.' She put the phone to her ear and walked slowly away down the path, her back to Ford. He watched her go, liking the way her backside moved in the thin nylon of her shorts, then he stepped into the cool of the room.

The blind was drawn on the narrow window and the TV was throwing flickering blue shadows on the bare brick walls. Grace was lying on the bed, pillows stacked behind her. She had the thin coverlet pulled up tight under her chin, her eyes wide and reflecting the light from the TV. Ford stopped between her and the screen, his shadow falling across her.

'Dad,' she squealed, managing to squeeze five different vowel sounds into a single syllable.

He sat down on the edge of the bed, waiting for her to look at him, but she had ducked her head around him and her eyes were fixed on the cartoon. He blew in her ear, ruffling the hair that hung in front of it, but she didn't flinch. 'You not talking to me?' he said.

He crept his hand under the coverlet until he found the warmth of her ribs, tickling her with his fingertips. She squirmed and slapped at his hand, looking at him now, her lips pursed, her eyes narrow. 'I want to go home,' she said.

He drew back his hand, then laid it gently over hers. She didn't snatch it away. 'We'll go back to Newman soon, when the police have finished at the house.'

She shook her head and her hair fell over her eyes. She pushed it away from her face with the back of her free hand, then glared at him again. 'Not that house. I hate that house. I want to go home to Perth. Our house.'

Ford had no words to say to her. He tried to gauge the expression in her eyes, how much of her anger was directed at him. 'We'll go home soon,' he said. They were the only words he had and he knew they were not enough.

'You always say that,' said Grace. He could feel her hand beneath his, slowly balling into a fist.

'This time I promise,' said Ford. 'We need to stay here for a while, and then we can go home to our house.'

'I don't like it here. There's only one channel on the TV.'

'We won't be here long.'

'It smells funny,' she said. 'Why do we have to stay here?'

He could think of no easy answer to that. He opened his mouth to tell her about her mother but the words would not come. He could not give her hope when he had so little of it himself.

'We'll have some fun tomorrow,' he said. 'You and me and Rose. Do you like Rose?'

'Why does she have a gun?'

It threw him. He let go of her hand, looked around the room.

'She tries to hide it from me, but I saw it,' said Grace, the anger in her eyes changing to fear. It was the same face he had seen in the aircraft hangar as she held her mother's hand, surrounded by men with guns, her own father holding one too.

'Rose is here to protect us,' he stammered. 'Like she did before.'

'Are those men coming back?' she said. 'The ones that shot you?'

He felt a twinge of pain in his shoulder, as he did whenever he thought of that day, and out of habit he put his hand inside the collar of his shirt and rubbed the scar. When he caught himself doing it he pulled his hand back, then placed it on her head, smoothing her hair, sweeping it behind her ear.

'No, sweetheart,' he whispered. 'They'll never come back.'

He heard a sniff behind him and turned to see Kavanagh standing in the centre of the room, fidgeting. 'I need to talk to you,' she said, tilting her head towards the door. Ford leaned forward and kissed his daughter, pausing with his lips against her forehead, taking in her smell, and then stood up.

Kavanagh reached under a towel folded neatly on the counter and pulled out the pistol, keeping Ford between her and Grace. She slipped it quickly into the waistband at the back of her shorts, and as she raised her singlet Ford saw the tattoo that stretched across the small of her back, bold gothic letters that read 'TRUTH BECOMES STRENGTH'.

He followed Kavanagh out the door and when she turned to him, her face was lined with worry.

'I called the local station,' she said. 'The call got redirected to Port Hedland. The sergeant and his senior constable are on a call, some drama at a remote community, three hours out. They're waiting for the flying doctor to get there. There was one uniform left in town and he got called out on a domestic on a cattle property up north somewhere. He won't open the station until tomorrow.'

Ford sat down heavily on the plastic chair beside the door, resting his elbows on his knees. 'So we're on our own?'

'I guess we've got these guys,' said Kavanagh, looking across the yard to where Reynard and Dussell were sitting on a pair of chairs in the gap between the pub and the residence. The space had been blocked off with air bricks where it faced the road, and covered with a corrugated-iron roof to make a breezeway between the buildings. Dussell was smoking, and Reynard was tapping the screen on his phone. Muddy was carrying a tool box across the yard to where Ford's LandCruiser was parked. The bonnet was already up, a square of old carpet draped over one wheel arch, and the spare tyre lay on a tarp stretched across the sand. Muddy dropped the toolbox next to the Toyota, leaned over the engine block and sucked his teeth.

Dussell walked slowly across the yard to the LandCruiser, then stuck his head under the hood to exchange words with Muddy. He wandered slowly around to the tailgate, leaned in to put his face to the glass, shielding his eyes with his hand. He straightened up, stretched his back, then walked back to his chair in the breezeway, sat down next to Reynard and started rolling a cigarette.

Kavanagh nudged Ford's elbow and set off across the yard towards Reynard. The landlord looked up from his phone and eyed them suspiciously as they approached. Kavanagh picked up a chair as she crossed the patio and put it down in front of Reynard, the back facing him. She straddled it and stared at him. Ford walked up with another chair and sat down, completing the small circle under the verandah. Reynard waited a few moments, expecting one of them to speak. When the silence became too much for him he said, 'You want to tell me who the fuck those guys in the under-taker suits were?'

When Kavanagh didn't reply, he looked at Ford, who shrugged. 'I don't really know who they are.'

'Or why they punched you in the face?' Reynard said.

Ford put a hand to the bruise and averted his eyes, so

Reynard turned back to Kavanagh. 'You reckon they're going to come back any time soon?' he asked. 'Because I'm going to open the pub again tonight, and if they walk back in and try that shit when the front bar is full, then it's going to kick off like you wouldn't believe.'

Kavanagh kept staring. 'So shut the place.'

'It's Saturday night. We've got a pool competition and footy on the telly. There would be a much bigger fight if I locked my regulars out. We open. Maybe it would be easier if you two weren't here.'

Kavanagh lowered her eyes and shook her head slowly. 'We're waiting for somebody. We arranged to meet them here.'

'You keep saying that, but the only thing that's arrived is trouble. You might try explaining yourselves, see if you can win me over.'

Kavanagh was still shaking her head. 'I'm a police officer,' she said, as if that answered everything.

Reynard didn't miss a beat. 'Great,' he said. 'When those two next show their faces, you can arrest them.'

'I'm not taking them on alone,' Kavanagh said.

'You don't have to,' said Reynard. 'I'll hold my shotgun on them and you can cuff them.'

Kavanagh looked down at her clothes, held her hands out wide in exasperation. 'I'm not carrying cuffs with me.'

'Then go to the station and call out the local boys in blue,' said Reynard.

'They're all out,' she said. 'The place is locked up.'

'Then call out someone from Hedland. That's not my problem.'

Kavanagh smiled at him, just a curl of her mouth. 'Sorry,

mate, but it is your problem. We're not leaving until we've finished our business.'

'Isn't that what the Maori said?' Reynard looked at Dussell, who grinned, smoke escaping from between his teeth. 'Everyone's got business to attend to, but nobody wants to tell me why it has to disrupt my business. How long will this take?'

'Don't know,' Kavanagh said. 'Could be this afternoon, might be tomorrow.'

She stood up and looked out over the yard, turning to check the line of the fence along the boundary. 'How secure can you make this place?' she asked.

'You reckon there's going to be a siege?' said Reynard, his eyes twinkling, enjoying it. Dussell tipped the wide brim of his hat forward so he could stare at Kavanagh's legs unnoticed.

'If they come back there might be more of them,' said Ford.

'Doesn't matter how many. We can lock this place down. We can make this place like the Eureka Stockade. The fence keeps most people out. If they get over the barbed wire then there's the dogs to deal with.'

Ford looked for the dogs. He hadn't seen them since he had driven into the yard. They were in the shade under his LandCruiser, lying on their sides, tongues hanging out, their eyes slyly watching Muddy. He was cross-legged on the tarp, the tyre resting between his knees, patching the puncture. 'They don't look like guard dogs,' said Ford.

'They're not,' said Reynard, 'but they make a hell of a racket if anyone they don't like comes in the yard, and then I come out with the shotgun.'

'What about the buildings?' asked Kavanagh. 'Are they secure?'

Reynard stood up and pushed his chest out. 'About once a year the tail end of a cyclone comes through here,' he said. 'They stray inland from the coast. We've got storm shutters on what few windows we have. We can lock all the doors too, so the only way in and out becomes the front door, and we can guard that easy enough.'

'You going to stand there all night?' said Ford.

'Nah,' said Reynard, looking pleased with himself. 'I just texted my man Curtis. He'll be here any second. Lives round the corner. He'll be working the door.'

'So you planned all this before we came over?' said Ford. 'You knew we wouldn't leave?'

'I hoped you wouldn't,' said Reynard. 'We don't get much excitement round here.'

Kavanagh sat back down and waved Reynard down into the chair next to her. She waited until she had his full attention. 'I don't like being bottled up in that room, only one exit,' she said. 'Especially with the kid.' She nodded towards the residence and raised an eyebrow.

Reynard smiled. 'Alright, you can stay in my place,' he said. 'Nice touch that, using the kid. You must know I've got a heart of gold. One condition, though, you tell me what this is about.'

Ford looked at Kavanagh and she nodded. 'We're supposed to meet my wife here,' he said.

Reynard looked from one to the other, frowning. 'Does your wife know you brought your girlfriend?'

'She's not my girlfriend,' Ford said.

Kavanagh laughed. 'He keeps saying that. I don't know why he finds the idea so offensive.'

Dussell coughed on his cigarette, then pushed his hat back so he could look at her face. 'If you were with me, I'd be happy for people to get the wrong idea.'

Ford watched her smiling at Dussell. An open, natural smile that creased her eyes and pulled the skin taut across her cheekbones. He noticed a blush of embarrassment in her cheeks, and realised that all three men were staring at her. She seemed to be enjoying the attention.

'So who are those guys?' asked Reynard.

Ford took a long breath before he spoke. 'My wife has been living with a guy in Macau. We think they work for him. She left him. They're here to take her back.'

There was a cough behind Ford and he turned to see a big man in the doorway. He was huge, filling the frame. Ford guessed he was at least two metres tall, maybe a hundred and thirty kilos, and had a belly that hung over his tracksuit pants. He stood there a moment, scratching at his bare stomach with one hand and at the stubble around his jowls with the other, before he nodded to Reynard.

'My man Curtis,' said Reynard, and raised an arm, palm outwards. Curtis took a couple of waddling steps into the breezeway and slapped the outstretched hand.

'This is your doorman?' asked Kavanagh.

'The best in the Bar,' said Reynard. 'Ain't that right, Curtis?' The big man just nodded slowly, the rolls of fat under his chin bulging in and out. He ran a hand over the cropped hair on the top of his head and gave a shy smile.

'Nobody gets past Curtis,' said Reynard. 'If the shit hits

the fan we just wedge the fat fucker in the doorway and nobody gets in or out.' Kavanagh still looked unsure but Reynard continued. 'It's all muscle under that blubber. He got shot in the belly one time, didn't feel the pain for an hour. When he did he just thought he was hungry. Didn't lose much blood. I think the skin and the fat just sort of rolled over itself and stopped the bleeding.'

'If this place is locked down, how did Curtis get in?' said Kavanagh.

'I let him in,' said Stacey, standing in the doorway.

'Just who we need,' said Reynard. 'I want you to show our guests round the house. They're squatting in there tonight. I'd better go put the shutters up and find a place to roll out my swag for the night.'

Stacey stepped across the breezeway, dodging between the chairs, and opened the door to the residence. She tilted her head for Ford and Kavanagh to follow her and led them into a corridor that ran down the centre of the house. Unlit, it was cool and dark. She opened doors on either side in turn to show them two bedrooms and a living room. They were sparsely furnished, the walls bare. Neither the double bed in the first bedroom, nor the old iron hospital bed in the second was made up. The living room had a sofa, a ripped leather armchair, a chipped coffee table and a large television. A sleeping bag was strewn across the couch and the coffee table was crowded with empty beer cans and food wrappers.

The corridor opened out into a kitchen that ran the full width of the building, with a laundry on one side with an old copper tub. A back door led into the yard. Kavanagh opened it, looked out to where Muddy was packing up his tools, the LandCruiser idling, then she closed the door and inspected the dead bolts. She walked to the opposite wall and pulled back the blind to check the window on to the street. Reynard was standing outside, the loose storm shutter leaning against his leg. He winked at her before lifting it into position over the window. Kavanagh turned to face Stacey, her eyes sweeping the room, taking it all in. 'This place is built like a battleship,' she said. 'Is that how the Ironclad got its name?'

Stacey leaned against the fridge, biting her nails and toying with the ends of her hair. 'It's named after the original gold lease that was on this block,' she said. 'They started this hotel and made more money selling grog than digging for gold.'

'You're a student of local history?' asked Kavanagh.

'Nah,' Stacey said. 'But you stand across the bar from Bobby Dazzler for long enough and you pick up a few things.'

'Like geology?'

'He took me out one time, to the hills. Showed me a few of the old workings.'

As she played with her hair, she stared idly at a series of photographs stuck to the fridge. Kavanagh stepped forward to examine them. There were twelve pictures, arranged in a grid, showing different women of Stacey's age and build, each one standing behind the bar. There was a mixture of blondes and brunettes, a single redhead, some with short hair and some with long, but all with the same curves as Stacey.

'Them's all the girls he's had working the bar in the last few years,' said Stacey, squinting at the nearest photo. 'Back-packers mostly. The girl before me was a German. He puts an ad on the internet, hires them that way. Most only stay a few months then move on.'

'Do they know what they're letting themselves in for when they come up here?' asked Kavanagh.

'What, Tom?' Stacey said. 'He's not so bad, once you get to know him.'

'I meant the heat, the isolation.'

'Some like it. Some turn and run after a week. You get all sorts.'

'But he seems to have a type. All the girls are similar.'

'You mean the tits?' Stacey said. 'Tom says he picks them that way because he sells more beer, but I don't believe him for a second.'

'You seem to know your way around the house pretty well,' said Kavanagh.

Stacey didn't take the bait. 'I live in one of the dongas out the back of the yard.'

'Is that where he'll be dossing while we're in here?'

'I dare say he'll come knocking on my door with that hangdog face of his.'

'That part of your job description?'

'Only as little as necessary to stop him drooling down my shirt front when we're behind the bar together.' She pulled herself upright and crossed the room. 'I'll go get you some clean sheets for the beds,' she said, and walked off down the corridor, her thongs slapping on the tiled floor.

Ford waited until she'd disappeared through the door before he said to Kavanagh, 'What do you reckon?'

She looked around the kitchen again and nodded. 'Best we'll get.'

Ford went to the back door. 'I'll go get Grace and the bags,' he said, leaving the door ajar.

Kavanagh did another tour of all the rooms. A bump on the outside wall made her peer out of the living-room window. Reynard was fitting the next storm shutter. She crossed the corridor to the main bedroom. She contemplated the double bed, and wondered whether Ford's wife would arrive before she needed to make a decision about where she was going to sleep.

She went to the window, checked the security screen and the locks, and heard laughter. Ford was pushing Grace on the swing, his back to Kavanagh, his daughter flying as high as his head, screaming every time he pushed her, her hair streaming out behind her on the down swing. Each time she reached the top of the arc, Ford would step to one side and try to kiss her on the cheek as she hung in the air, his loud smooch followed by her high-pitched cackle, her hair flying out in a halo before she dropped down again.

Kavanagh thought about her own father, trying to retrieve memories of them playing together, but she could remember little. Her father was not that much older than Ford, only a dozen years or so, yet they seemed from different eras. She had always compared the men she knew to her father, the one constant in her life: strong, reliable, protective and stern, but watching Ford she wondered whether she had the wrong idea about the sort of man who made a good father.

FIFTEEN

It was an hour after sunset and Ford was pacing the kitchen barefoot, his feet slapping on the lino. He had two cigarettes going, one in his hand and another that he'd forgotten in the ashtray on the table. He'd found a bottle of vodka in the laundry cupboard among the washing powder and it sat next to the ashtray beside a single shot glass, and every few laps of the kitchen he would stop and stare at it but not dare lift it.

Kavanagh sat at the kitchen table reading a fly-spotted paperback she'd found on the shelf above the toilet. She was still dressed in the singlet and running shorts, her bare legs stretched out in front of her. She seemed unperturbed by Ford's pacing or the noise of the television in the next room, or by the distant jukebox and hum of voices from the bar. She saw Ford looking at his watch. 'I'm starting to think somebody picked her up,' she said. 'Diane said she saw men watching her. Maybe they caught up with her on the road.'

'Why are Bronson and Wu still here?' he said. 'They should have gone to join up with the others, or headed back to Macau.'

Kavanagh put her book face down on the table. 'What if someone else found her first?'

Ford sat down heavily on the chair opposite her and stared at the bottle. 'Roth? You think it's him? I thought he and Bronson both worked for McCann.'

'I don't know about that,' Kavanagh said. 'Bronson doesn't seem to like Roth. Maybe Bronson's working for someone else.'

'You seem pretty sure Roth is close.'

Kavanagh looked at the vodka bottle, frowned, and got up to see if there was anything else to drink in the fridge. 'Diane says she knows where the gold is, and it's somewhere round here. Roth will want to intercept her before she can tell me, and if he can't find her he'll move the gold. Either way, he's going to show up.' She opened the fridge door, but there was only a single carton of milk, a box of eggs, and a couple of bottles of mineral water. She looked at the cooker, which looked unused, as did the sink, and wondered if Reynard had all his meals in the bar.

Ford had paced another line across the kitchen and stood by the back door. 'In the bar this afternoon, Bronson said he still had business in Marble Bar.'

'Maybe he's after the gold as well,' Kavanagh said.

Ford walked back to the table and stubbed his cigarette in the ashtray. He saw the second cigarette still burning there, and picked it up. He took a long drag. 'So what do we do?' he said.

Kavanagh leaned against the fridge and folded her arms. 'We've got no choice but to hang around here and see what happens. Wait for Bronson to make his next move.'

Ford drank from the shot glass, then picked up the vodka bottle and unscrewed the cap. As the bottle hovered over the glass, he caught her staring at him. 'You want a drink?' he asked.

'All the time I've known you, you've only offered me shots of vodka or whisky,' she said. 'Won't you ever buy a girl a glass of wine?'

Ford caught the look in her eye and hesitated for a few seconds, then made a decision. He put down the bottle and strode down the corridor towards the bar. He put his head around the door of the living room to check on Grace. She was asleep on the couch with a smile of perfect beauty, the TV flickering in the dark room.

When he opened the front door, the noise from the bar got louder. There was a knot of people sitting in the breezeway smoking, and they watched him as he stepped between the chairs. The bar was full, the jukebox booming, the footy playing on the TV, and a group of men were clustered around the pool table watching the game. Most were dressed in T-shirts, shorts and thongs. A few had their wives with them for dinner, and wore a freshly ironed shirt with a collar. Reynard and Stacey stood side by side behind the bar, talking with Muddy and an old Aboriginal man with white hair and a round belly. Muddy smiled at Ford as he stepped up to the bar.

'Did you fire up the LandCruiser, bro?' he said. 'She sweet or what?'

Ford nodded, tried to return the smile. 'Purred like a sleeping lion,' he said. 'What do I owe you?'

'Well, the going rate for a puncture is a cold carton of tinnies,' said Muddy. 'And I reckon you could give us a hundred for the racing tune-up.'

Ford whistled, his eyebrows raised. Reynard laughed. 'When you travel in the Pilbara, you need to bring plenty of tyres and lots of money.'

Ford nodded to Reynard. 'Give him his carton,' he said, opening his wallet.

'You owe me for the room, too,' said Reynard.

Ford started pulling notes from his wallet and placing them on the bar. Reynard kept nodding until the wallet was empty.

Ford sighed. 'I reckon all that might buy me a shot of that good whisky from the top shelf, and some sort of wine for the lady next door.'

Reynard took down the bottle and splashed whisky into a glass, then drew a bottle of white wine from the coolbox. He looked suspiciously at the label. 'This is the only wine we got,' he said. 'No idea if it's any good, but haven't had any complaints. How are you going with that cop?'

'It's not like that,' said Ford, taking the bottle and examining the label.

'The colder they are, the hotter they get,' said Reynard. 'When a cold chick gets hot, man, how she sizzles.'

Muddy joined in. 'Hey, bro. You know what the difference is between a cop and a sperm?'

Ford picked up the whisky glass and sniffed it, shaking his head.

'A sperm has a one-in-a-million chance of becoming a human being.' The three of them watched for Ford's reaction. He ignored them and drank the whisky. It was better than he expected. They were all smiling at him.

'Any news?' he asked.

'Those two guys cruised past about half an hour ago, driving an old ute,' said Reynard. 'We haven't seen them since.' He nodded towards the front door. Curtis was sitting in a chair beside the door, his arms folded, cuddling his beer.

'I've got something else for you,' said Reynard. He reached under the bar and pulled out a T-shirt, holding it up so Ford could read the words 'Ironclad Hotel' printed across it. 'It's clean,' said Reynard, 'which is more than I can say about that shirt you're wearing.'

He threw it at Ford. 'Just trying to give you a fighting chance with the blonde,' said Reynard. 'And besides, I don't like you FIFO types coming into my bar in your work clothes.'

Ford raised the wine bottle and the T-shirt in salute and turned to go. He gave a small wave to Curtis and returned to the house the way he had come, pulling on the clean shirt before he stepped into the kitchen.

Kavanagh was sitting at the table reading when he came back in. She looked up and when she saw the T-shirt she raised an eyebrow. It was a size too small for him, hugging his long torso so she could see how wiry he was. She wondered how he might look if he ever made any effort with his appearance, but decided she liked him for not knowing how good-looking he was.

Ford put the bottle on the table in front of her and said, 'You find some glasses for that while I put Grace to bed.'

He went to the living room, turned off the TV, and lifted his daughter off the sofa. She rested her head on his shoulder, her arms creeping around his neck, her legs wrapping round his torso as he carried her across the corridor to the second bedroom and laid her on the iron bed. He pulled the single sheet over her and kissed her forehead, then walked softly out of the room.

He sat down at the table opposite Kavanagh and looked at the two glasses of wine she had poured. Kavanagh cradled hers between her hands, half of it drunk already. 'How is it?' he said.

'Classy,' she replied.

Ford took a mouthful and swilled it round his mouth. 'Another few years and this will be ready for pouring down the sink,' he said. He smiled at her. She smiled back, a glow in her eyes. Ford let the silence fill the space between them. Finally, he asked her, 'Why did you come here?'

She contemplated the bottom of her glass. 'You know the answer to that,' she said. 'I'm here for the gold.'

'You're not going to let me imagine that you might be here to see me?'

She smiled at that. 'You really don't see what's happening right in front of you, do you?'

'So me and Grace, we're just a means to an end?'

Her smile dissolved and she took another sip of wine, making him wait, staring at him over the rim of the glass. She licked her lips. 'I think you should be asking yourself why you came up here.'

'Because Diane asked me to.'

'So you're thinking about her. You think she wants to get back together?'

'I think that's probably not what she wants, but it's a possibility.'

Kavanagh looked at him hard now. 'Why would you go back to her?'

Ford tried not to avert his eyes. 'For my daughter's sake.'

'Seems a big sacrifice.'

It was Ford's turn to drink now, a big swill that he let run down his throat. He'd had enough to drink to start to feel relaxed, or at least to fake it. 'I was doing a ten-hour shift,' he said. 'Six days a week, in the world's biggest hole in the ground. Forty-degree heat, middle of nowhere. Don't talk about sacrifice. Putting up with the woman I used to love, the mother of my daughter, that sounds like a doddle compared to living up here.'

'I feel obliged to remind you that she conspired to have you killed.'

Ford smiled, intent on not letting her upset him. 'Yeah, well,' he said. 'That can have an awful effect on a man. Make him lose faith in himself. Almost gives him a feeling he isn't wanted.'

She smiled too now. 'You fought pretty hard to get your daughter back. Now you're going to give her up again?'

He looked down at his hands. He couldn't stare at the blank tin wall and he couldn't look at her for more than a few moments. He spoke down into the glass, watching the vibrations of his voice move the surface of the wine. 'It's not until you have children that you understand how to give and expect nothing in return. I'm not giving her up. She's not a possession. Whatever we can work out, Diane and me, has got to be better for Grace than what she has at the moment.'

'So this is what you want?'

'It's not what I want,' he said, 'it's what Grace wants. She wants her mother. You talk about the law being the one constant in your life. For me now, it's love. It's all I've got. But it's not like the law. There's nothing written down, no right and wrong. Most of the time I'm trying to guess the right thing to do and then I end up doing the wrong thing. I envy you your certainty.'

She emptied her glass and picked up the bottle. 'You really are a glass-half-empty kind of guy, aren't you?' she said.

'So top me up,' he said, holding up his glass. She refilled their glasses and he watched the light refracted through the golden liquid dancing across the table. 'We used to talk about her mother. Grace used to ask me about her every day. We used to go to sleep together wondering where she might be. Me making up lies about how her mum would be thinking about her.'

'So how do you think this is going to work out? Some perfect picture you've got in your head of you back as a family?'

'Three years ago Grace's future seemed mapped out for her. We had the house in Shenton Park, both of us working hard, had her name down for a good school, money set aside. Now I see nothing in her future. A blank page. I'm just trying to rewrite something for her.'

'Wasn't it you that screwed up the marriage in the first place? You're not an easy man to love. Are you going to change?'

Ford sighed. 'I can't be something I'm not. Grace would see straight through that. I had to let her come to me and take what she wanted. Now I have to let her do the same thing with her mother. I'm not sure I have the right to get between that.'

'What about you? Are you going to be able to forgive Diane? You reckon you can rekindle the flame?'

'When you've been together twelve years, that's not the most important thing,' said Ford.

Kavanagh stood up, stretched her back, walked to the fridge and took out one of the bottles of water and filled her glass. 'You could live without passion?' she said, staring at the tiles above the sink. 'I'm not sure I could do that.'

Ford turned his chair to face her, put his elbows on his knees, nursing the wine glass in his hands. 'Infatuation is the exciting bit at the beginning,' he said. 'Real love is the boring part that comes later. Kids change everything. You want to have children?'

She shrugged. 'Some day.'

'Well, until you do, you should enjoy this time when you know all the answers. When you have kids, you'll find the world isn't so certain anymore. The world shrinks. You stop caring about yourself, or other people. The world gets smaller until it's just a small circle about six feet in diameter centred on your kid.'

She sighed. 'We are all capable of telling ourselves all sorts of lies in order not to face the truth.'

'I know that better than anyone,' said Ford. 'I'm giving up one thing for something else. I learnt that we lose ourselves when we try to deny these changes, when we deny that life involves loss.'

She turned to him and her eyes shone with a determination,

a decision made. She took three quick strides across the floor towards him, put her hands on his shoulders and straddled him on the chair. She sat down in his lap and looked directly into his eyes. 'You really can't read any kind of signal a woman gives you, can you?'

'I can read this one,' said Ford. 'No ambiguity here.'

That made her smile, relax a little. 'What I like about you is that you don't have any moves. No lines.'

'I don't understand much about women.'

'It's sweet that you say that as if I don't already know.'

Ford shrugged under her hands. 'I know guys are supposed to have the patter, but I can't. The moment I think I know what a woman wants, she wants something different. You're hard to read, and I made a mistake once already, remember? I figured you were impervious to flattery and humour and flirting.'

She tightened her grip on his shoulders, her fingers digging in. 'All women want flirting,' she said. 'It's just a matter of the degree of subtlety.'

'This is subtle?'

She laughed now, having fun. 'It needed drastic action. If I'd waited for you, it might have been a long weekend. Is this how fast you work?'

Ford put his hands on her waist, feeling the taut muscles under his fingers. 'I wait to see what the woman does. I try to react to that.' He slid his arms around her, but stopped when he felt the hard metal of the gun in the back of her waistband. 'I learnt something today,' he said. 'All about the Chinese concept of *wu-wei*. It's about letting things happen. I'm a bit like that. Action through inaction.'

'And do you get a lot of action?'

'Not so much.'

She leaned forward and kissed him, just the lightest pressure, her eyes closed. He could taste the wine on her lips, recognised the sandalwood and jasmine of her perfume.

She leaned back. 'I wanted to kiss you the first time you made me laugh.'

'But you didn't.'

'The moment never seemed right.'

'I'm not sure it is now.'

She didn't answer that, looking past his shoulder at the blank window, then she ruffled his thick hair, plucking at the strands of grey around his temples. 'I'm curious about your wife,' she said. 'I only saw her once, from a way away in that hangar, but I've seen the chaos she left behind, especially the mess in your head.' She tapped him on the forehead with her knuckles, then smiled when he winced. She put her other hand to his head, held it still and kissed him hard, pressing her body into him, crushing her lips against his, opening her mouth now. She kissed him in a way he hadn't been kissed in five years.

When she released him he sat stunned, his breathing shallow.

'Even now, you're not here,' she said, her eyes misting. 'You're not in the moment. You're thinking about her. You don't know what you want. Your head's telling you one thing, but your body's telling me something different.' She picked up his glass of wine and finished it in one gulp, grimacing as she swallowed. He looked at the slender nape of her neck, exposed where her hair was cropped short, the bleached white hairs against her pale skin, almost invisible, and he put his face to her and kissed her behind the ear.

'Do you have a condom?' she said quietly.

'You worried about pregnancy or disease?' said Ford.

'You really don't have any patter, do you?'

'It's just that I had the snip,' he said, 'so you don't need to worry about that.'

'Vasectomy?'

'Diane's idea.'

'She took your house, your daughter and even your balls,' she said. 'She didn't leave you with much.'

'She let me keep my scooter.'

'That old Vespa? Where is it?'

'Still in Perth,' he said. 'That air-cooled motor can't cope with the heat up here. And have you ever sat on a vinyl seat that's been in the sun all day?'

'I ride a motorcycle,' she said, 'and I live in Kalgoorlie. It gets plenty hot enough there.'

'Easier for you. You have no balls to burn.'

'Neither do you,' she said.

'Can we change the subject?' said Ford. 'It's doing nothing for my mood.'

'I can feel that,' said Kavanagh, and kissed him again. Longer this time, tender. She stood up, picked up her glass of water from the table, and held out her hand for him. He took it and she pulled him out of the chair and led him down the corridor to the bedroom.

The room was dark except for the light that spilled in from the hallway, and he stood in the open doorway watching her as she pulled the gun from her shorts and placed it next to the glass of water on the table beside the bed. She pushed down her shorts, pulled her singlet over her head and dropped it to the floor, then slid naked under the sheet.

Ford sat on the edge of the bed and leaned over her, looking into her face clean of make-up. He had thought of her as much younger than him, but looking at her now he noticed her age for the first time. He wondered whether she had been through the same sort of pain he had, whether it showed in her eyes. In that moment he recognised her pain and he wanted to reach out and touch her hair, to give her solace and hope. She looked back at him, waiting, waiting for him to move in. He stood up and undressed quickly, pulling back the sheet and lying next to her.

They made love as soon as their bodies touched. She wrapped her legs around him, pulling him into her, her eyes closed, her head thrown back on the pillow, showing him her neck. He wanted the feeling of her to take him away, stop him thinking of the men outside in the street, maybe watching the house now. He wanted her to open her eyes and look at him, join him so they could be carried away together.

They were quiet, both thinking about Grace in the next room, and the crowded bar across the breezeway, the sound of music and voices mingling with the rattle of the air-conditioner.

It was far more tender than he had ever imagined it, a slow embrace, neither daring to speak and break the unspoken pact of silence. When she came she bit into his shoulder, stifling a moan, and afterwards they lay clinging to each other, the sheet damp with sweat around them, their chests pressed together until their hearts slowed and their breathing eased.

They released each other and lay apart, the sheet thrown off, her head on his shoulder, feeling the cold blast of the air-con across their bare skin. Ford felt relief. He had known one way or another they were going to reach this point, and now it wasn't something he had to think about any longer. It was done.

Kavanagh lifted her head from his shoulder, rolled onto her belly and put her face close to his. 'You're quiet,' she whispered.

'When am I noisy?' he said.

'It's good to get all that out of the way,' she said. 'The next one, that's the fun.'

She ran a hand through his hair, stared into his eyes. 'You have such long lashes,' she said. 'Grace has the same big eyes as you. Very soulful. I look at her and I can see what you must have looked like as a boy.'

Her hand moved across his shoulder, her fingers finding the teeth marks where she had bitten him. Her fingers walked across his skin until she found where he had been shot, the rosette of puckered scar tissue from the bullet that had passed clean through his shoulder.

'Chicks dig scars,' said Ford, his voice sleepy.

'Does it still give you pain?'

'Not often,' he said, 'but every now and then it reminds me it's there.'

He stroked her back, moving his hand up until he found the scratch marks down her shoulder blade, feeling the raised skin. 'And what's this?' he said. 'It looks like you've been mauled by a cat.'

'It's the *yant ha taew*,' she said.

It meant nothing to him. He waited for her to explain.

'It's Thai scripture,' she said. 'The Five Sacred Lines, a Buddhist prayer. I had it done when I was travelling in Thailand, at a temple, the Wat Bang Phra. It's a special place. You can feel it when you go there. The prayer protects me from danger.'

'Has it worked?' said Ford.

'This from the man who got shot three times in a weekend?' she said.

He could feel her chest moving against him as she laughed silently. He shrugged her off and sat up, reaching for the glass of water on the table. His fingers found the cold steel of the gun and he snatched his hand away. 'You know,' he said, 'when I fantasise about making love to a beautiful woman, she's not normally packing a gun.'

'What boring fantasies you must have,' she said, and pulled him back down onto the bed. She straddled him, grabbed his wrists and pinned him to the bed. 'You told me you felt your wife was a living ghost, haunting you,' she said. 'Consider this an exorcism.'

She kissed him and for a while it didn't matter who might be outside. They were together and there wasn't anything else.

SIXTEEN

Ford woke up on his face. It took him a few moments to work out whether it was still dark, but with sustained effort he managed to open his eyes. The room was shaded, but there was enough light leaking around the storm shutter to let him know it was morning. He had slept on his arms, and they refused to move. He rolled onto his side and curled up, waited for the sense of vertigo to cease and for the feeling to return to his limbs. He felt a breeze across his backside, a cool draught from the air-conditioner, and was disturbed to discover he was naked. He poked around with his toe until he found the sheet bundled up at the foot of the bed. He pulled it over himself and curled up tighter into a foetal position. As he lay there he became aware that he could map the exact dimensions of his liver, and it felt as swollen as his tongue. He opened his eyes again to look at the person beside him. He recognised the cloud of blonde hair, but there was something wrong with the scale, a trick of perspective or maybe a failing of perception. He squinted until his eyes came into focus and he realised it was Grace lying beside him.

He sat up and as his eyes adjusted to the gloom he could make out Kavanagh silhouetted against the outline of the window. She was sitting on a plain wooden chair, her back straight and her head level. She had a blanket spread across her legs, and her hands were hidden beneath it. Ford couldn't tell if she was sleeping or meditating, until she spoke.

'Good morning,' she whispered.

Ford dropped his head back onto the pillow and groaned. 'What time is it?'

'After seven,' said Kavanagh, putting her hands high above her head to stretch.

'What time did Grace come in?'

'A couple of hours ago. She had her eyes closed, walking in the dark. I was already up. She didn't see me.'

'You've been in that chair all night?'

'Most of it. I heard noises outside, got up to check it out and couldn't get back to sleep.'

'I could have helped with that.'

'You were dead to the world.' She stood up and the blanket fell away, and he saw she had been cradling Reynard's shotgun in her lap.

Ford swung his legs off the bed, looking around on the floor for where he'd cast off his clothes. As he pushed his head through the neck of his shirt he caught the half-smile on Kavanagh's face. He put his right foot into the leg of his pants and pulled them to his knee, then snagged his left heel in the waistband, lost his balance and sat down heavily on the bed.

Kavanagh stifled a laugh, stepped around him and opened the bedroom door.

'Any sign of our friends?' asked Ford.

She stopped in the doorway and thought for a moment before she spoke. 'They're out there somewhere. We'll need to make a move pretty quickly.'

'You have some sort of plan?'

'Yeah,' she said. 'Breakfast.'

Ford went to the bathroom and showered, and when he returned to the bedroom Grace stirred, her shirt riding up to expose her belly. She scratched it and rolled over, then lifted her head from the pillow to look at him, her eyes sleepy and confused. He carried her to the bathroom and sat her on the toilet, and when she had finished she looked up at him and said, 'What day is it today?'

'Sunday.'

She thought for a moment, then her face lit up. 'Can we have pancakes for breakfast?'

Ford picked her up, stood her in front of the basin and put her toothbrush in her hand. She held it steady while he squeezed toothpaste on it and turned on the tap. She stretched up onto her toes to put the brush under the running water.

'I'll have to see what's in the fridge,' said Ford as she brushed her teeth. He picked up his own brush and started to clean his teeth, and they stood side by side, looking at each other in the mirror. He held her up so she could spit in the basin and then carried her into the kitchen and sat her in a chair at the table. Kavanagh was leaning against the fridge, a phone to her ear. The shotgun lay on the counter, wrapped in the blanket.

'Is that my phone?' asked Ford.

'I've been trying her number at fifteen-minute intervals since the sun came up. No reply.'

Ford nodded towards the gun. 'How did you get that off Reynard?'

She showed him her teeth and pushed her chest out at him.

Ford went to the fridge. There were three eggs in the carton and half a litre of milk. He carried them to the counter and pushed the shotgun aside to make room. In the cupboard he found some flour and sugar and a crusty tin of golden syrup. He discovered a bowl and a rusted hand whisk under the sink and put some flour in the bowl and broke the eggs into it. He put the bowl under his arm and started to whisk it, all the while watching Kavanagh.

'So what have you been doing all night?' he said.

'Thinking.'

'And did you reach any conclusions?'

'If Diane didn't arrive here yesterday, she won't get here.' She was keeping her back to Grace, her voice a whisper. 'We can't sit here another day waiting. We need to get out there and search for her.'

Ford watched the lumps rise in the batter, trying to break them up with the whisk. 'Where do you reckon we should start?'

'If the gold is around here, then it must be because McCann has some link to this place. We'll go talk to the local uniform and see what they know.'

She put his phone on the counter. 'I'm going to take a shower.'

'You want a pancake?' said Ford.

She looked at the lumpy batter in the bowl and scrunched up her nose, then kissed him lightly on the cheek and turned towards the bathroom.

Ford put a cast-iron frying pan on the stove and thought about his wife as he made pancakes. The batter spat, mingling with the hiss of the shower from down the hall. He stacked the pancakes on a pair of plates and remembered the lemon tree in the yard. He turned off the cooker and stepped outside into the bright sunshine. Stacey was walking across the yard from her donga carrying a plastic bucket full of cleaning products. She waved to him and he waved back. He picked a large lemon off the tree and put it to his nose. When he returned to the kitchen, Grace was looking at him and frowning. 'I'm hungry,' she said.

'Good,' said Ford. 'Look what I made you.' He put the plates on the table, sprinkled sugar on the pancakes and squeezed the lemon over them. They sat in silence, eating and watching each other across the table.

By the time Ford had finished washing up, Kavanagh had come back dressed in her jeans and boots, the cowboy hat pushed far back on her head. She picked up the gun, still wrapped in the blanket, and put it under her arm, then swung her backpack over her shoulder. She leaned against the back door and watched Ford pull on his work boots and dress Grace. She opened the door to let them out, then followed them to the car.

'Where are we going?' said Grace.

'To meet a friend of Rose's,' said Ford. 'Another police officer.'

He drove out into the street and stopped to let Kavanagh close the gates behind them. He looked up the street and checked his mirrors, but the town seemed deserted. Rising in front of him was a hill, red dirt sparsely covered with parched yellow grass. A white building stood alone on the crest, a simple rectangular hall of weatherboard planks with a high-pitched roof of corrugated iron and boarded-up windows. There was a tall arched door at the front, and above it, on the ridge of the roof, was a small wooden cross. A man was standing in the shadow that the church cast across the hillside, and as Ford watched he stepped into the sunshine. It was Wu, and Ford could see the small plume of smoke rising from the cigarette in his hand.

'Got a good view of the town from up there,' said Kavanagh as she sat down next to Ford. If she was unnerved by Wu's presence she didn't show it. Ford drove off, turned right into the main street, and pointed to the police station on the low rise ahead of them, a marked police ute parked outside. The digital sign in the street registered thirty-eight degrees.

Ford parked next to the blue checkerboard sign. There was a single white panelled door, the last one in the long façade, shaded by a low roof that cut between the tall gables. The police ute was parked in front of a humble white house, which seemed to cower beside the imposing stonework of the station. A radio mast stood in the narrow front garden of the house, rising high above both buildings.

Kavanagh stepped down from the car and waited for Ford while he unstrapped Grace and lifted her down, then held her hand as they walked up the stone steps to the door. Grace looked up at the blue sign and her lips moved as she silently read each letter to herself and formed the word in her mind. 'Is this where Rose works?' she asked. Ford looked at Kavanagh and she shrugged and nodded. She took Grace's free hand, the three of them walking together through the broad doorway and into the cool corridor beyond.

There was no obvious front desk; a series of doors led off either side of the corridor, and the first open door revealed a small office with two desks, one either side of a carved timber mantelpiece above a blocked hearth. A young officer in a blue uniform was sitting at a desk staring at a computer screen. Kavanagh stepped into the doorway and coughed; he looked over his shoulder at them and waited for them to speak. He was slender, his fine brown hair hanging straight on his forehead, an alert pair of eyes above a narrow nose and sunken cheeks. His nametag read 'Saxon'.

Kavanagh took off her hat and held it by the brim, turning it slowly in her hands. 'My name is DC Rose Kavanagh,' she said. 'Gold Stealing Detection Unit.'

He spun on his chair to face them, his hands flat on his knees, and looked Kavanagh up and down before staring past her to where Ford and Grace were standing in the corridor. His expression remained blank. 'All the way from Kalgoorlie?' he said, his voice a flat monotone.

Kavanagh shifted uneasily, leaning on one side of the doorframe then the other. Saxon's expression didn't change. 'What can we do for the Gold Squad?' he asked, picking up his phone and notebook from the table. He slowly undid the button on his shirt pocket and slid them inside.

'I'm looking for two men, persons of interest connected to the recent homicide in Newman,' Kavanagh said.

'You got identification?' asked Saxon.

Kavanagh took out her wallet and showed Saxon her badge, and he studied it for a few seconds before glancing at Ford. 'What about your partner?' he said.

Kavanagh shook her head. 'He's a witness. Helping with enquiries.'

Saxon frowned. 'Why are the Gold Squad interested in a homicide?'

'It's linked to something else we're working on,' said Kavanagh.

Saxon waited for her to elaborate. She stared straight back at him, daring him to challenge her. He wore her stare for a few seconds before Grace stuck her head around the side of Kavanagh's legs and broke his concentration. Saxon leaned forward on his chair to get his face closer to Grace's, but she took a step back, pushing herself into her father's legs. 'Hello,' he said, his manner changing instantly, friendly now. He wrinkled his nose. 'My name's Matthew. What's yours?'

Grace hesitated, and then looked up at her father. Ford smiled at her and nodded so she turned to the policeman, lifted her chin and said slowly and precisely, 'My name is Grace.'

Saxon smiled. 'My wife is baking some biscuits in our kitchen next door. Would you like to help her?' He looked up at Ford and Kavanagh and waited for them to nod their acceptance, both realising it would be better for her not to hear what they wanted to say. Grace nodded shyly and Saxon held out a hand to her. When she took it he stood up, stepping between Kavanagh and Ford. 'Is this your daddy?' he asked softly. She nodded, the smallest movement.

Ford held out his hand. 'Gareth Ford,' he said, and when Saxon took it, the pressure was firm and the eye contact direct.

Saxon led the little girl down the corridor and back out into the sun with Ford and Kavanagh following. As she stepped outside she looked over her shoulder at her father and was happy to see him behind her. They walked up the street to the house next door. It was low and white, weatherboard and corrugated iron, the windows shuttered against the heat. They walked through the small neat front garden dotted with yucca and frangipani, and in through the front door. 'Only me,' called Saxon in a sing-song voice. A young woman stepped into the corridor at the far end. She was as small and neat as the house, dark hair pulled back and pinned in a bun, her face as pinched and lean as her husband's. She held her hands out from her sides, her fingers coated white, and she wore a black apron dusted with flour. The apron was pushed out by the curve of her pregnant belly and Ford guessed that she only had a couple of months to go.

'This is my wife Anna,' said Saxon. 'And this is Grace,' he said to his wife. 'She'd like to help you with your baking.' Ford watched the expression change in Anna's eyes though her smile remained fixed, and he saw her communicate silently with her husband, as if it was a routine they had repeated many times with many different children. 'I just need some time to speak to the grown-ups,' said Saxon quietly.

His wife acknowledged him with her eyes and then crouched down to Grace's level. 'And how old are you, Grace?' she said.

'I'm six,' said Grace. 'Are you going to have a baby?'

The policeman's wife nodded and took Grace's hand and led her into the kitchen, speaking softly to her as they disappeared through the door, a vision of domestic stability that Ford had forgotten. Saxon turned to wave Ford and Kavanagh back through the front door.

They walked back to the station in silence, Saxon returning to his chair in the office, swinging on it impatiently as they stepped into the room.

'Do you normally take children with you on an investigation?' he said.

Kavanagh pulled out a chair from under the empty desk and ignored the police officer's question. 'Where's your sergeant?' she asked.

Saxon hesitated. 'He's still on a call out east. Trouble at one of the remote communities. He's out there waiting for the flying doctor, and they'll need social services as well. Clusterfuck. He might be back tomorrow, but it's a long drive.'

'Everything happens slowly around here.'

'The locals live on Bar time here,' said Saxon. 'You'd better get used to it. Judgement Day itself will be a day later in Marble Bar.'

'Wouldn't your sergeant normally be living in the station house?' asked Kavanagh.

'He's single. He gave up the house to us, what with the baby and all. He's got lodgings in the town, which worked out well for him now he's knocking the landlady.'

'What about the senior constable?'

'He's in lodgings too, but without the benefits.'

'I mean, where is he?'

'On the same call as the boss.'

'So you're in the chair?'

'That a problem for you?'

Kavanagh let the pressure drop before she said calmly, 'These two guys we want, one is huge, Maori, facial tattoos. Built like a rugby player. The other one is Chinese, small, pudding-bowl haircut. Both dressed in black suits and ties in this heat.' She waited for Saxon to take that in and then she said, 'Have you heard any reports of these guys in the last couple of days?'

Saxon didn't break eye contact with her. 'You got names for these characters?'

'Only first names, Bronson and Wu, although those could be last names, I don't know.'

Saxon looked at his computer and shrugged. 'That's not much help.'

Kavanagh sighed. 'I reckon if these guys had made any trouble in Marble Bar, you'd have heard about it.'

'I was out of town yesterday,' said Saxon. 'You sure these guys are here?'

'I know they are. Both were in the Ironclad yesterday, and we saw the Chinese guy on the way here,' said Kavanagh.

'So what are you asking me?'

'I'm trying to find where they are staying, and whether I have grounds to bring them in. They may have stolen a vehicle to get here, a ute, but I don't have the index. Probably flogged it in Nullagine.'

Saxon's face brightened and he swivelled his chair to face his computer. He tapped at the keyboard and stared at the data scrolling across the screen. He leaned back in his chair when he found what they wanted. 'Old Bill Webster reported his ute missing from outside the Conglomerate yesterday,' he said. 'Battered old Nissan tray-top. He was having his lunch at the hotel, mostly liquid. Silly old bugger always leaves the keys in it in case someone else needs to drive him home. Constable at Nullagine reckoned it was just some kids joy riding. It happens regularly. Ute normally shows up a couple of days later with goon bags on the seat and used condoms on the floor.'

'And if Bronson and Wu are in town, where might they stay?'

'There's only the Ironclad and the Traveller's Rest, or the caravan park.'

'You done your patrol this morning?'

'I thought you said you saw them already?'

'I need to know why they are in Marble Bar, who they know here.'

'That's not the sort of data they keep on the server.'

Kavanagh thought for a moment. 'Does the town have any links with Alan McCann?'

'That millionaire bloke?' said Saxon, scratching his head. 'Didn't he skip the country? Went broke or something, after that robbery out at his mine?'

His eyes widened. He looked at Ford and back to Kavanagh, then his face cracked into a broad smile that showed his teeth.

'You're still chasing the gold from that robbery,' he said. He looked at Ford again. 'I thought your name sounded familiar. Here's me wondering why she's dragging a civilian round with her and now I know. You were the dropkick they set up as the inside man.'

Ford leaned against the doorframe, staring at his feet. When he looked up Saxon was still grinning at him. 'Well done,' he said, 'you pieced it together.'

'Yeah,' said Saxon. 'We're not all stupid out here in the country, eh?' He turned to Kavanagh. 'Eight more months of my country service and I'll be back in the city and sitting my detective exams. Then I'll be a DC like you.'

Kavanagh forced a smile. 'Keep up the good work with us and I'll put in a word for you,' she said. 'Now what do you know about McCann? Any links around here?'

'You reckon this homicide is linked to the robbery?'

Kavanagh sighed, blowing out her cheeks. 'Let's go with that. I need you to check whether there was anything discovered on the post-mortem.'

Saxon spun back to the computer. 'What's the name?'

'Joshua Harding. Died in Newman the day before yesterday.'

He tapped furiously at the keyboard, his face close to the screen, his head moving side to side as he searched the data.

'Here you go,' he said, triumphant. 'The doctor in Newman still hasn't signed a death certificate. Can't determine the cause of death. No trauma except for some bruising to the face, chest and arms consistent with a fistfight. No head or neck injury. Heart and lungs appeared normal, initial tox screen only showed high blood alcohol. They've shipped the body to Perth at the request of the investigating officer.'

Kavanagh stood up and leaned over Saxon's shoulder to read the screen, her forehead scrunched, her eyes squinting in confusion. She pulled her phone from her pocket and thumbed the screen, then turned and pushed past Ford into the corridor.

Ford followed her out the front door. She was leaning against the rough stone wall of the building, listening to her phone ring. Ford waved his hand in front of her face to get her attention and pointed to his ear to let her know he wanted to listen. She scowled at him, then tapped the phone to put it on speaker.

'*Perth Gazette*,' said a voice on the phone.

'Alannah Doyle, please.'

The receptionist didn't reply; there was a click followed by a different ring tone.

'Doyle,' said Alannah, her voice muffled, the general murmur and clatter of a newsroom behind her.

'Alannah, it's Rose,' said Kavanagh, her voice brusque. Ford wondered what threshold he needed to cross before she allowed him to use her first name.

'Why don't you ever call me at home?' said Doyle, a laugh in her voice.

'Sorry, this is business. Have you made any progress finding McCann's assets?'

The line went quiet, muffled again, and then Doyle was back.

'We thought we were close,' she said. 'We tracked down most of his money and share holdings to an account in Liechtenstein, but as soon as we started talking to the local authorities McCann shifted it all to Macau. We haven't been able to find it there.'

'Is McCann still in Macau?'

'He is, but he's making noises about coming back to Australia. His lawyer's been sending out press releases saying that the Securities Commission has no evidence against him, and that he's going to refloat his company.'

'Using his overseas money?'

'He's still denying those funds ever existed. We reckon he laundered it all in Macau. He's staying at the Penglai Island Casino over there, the personal guest of the Lau family, and we think they've converted all his assets to cash through the casino, or through their other businesses. They are one of the big families over there, into everything. They have a couple of casinos, and all sorts of stuff on the Chinese mainland. Shipping, steel, electronics, plastics. They've even got into sheep and beef imports. McCann's been boasting that the Lau family are his new partners. They're putting up the cash to help him refloat. We just can't work out if it's their money or his. What's your sudden interest after all this time? Where are you?'

Kavanagh looked at Ford. 'I'm in Marble Bar,' she said. 'With Gareth Ford.'

'Have you found something up there?'

'Not yet, but I reckon we're close. Do you know of any connection between McCann and Marble Bar?'

'There's bound to be something,' said Doyle. 'He has gold and iron ore leases all over the Pilbara, all of which are still owned by his Glycon Corporation and are in receivership. He's got some pastoral leases and some parcels of land adjoining the harbour at Hedland.'

'I didn't know he was into farming.'

'Shit yeah,' said Doyle. 'They go way back. McCann grew up on a cattle property west of Newman, place called Jarra Jarra. He still considers himself a simple farm boy at heart, likes to have his picture taken in a big hat, mustering cattle, show his common touch. When he first made his money he bought up a heap of pastoral leases in that country and started talking about restocking them, but then he got into property development and forgot about it.'

'Are those leases held by Glycon?'

'No,' said Doyle, 'he has another company called Ophion that escaped the receivers because it was held by a family trust.'

'And does that company own anything in Marble Bar?'

'I can answer that one for you.' The voice came from behind them, and both Ford and Kavanagh turned to see Saxon standing in the doorway. He had his hands on his hips, the fingers of his right hand resting lightly on the butt of his pistol. Ford noticed that the strap across the top of the holster was still fastened. 'Kill the phone,' he said. His voice was calm, but his eyes were alert, swinging from Ford to Kavanagh and back again. 'Come back inside,' he said. He stepped out of the doorway to let them past, then followed them down the corridor to the office.

Ford and Kavanagh leaned against the mantelpiece trying to look relaxed. Ford raised an eyebrow and she gave him a small shake of her head, holding a hand out level, the fingers splayed, letting him know he had to keep cool. Saxon blocked the door, his hands still on his hips, thumbs tucked in his belt, his fingers trembling slightly next to his gun. Ford wondered how many times he had drawn it.

'I just phoned Newman to ask about the homicide,' said Saxon. 'Spoke to the sergeant there.'

'Eley?' asked Kavanagh.

'That's him. He said you were there the day before yesterday. After you left he phoned the Gold Squad, see if they could tell him what the fuck you were doing poking your nose around a suspicious death.'

Kavanagh was restless now, shifting her weight from one foot to the other, avoiding Ford's gaze. 'They told Eley you are currently under suspension.'

She looked at Ford now, tilting her head to one side, raising her eyes to the ceiling and biting her lip. It was the first time Ford had seen her try to act coy, and she couldn't pull it off. Ford's eyes moved down to the bulge that the Russian pistol made in the back of Kavanagh's jeans. She pulled her shirt down over it and tried a dismissive shrug, but when she saw what little effect it had, her face turned hard.

'So what are you going to do, kiddo?' she said. 'You going to help me or are you going to play boy scout and wait for your sergeant to come take care of you?'

'I can't help you,' he said, dropping his hand from his hip, his voice quiet.

'You already did,' said Kavanagh. 'You accessed those files for me. You're into it now. Best tell me what you know of Ophion.'

Saxon sat down in his chair and put his head in his hands. 'They own quite a bit of pastoral property round here. Absentee landlords. I knew the name, but not that they were linked to McCann until I heard you on the phone.'

'What's the closest property of theirs to Marble Bar?'

'Corunna Downs Station,' said Saxon. 'It's an old rundown homestead about forty kilometres south of town.'

'And who lives there?' said Kavanagh, enjoying having control of the situation again.

'A couple of guys. They're supposed to be looking after the place, but the homestead has gone to shit.'

'When was the last time you went there?'

'Maybe six weeks ago. We had a complaint about stock wandering on to neighbouring land looking for pasture. That was the start of the dry season. They should've been putting fodder out for them.'

'So that's where we'll start,' said Kavanagh.

'Not me,' said Saxon. 'I've made enough trouble for myself without wandering on to the property without a warrant.'

'I'm Gold Squad. I don't need a warrant,' said Kavanagh, standing taller, walking slowly to the door.

'That's right,' said Saxon, looking up, his face defeated. 'You and the Fisheries Department, you guys can walk in anywhere you like. Does that privilege extend to officers that are suspended?'

Kavanagh ignored him and waved at Ford to follow her.

'It'll be forty degrees out there before midday,' said Saxon. 'You can't take that little girl out there in this heat. You can't put her in the way of whatever shit you think will clear your name.'

'He's right,' said Ford. 'She's seen enough.'

'She can stay here,' said Saxon. 'Anna is used to blow-ins. We get all sorts of kids stopping with us. Welfare mostly.'

Kavanagh looked at Ford and he nodded. 'I'll go back to the house on the way out. Tell her we'll be back before the biscuits have cooled.'

As they stepped through the door Saxon called them back. 'You guys ever been out bush on a day as hot as this?'

Kavanagh smiled. 'I'm from Kalgoorlie, buddy.'

'Even so, you get lost out here without water you've got less than an hour. Make sure you have plenty of fuel, water and spare tyres.'

'We know all about tyres,' said Ford.

'You're a Pom, right?' said Saxon. When Ford nodded he said, 'Mad dogs and Englishmen go out in the midday sun.'

Kavanagh glowered at him. 'You calling me a dog?'

SEVENTEEN

Ford looked through the windscreen to where the road ended just beyond the station house. 'This road is a dead end,' he said, starting the engine and turning up the air-conditioner to its highest setting. 'I hope that cop gave you some decent directions.'

She stared at him over the top of her sunglasses. 'Head east out of town, then take the first road south. It's signposted to Corunna Downs. I think we'll get there without a GPS.'

Ford drove back down to the main street. He turned right and looked up the hill towards the church, but there was nobody around. As he passed the gas station he checked his fuel gauge and was happy to see it nearly full, the temperature gauge reading normal. The door of the Ironclad was closed when they passed, the storm shutters still on the windows. As they crawled slowly through the town both Ford and Kavanagh looked right and left. Kavanagh picked up the shotgun and pulled off the blanket, resting the gun upright between her knees, her hand grasping the barrel. 'This town seems even more dead on a Sunday,' she said.

'Looking at the state of the church, I don't think this town pays any heed to the Sabbath,' said Ford.

'God abandoned them a long time ago.'

They reached the edge of town without anything moving apart from the heat haze rippling off the bitumen, and Ford could sense Kavanagh relaxing in the seat beside him.

She laid the shotgun flat along the dashboard, then took the pistol from the back of her jeans and put it in the glove box.

Ford looked across at her. 'Why didn't you tell me you were suspended?'

She took off her hat, laid it flat on the seat beside her, and ran a hand through her hair. It looked damp with sweat, and lay slick against her head, her fingers leaving ridges in it. 'Because it was none of your business.'

'Was that why you couldn't bring a gun or handcuffs with you?'

She didn't answer, instead slapping the dashboard and waving at the narrow sign that pointed off to their right. 'That's our road,' she said.

Ford made the turn on to the gravel road, centred the steering wheel, and waited to see if she would answer.

They were already into dry rocky country before she spoke, the road winding between sharp outcrops, stunted trees clinging to the slopes, spinifex and buffel grass struggling upwards between boulders. 'It's bullshit,' she said, looking out the window at the barren landscape, holding the handle above the door and swaying with the motion of the cab as

Ford negotiated the potholes in the road. 'The stories that Alannah was running about McCann, there were little details in there about the police investigations, or lack of them. The top brass figured someone in the department was leaking stuff to the newspaper. They looked at Alannah, found out that we were friends, and decided I was the culprit. Then they suspended me.'

'So it wasn't you?'

'No,' said Kavanagh, 'it was me, but the bastards never had any proof.'

'Why'd you do it?'

'Because the police and the Securities Commission were going to drop the case against McCann. They weren't able to come up with any evidence, had McCann's lawyers badgering them and blocking them at every step, and they were under pressure from the receivers to drop it.'

'I'd have thought the receivers would want to keep chasing him. Get their money back.'

'Nah,' she said, 'exactly the opposite. Once they couldn't get their hands on any easy money, they gave up the chase. The best way for the shareholders to get any of their money back is to let McCann re-float his company. I reckon they'd even let him use the defrauded cash to do it.'

'And you don't want that?'

'The bastard is going to walk right back into the country as if nothing's happened, and they are going to treat him as if he's the saviour of his own company.'

'Why you?'

'Why not? Somebody has to take the bastard down. But mostly I just want to get that gold back. Do my job.'

As they passed a clump of melaleuca, a startled flock of budgerigars burst out of the bushes and swarmed in front of the car. Ford stopped and watched them bob and dart across the ground, their green wings turning in the air, their screech and chatter slowly fading as they passed over the nearest rocky outcrop. He turned to Kavanagh. 'Do you trust Saxon?' he said.

'You're the one who left his daughter with him.'

'You reckon he'd call it in? That he'd seen you here?'

'Probably not. He knows he's out of his depth. He'll sit in that station babysitting your kid until his sergeant comes back to babysit him.'

'You don't seem to have a high opinion of him. Not much brotherhood evident in that big blue gang of yours.'

'I don't have much time for his sort.'

'Uniform?'

'Nah, the young ones,' she said. 'I'm sure he joined for all the right reasons, but the academy would have squeezed that out of him, taught him that it's "them and us". Then he comes to a place like this for his country service, and he's apart from the rest of the town, just running down the clock till he can get back to the city. No wonder he doesn't know what's going on round here.'

Ford let it drop and concentrated on the road, which had deteriorated to a series of ruts between boulders and potholes. He stopped the Toyota and engaged four-wheel drive. He started off again slowly, weaving across the road to find the smoothest ride. The road dipped down into a dry river bed, soft sand between stands of paperbark trees. Ford let the car snake across the dry sand. A small mob of cattle was huddled in the sparse shade provided by the trees. They were so thin their ribs were showing, their tails flicking at the cloud of flies that hung around them.

After the river bed, the country opened out into broad grasslands. They could see the high ranges along the western horizon, and in front of them was a line of small round hills, dark at the top where black rocks poked through the yellow grass, marching away to the south. The road seemed to follow the black hills until it veered off east towards a fence line. A gate marked the place where the fence crossed the road, and a pair of horses stood on the far side, their heads hanging over the gate, watching them approach. One grey, the other chestnut, they were short and stocky brumbies, left to run wild on the property. Thin as the cattle, their coats were long and shaggy, their manes hanging long and covering their eyes. Kavanagh watched the horses as they approached, leaning forward in her seat. 'Slow down,' she said. 'Don't startle them.'

She opened the car door before they got close to the gate, waved Ford to a stop, and then jumped down, leaving her hat and glasses on the seat. She walked calmly up to the gate, both hands held out in front of her, palms out. The grey pawed the ground as she got closer, threw back its head and tossed its mane, but didn't move away. Kavanagh reached the gate and put a hand on each horse, close to the nose, stroking gently. They stayed that way for a minute, then the grey got spooked, kicked out its hind legs, turned and cantered away along the fence line. The chestnut watched it go, turned briefly to Kavanagh as if to say goodbye, then followed its partner at full gallop.

Kavanagh didn't move until they were out of sight among a stand of cajeput near the horizon, then turned her attention to the gate. It was secured only by a loop of bailing wire slung over the adjacent fence post, and Kavanagh had to lift and drag the gate, its hinges rusted and twisted. A small enamel sign, secured to the gate with wire and peppered with gunshot, announced that they were entering Corunna Downs Station. Kavanagh waved the car through and closed the gate behind it. When she climbed back into the car her face was pink and her shirt stained with sweat under her arms. She picked up her hat and swatted at a fly, then leaned forward to put her face to the air vent in the dash.

'How far is the homestead?' asked Ford.

'Five kilometres, maybe,' she said, lifting the hem of her shirt to wipe her face, showing Ford the tattoos across her back. He tried to read the expression in her eyes, something more than simple apprehension, but she put on her sunglasses and waited for him to drive on.

Each was lost in their own thoughts for the remaining distance. The road curved around a fold in the landscape and Corunna Downs Station spread out in front of them. Ford stopped when he saw it, put the car in neutral and gazed out across the homestead. The dust kicked up by the car's tyres drifted slowly past them towards the buildings.

The homestead itself was a broad colonial building with walls of thick stone, rendered and lime-washed. Small windows were punched into the walls, some boarded up with plywood sheets dried and split by the sun. Other windows were shaded with tattered curtains. The high tin roof overhung the walls on all four sides to form a broad verandah. The roof sheeting was old, individual sheets lapped over one another, patched in places. What had once been a grand house, home to wealthy landowners, had become a symbol of the decline of the region's dependence on farming. Mining had taken over, and the animals and pasture had been neglected. A narrow strip of garden surrounded the house, the only belt of green in a desiccated landscape, ringed by a timber picket fence that had rotted. Its missing posts gave the house a gap-toothed smile. A line of rose bushes pushed against the fence, grown straggly and choked with weeds, a few stray red petals hanging among the thorns. The garden was still irrigated, the water coming from an old wooden tank propped up on rusted steel legs. Moss bloomed on its sides, where water dripped from the gaps between the timber planks. An iron windmill stood beside the tank, creaking loudly as it turned in the breeze.

The house was surrounded by a dozen other buildings: sheds and workshops, stables and garages. Several transportable dongas had been left on the edge of a broad circle of compacted dirt in front of the house, which acted as a storage yard. There was an old caravan too, and a collection of vehicles in various states of disrepair: trucks, utes and tractors, and a cattle trailer hitched to an old prime-mover. They were all caked in dust, and most were without wheels, sunk to their axles in the dirt. The only two vehicles that appeared roadworthy were a white ute, the aluminium tray stacked with galvanised tool boxes that shone in the sun, and a fuel tanker, painted a dull desert yellow, sitting high on off-road tyres. The cab was boxy, welded together from flat steel panels, and it looked military. Fresh tyre tracks in the sand led up to the ute.

'Looks like somebody is home,' said Ford.

Kavanagh nodded slowly but didn't speak.

'That's not the ute that Bronson was seen driving,' said Ford, trying to coax her into speaking. She only shook her head. She was looking from side to side, taking in the open ground. The only trees were a handful of eucalypts near the house, taking advantage of the bore water. The rest of the country was parched sand and tall yellow grass, the occasional stunted bush. They could not approach the house unseen, even if they had not been spotted already.

Kavanagh pulled up her backpack from the footwell and put it on the seat beside her. She opened it and pulled out a plastic supermarket bag. She laid it in her lap and reached inside, taking out two shotgun shells. She lifted the shotgun off the dashboard, broke it, and pulled out the shells. She tossed them over her shoulder onto the back seat. 'Sporting shot,' she said, as she fed the new shells into the gun. 'These are double-ought.' She snapped the gun shut and put it back on the dashboard, then pulled a handful of shells from the bag and held them out towards Ford. 'Fill your pockets,' she said. Ford stuffed the shells into the patch pocket on the leg of his work pants and she passed him another handful.

Kavanagh opened the glove box and took out the pistol, checked there was a round in the chamber, then leaned forward to poke it into the waistband at the back of her jeans.

'Who do you reckon is in there?' said Ford.

'I'm hoping it's Roth,' she said. 'If we get lucky, your wife is with him. There's only that ute, and that carries two, so we're not likely to be outnumbered.'

She turned and looked at him now, her eyes cold and

blue. 'I want you to drive up to the house nice and slow. Confident, like it's a casual visit. Don't hesitate. Park on the right of the house, in front of the ute. I'll get down and go up to the door. I don't want you to leave this vehicle. I want you ready to drive. Do you understand all that?'

Ford nodded and put the LandCruiser in gear, driving slowly forward. Keeping his eyes on the windows of the house as they got closer, he drove in a wide arc around the yard, stopped in front of the house, then backed up towards where the ute was parked. As he pulled up the handbrake and killed the engine he saw the curtain twitch in the window next to the front door.

Kavanagh stepped down from the Toyota, leaving her door open, and walked calmly along the fence in front of the house, heading for the open gate at the far end. As she passed the front door it opened and a man stepped out onto the verandah and leaned against one of the timber posts supporting the roof. 'Mornin',' he said, his voice loud enough to carry to Ford.

He was young, late twenties perhaps, tall and athletic. He wore a white polo shirt, which was a size too small and clung to his flat stomach and broad shoulders, with dark blue jeans and white tennis shoes. He had a blue baseball cap pulled down low to shield his eyes. Where the house was old and tired, everything about this man was young and clean-cut.

Kavanagh turned to face him, tilting the cowboy hat back on her head and pushing her chest out, smiling broadly. 'Good morning,' she said, breezily. 'I'm looking for my horses.' He didn't answer, just stood watching her, his eyes in shadow beneath the cap. Kavanagh raised her voice. 'Haven't seen them since the day before yesterday. Wondered if they'd strayed on to your place.'

They stood facing each other, ten metres apart, with the broken picket fence and the garden of weeds between them. The man didn't speak. He looked Kavanagh up and down and then turned to the car. He shook his head, and Ford thought about the mining company logo on the door and the hazard lights on the roof.

'Where you all from?' he asked. Ford heard the accent now. North American.

Kavanagh stood with her hand on her hip, took off her hat and used it to fan her face, then waved it vaguely in a northerly direction. 'Two piebald ponies,' she said. 'They'd be looking better fed than any of the animals on your land. I saw some brumbies over by the fence line, wondered if my pair had taken to running with yours.' She nodded in the direction of the gate and started walking towards it.

'I wouldn't know about that,' said the man, and Ford picked the accent as Canadian. He'd worked with enough men from the big Canadian gold-mining companies to recognise it. The man pushed himself off the roof post and turned to follow Kavanagh, the two walking away from Ford, matching each other step for step either side of the fence.

Ford could see the bulge of the pistol in the back of Kavanagh's jeans and, looking at the Canadian, he saw a similar outline in his pants. His shirt was so tight Ford could make out the outline of the butt of the gun and the straight squared-off barrel of a big automatic. Ford swung open the car door and stepped down, then reached back inside to slide the shotgun off the dashboard. He put the stock in the crook of his elbow and rested the barrel on his shoulder, pointing to the sky, then said Kavanagh's name.

She turned first, looking at Ford and taking in the shotgun, waving him back with a flick of her hand. The Canadian turned more slowly and, when he raised his head to look at Ford, the sun hit his face and Ford could see his eyes under the cap, watching them widen as he took in the situation. He took two steps backwards under the verandah, looking from Ford to Kavanagh, his body tensing, his weight on the balls of his feet.

Ford lowered the barrel of the shotgun and pulled the stock into his shoulder and, when Kavanagh reached behind her back for her pistol, the Canadian broke into a run, bending low and pulling the automatic from his pants. He raised the gun as he ran back towards the front door of the house, firing two rapid shots at Ford. Ford ducked behind the driver's door, and the first shot punched through the sheet metal next to his head, the second shattering the window and showering Ford with glass.

When Ford raised his head, he saw the Canadian disappear inside the house. Kavanagh was up and running, tossing her hat aside, her gun held out in front of her. She hurdled the fence and stumbled through the weeds, then sprinted along the verandah towards the door. As she passed the window the glass exploded outwards, the gunman firing from inside the house. Kavanagh flattened herself against the wall between the window and the door and looked for Ford. She saw him crouched behind the car door, his eyes peering over the sill, and she waved him forward.

Ford ran around the back of the car to the passenger door,

putting the big Toyota between him and the house. He reached across and turned on the engine, slipped the car into low gear, and released the handbrake. The car began to creep forward across the front of the house, Ford crouched next to the passenger door. When he was level with the window he stood tall and fired twice through the shattered window. He reached inside the car and took it out of gear, then fumbled in his pocket for two more shells. His fingers trembled as he fed them into the breech, and as he snapped the gun shut he heard the boom of the Canadian's gun and felt the vibration through the car as the bullet slammed into it.

He took a deep breath and peered over the hood at Kavanagh. She was still flat against the wall, her gun raised. With her free hand, she pointed to the window, her fingers making the shape of the gun. She mimed firing the gun at the window, then spread her palm and counted down from five on her fingers, then mimed a second shot through the window. Ford nodded that he understood, and she started another countdown on her fingers.

Ford counted the last two seconds in his head then threw himself flat across the bonnet of the Toyota. He fired the first barrel through the window as Kavanagh crept through the front door. There was an immediate muzzle flash from inside the house and again he felt the car vibrate beneath his chest. He had lost count; he tried to start again, realised his error, so pulled the trigger, feeling the shotgun kick into his shoulder. He rolled off the car and landed on his side in the dirt, clawing at his pocket for more shells. He heard two quick cracks of gunfire from inside the house, then a single boom from the big automatic, then silence. He pushed the new shells into the shotgun, snapped it shut and then he was running, vaulting the fence and rushing to the door.

'Rose!' he yelled as he kicked open the door, the shotgun wedged low against his hip. He spun around in the front room, searching for her. She was standing near the window, staring down at the body of the Canadian slumped against the wall, two crimson rosettes blossoming across his shirt from the bullet holes in his chest. She looked around at Ford, her face ugly with anger. 'I told you to stay in the car,' she hissed.

Ford put the butt of the shotgun on the floor and leaned on it, bent double and fighting for breath. 'Why didn't you answer me?' he said.

'Don't ever call me by my first name,' she said.

EIGHTEEN

The Canadian's eyes were still open. Ford sat on an upturned milk crate as he tried to discern the expression in them. He decided it was a mixture of surprise, fear and anger. A trail of blood trickled from the corner of the dead man's mouth and, from the bright red stains on the front of his shirt, Ford figured that both bullets had hit a lung. His body was slumped against the wall, his legs twisted. The floor around the body was strewn with shards of broken glass, splinters of wood and chunks of plaster that Ford's shotgun had scattered. The room was bare except for a trestle table stacked with the Canadian's belongings and, next to it, in front of an old pot-belly stove, was an army cot with a sleeping bag neatly rolled at its foot.

The pistol was still in the dead man's right hand, a big chromed automatic with pearl inlay in the grip. His left hand held a telephone and Ford leaned over to prise it out of his fingers. It was larger than any phone Ford had seen for some years, with a rubberised case and an extended number pad.

Kavanagh had walked back to the doorway, her hand on the frame, her fingers probing where the Canadian's bullet had splintered the timber. She sighed and looked at Ford. 'I felt the air move as it went past my ear,' she said. 'Could have only been a couple of inches.' She was short of breath, her face wet with sweat, her eyes still darting nervously around the room. She waved her hand beside her ear, as if swatting away an insect, then walked to the trestle table.

Ford stepped up behind her and laid a hand on her shoulder. She shrugged it off, so he showed her the phone. She took it, turning it over in her hand to examine it, and he noticed that her hand was shaking. 'Satellite phone,' she said.

'Was he using it when you came in?'

She pointed to the screen. 'He sent a text just before I shot him. One word: *vulture*.'

'What does that mean?'

'Maybe some sort of distress code. Somebody will be coming to find out. We're lucky he reached for the phone and not that thing.' She used the phone's antenna to point to the assault rifle laid out on the table, a small stack of distinctive curved ammunition clips beside it. It was a stubby carbine, a Russian AKS-74u of the same type that had been used in the Gwardar robbery. The same gun carried by the mercenaries who had ambushed them on the road from Kalgoorlie, and the one used to shoot Ford. He felt a twinge in his shoulder at the memory. He had stopped wondering if the pain was real or an echo in his mind; it didn't seem to make much difference anymore.

Kavanagh put the phone down and leaned over to examine the items laid neatly on the table. There was a carefully folded pile of clothes next to an olive green duffel bag. At one end was a plastic bowl and a shaving mirror, and at the opposite end a Primus stove and a nested set of aluminium cooking pots. Beside the AK were a two-way radio and a small rectangular screen that appeared to be some sort of tablet computer. Under the table a carton of tinned food sat beside a cardboard tray of bottled water shrink-wrapped in plastic. The edge of the plastic was torn where several bottles had been pulled out. Kavanagh bent and helped herself to a bottle, twisting the cap in her teeth and sucking greedily.

'Doesn't look like he's been camping here very long,' said Ford.

Kavanagh nodded as she swallowed, but didn't speak. She put down the bottle, pulled her gun from her jeans and walked off through the door. Ford made to follow her, but she stopped him with a wave of her gun.

Instead he found his cigarettes and tapped one out of the packet. It quivered between his lips as he flipped his lighter open and held the flame. He took a long drag and held down the smoke, keeping it in his lungs and watching the cigarette dance in his shaking fingers.

Leaning across the table he picked up the computer tablet and examined it, looking for a switch to turn it on. Beneath it, still lying on the table, was a broad leather wallet. He undid the long zip and found a Canadian passport inside. The face of the dead man stared back at him, paler in the photograph. Grant Collins; thirty-two years old. Next to the passport in the wallet was a billfold. Ford pulled off the brass money-clip and counted out a thousand dollars in new fifties, and beneath it another thousand in American greenbacks. He folded them and slipped them into his back pocket.

The only other item in the wallet was a laminated photograph of a small girl. She looked the same age as his own daughter: pale skin and freckles, curly brown hair spilling from a woollen cap, smiling at the camera and squinting in bright sunshine. What little landscape could be seen behind her was pine trees and snow. It occurred to Ford that Grace had never seen snow, and he thought about why this man had also left his little girl behind. Maybe she was with family, rather than trusted to strangers, and Ford wondered how long it would take before the girl was told about her father. She would not understand what her father was doing on the far side of the world, in a place that had never seen snow.

He was still lost in those thoughts when Kavanagh returned, her boots scraping on the floorboards. 'Nobody else in this place,' she said. 'Your wife was never here.'

Ford showed her the passport. She flicked through it, her shaking hand making the pages flutter.

'It doesn't tell us much,' he said.

'If you'd stayed in the car, I might have got the drop on him and been able to question him,' she said, her face set firm, her jaw locked.

'I saw his gun,' said Ford.

She closed the passport and tossed it on the table. 'It lists his profession as pilot,' she said. 'That tanker truck out the front is marked as carrying aviation fuel. I want to find his plane.' She toyed with the two-way radio and then picked up the computer tablet. It was a matte black screen, with a series of switches and dials set into the frame.

'What is this?' she said, then found the switch and the screen grew brighter, resolving into a brightly coloured pattern that Ford recognised as a map.

'It's a navigation computer,' he said. 'Some sort of GPS. Never seen one this big before.'

Kavanagh passed it to him. 'You're the computer nerd,' she said. 'See if you can work it.'

Ford played with the buttons in the frame and watched as the map on the screen zoomed and scrolled, various dials and gauges appearing and vanishing. After a minute he thought he had a feel for it. He zoomed the map out until he could recognise the coastline. 'There's a few markers programmed into this,' he said, tilting the screen for her to see. 'Airports at Hedland and Broome are marked, and there's a pair of markers south of Marble Bar.' He pointed to two glowing green diamonds at the bottom of the map, then zoomed in on them.

'This little picture of an aeroplane is a cursor marking our position. The other two markers are northwest of here, close together, maybe ten kilometres away.'

'Then that's where we're headed,' said Kavanagh.

'Shouldn't we search the homestead first?'

'Roth wouldn't have stashed anything here. It could be tracked back to McCann. He'll have it out bush somewhere. One marker will be the plane, and I want to know what the other one is. I'm not going to hang around here waiting to see who responds to that distress call.'

She walked to the door and opened it. 'Come on, the clock is ticking.'

Ford motioned towards the Canadian. 'You just going to leave him?'

Kavanagh yawned. 'Whoever he called will take care of him. Remove all trace of him from this place. I'm not doing their housekeeping for them. Don't leave that butt behind.'

The cigarette between his fingers had burned down to the filter. He pinched the end of it and put the butt in his pocket, then picked up the AK and began to follow her. 'Leave that,' she said. 'I don't trust you with it. Just bring the shotgun and the GPS.' She turned and stepped through the door and he heard her boots receding along the verandah.

When Ford emerged into the heat and flies, Kavanagh was walking through the weeds searching for her hat. She found it, looked up to gauge the height of the sun, then screwed the hat down onto her head. Ford walked to the LandCruiser and assessed the damage. There were two bullet holes above the front wheel arch, and another in the driver's door. He felt under the wheel arch to where the slugs were embedded in the engine insulation.

'Anything serious?' Kavanagh asked as she walked to the passenger door.

'No,' said Ford. 'She's good to go.' He brushed the broken glass off the driver's seat and slid the shotgun along the dash. He set the GPS on the centre console and started the engine, staring at the GPS screen, trying to get his bearings.

He pulled out and circled the yard until he found a sandy road that headed west. He kept one eye on the road, the other on the GPS, and soon they were out in the dry country again, among the stunted trees and parched yellow spinifex.

Ford wiped the sweat from his brow. With the window

gone, the air-conditioner was struggling but he left it on, if only for the slight trickle of cold air that blew from the dash in contrast to the hot rush of baking air from outside, bringing with it dust and flies. Ford powered down the windows in the back to create a through draught. Kavanagh fanned herself with her hat.

The road passed through a fence line and Ford slowed to read a rusted sign fixed to a fence post. It had faded in the sun so completely that the words were only visible because the paint had stopped the letters from rusting as much as the rest of the sign. It read: 'CORUNNA WARTIME AIRSTRIP'. Ford looked at Kavanagh as he moved off and she nodded, a small smile curling her lips. She sat upright in the seat, leaning forward, one hand grabbing the handle on the dash, the other grasping the handle above the door, her body swaying back and forth with the movement of the car on the uneven road, willing them forward. She looked down at the GPS. 'How accurate do you think that thing is?'

Ford fiddled with the controls as he drove, zooming in on their location. The screen didn't show any kind of runway, just blank country bounded by a river to the west.

'These things read to the nearest few metres,' he said. 'It'll take us right to it.'

She wasn't listening. She was scanning the bush, her eyes drawn to the row of blue hills that shimmered in the heat haze along the horizon. Ford drove on, one eye watching the cursor on the screen creep closer to the nearest diamond marker. The trees had disappeared, the country changing to open grassland of buffel and spinifex, almost as tall as the bonnet of the car and brittle yellow. A pair of small black-topped hills stood above the plain to their left, and the way-marker indicated that their destination lay on the far side of them.

The road grew wider and the grass withdrew on either side until they were on a broad expanse of bare red sand that stretched away ahead of them in a straight line. 'It's a runway,' said Kavanagh.

Ford nodded and checked the screen. He found a narrow track that curved away towards the black hills and followed it, just a pair of wheel ruts through the grass. It led him to the base of the hills and when the cursor on the screen passed over the diamond marker, he stopped. 'This is it,' he said, and turned off the engine.

The heat and the silence rushed in through the window and smothered them. They gazed at the featureless landscape, sweat beading on their foreheads, until Ford spotted something in the grass and opened his door. He found a cap under the seat, a company hat with the logo sewn on to it, and put it on, pulling the peak tight over his eyes. He walked away from the road to a rectangle of concrete devoid of grass. The perimeter of the slab was strewn with sheets of rusted corrugated iron and flakes of asbestos sheeting, the remnants of a long-demolished building. He stepped off the concrete into the grass, and tripped over something. He reached down and found a rusted steel cylinder; looking around, he saw that the ground was littered with scrap metal. Kavanagh, just behind him, pushed the rusted steel with the toe of her boot, turning it over in the grass, swatting away the flies with her hand. She walked over to an open steel frame, the size of a refrigerator, lying on its side in the grass. 'What is all this?' she asked.

Ford stooped to pick up the rusted cylinder he had tripped over. 'Wartime stuff,' he said. 'This looks like a bomb casing, an incendiary maybe. That frame in front of you is a bomb crate, used for transporting the bombs to the plane.'

Kavanagh squatted and sifted through some of the metal. She lifted a small propeller, not much bigger than the palm of her hand.

'Bomb spinner,' said Ford. Kavanagh looked puzzled. 'It rotates in the rush of air as the bomb falls, pulls out the fuse and arms the bomb.'

Kavanagh shrugged and pitched it into the grass, watching it spin as it flew away from her.

Ford picked up a handful of slug-shaped metal pieces from the ground and dropped them again, too hot to touch from lying in the sun. He pulled his sleeve down over his hand and tried again. 'Fifty calibre bullets,' he said, holding them out for Kavanagh to see.

'Careful they don't go off,' she said, her voice not expressing any concern at all.

'These are just the projectiles,' said Ford. 'The cartridges are those longer hollow brass shells on the ground.'

She eyed him from under the brim of her hat. 'More weird stuff that you know too much about.'

'I was fascinated by planes as a kid. All sorts of military gear. Tanks, battleships, all that.'

'Did you used to build those little plastics kits?'

He smiled. 'I considered joining the Royal Air Force when I was a teenager.'

She laughed at this. 'I can't imagine you in uniform taking orders.'

'Neither could I,' he said.

She turned and started walking away through the grass, stepping carefully between the twisted metal. Ford called after her. 'So what are we looking for?'

'Something more than we can see here,' she said. 'Something the pilot needed to find.'

'His plane's not here.'

'There were two markers.'

Ford's eyes followed her as she receded into the grass. He took a couple of steps in pursuit but a bright flash of light from the ground, a reflection, caught his eye. Taking a step backwards, he turned towards the sun and moved until he caught sight of the reflection again, a white flash through the long grass, bouncing off something lying among the scrap metal. He walked towards it and found the source, a sheet of glass lying flat within the rusted remains of an iron window casement. At first he thought it was part of the window, a remnant from the demolished building, but when he stepped closer he realised that was what he was meant to think. The rectangle of glass was new, only the size of a TV screen, and the black hexagonal pattern bonded to the back of it appeared to be a solar panel.

'Over here,' he said to Kavanagh, and knelt down. He lifted the glass, and saw where the electrical cable was connected to the panel. He took the wire in his fingers and followed it to where it disappeared into the grass. When Kavanagh reached him he had traced the wire five metres towards the foundations of another demolished building. Her eyes followed the cable back to the solar panel and she smiled again. Kneeling down next to Ford, she took the cable from his hand, the tips of her fingers grazing his palm. She then pulled hard on it and the cable sprang from the grass, revealing another five metres stretching to where the wire disappeared under a large sheet of corrugated iron. Kavanagh strode across to the spot where it disappeared and squatted down. She tried to lift the sheet, wincing at the touch of hot metal. 'Give me a hand,' she hissed.

The corroded iron was covered with stones and dried grass. Ford took the side opposite Kavanagh and together they lifted it onto its end, then pushed it over to let it fall into the grass. Beneath the iron there was a flat timber trapdoor. Kavanagh pounced on it, her fingers clawing at the edge of the rotted timbers. The door came up, pivoting on rusted hinges, then landed with a crash onto the sheet of iron.

A set of concrete steps led down into darkness. Kavanagh skipped down them until she had disappeared into the gloom. 'Shit,' she grunted. Her voice echoed back from below.

When Ford reached the bottom of the steps Kavanagh was pushing at a door, aged timber like the trapdoor, secured on one side with a bright new steel hasp and a heavy brass padlock. Kavanagh pushed Ford back up the steps, pulled the pistol from her belt and took aim at the padlock.

'No!' shouted Ford, grabbing her gun hand, pushing her arm down. 'Did you ever see that work anywhere but the movies? In this tight space you're more likely to shoot yourself with the ricochet.'

He went back up the stairs. 'Wait here,' he said. 'I've got gear in the car.'

He returned with a tyre lever and a rubber torch. Kavanagh stepped aside so he could examine the door's timber. It was old, of wartime vintage, built from heavy planks that had warped and shrunk with age. The hasp and the padlock looked sound but whoever had fitted the hasp had ignored the hinges, which were secured to the timber by brass screws, green with age. The hinges were welded to a steel frame, which was cast into the concrete and corroded and flaked. Ford jammed the chisel end of the tyre lever under the metal plate of the upper hinge and leaned into it. He felt it give. It took him three hard pushes before the screws gave, the wood splintered, and the hinge peeled away from the door. After he'd done the lower hinge, he tried pushing the door. It moved slightly. He looked at Kavanagh and they both put their shoulders to it; at the fourth attempt they heard the timber split and the door swung inwards, pivoting on the hasp and scraping along the concrete floor.

Ford turned on the torch and stepped past the shattered door. The room he entered was dark, the air cool and dry, and it smelled of rat droppings. The sound of his shallow breathing filled the narrow space. The bunker was four metres long and two metres wide, the walls made from corrugated iron. Ford shone the torch around the walls. 'Air-raid shelter, maybe,' he said.

The wall along one side was lined with steel shelving, each shelf packed with cardboard archive boxes. The opposite wall was stacked with wooden crates and steel boxes, some of them with lettering stencilled on the side that identified them as military. The space down the middle of the bunker was barely large enough for the two of them to stand.

'There must be a light around here,' Kavanagh said. 'I can't see what I'm doing.'

Ford swept the bunker wall with the torch but could not see a switch.

'What was the solar panel for?' said Kavanagh. 'Must be for light.'

Ford played the beam along the curved roof, corrugated iron like the walls, and calculated there must be at least a metre of earth above their heads. He turned around and shone the light on the arched segment of wall above the door. A crude wooden shelf had been fixed to the wall high above the door, and on it was a pair of lead–acid car batteries. Above them were a caged light bulb and a small white box with a tiny winking red light.

'Shit,' said Ford, under his breath. 'Movement sensor.' He found the point in the roof where the plastic pipe entered and followed the cable out of the pipe to the batteries, and then to a conduit that passed down the wall until it was hidden behind the open door. Ford pulled the door away to reveal the light switch, and flipped it. The light from the bulb was weak, but enough for Ford to see the equipment on the shelf, previously hidden in the shadows. The white box was a movement sensor pointed down at the door, and it was connected to a large satellite phone similar to the one the Canadian had been holding when he died.

'We just triggered it,' said Ford. 'Someone will know we are here.'

'Then we haven't much time.' Kavanagh snatched the tyre iron from Ford's hand and jammed it under the lid of the nearest crate. The lid flew up and she thrust her hand into the polystyrene packing chips inside. She came up with a gun, the same stubby AK they had seen at the homestead.

She opened the lid of the steel box beside it and found it full of ammunition, bullets lined up neatly in rows. She pulled out the handles recessed into the sides of the box and lifted it onto the crate so she could open the box beneath it.

'Shine the torch here,' she said, peering into the shadows. Ford angled the beam down and was dazzled by the yellow light that reflected up from the box and filled the bunker. It was gold: flat discs the size of large coins, piled to half the depth of the box. Ford looked at Kavanagh's face, lit up from beneath with a golden glow. She was grinning, her lips drawn back, her teeth bared, her eyes wide and shining as bright as the discs. She picked out one of them and tossed it, watching it spin in the air. She caught it and put it in her pocket, then flipped out the box's handles and hefted it for weight. 'Twenty kilos,' she said breathlessly. 'One hundred and sixty kilos were stolen from Gwardar, so I'm hoping there's seven more of these.'

The ammo boxes were stacked three high, in four rows. Kavanagh stripped the lid off the top box in the second rank and found bullets. The box below it had gold, as did the one on the bottom. She leaned over with her hands on her knees, panting hard. 'It's all here,' she said, as if to herself.

Ford turned to the shelves. 'So what's all this?' he said, lifting the lid off the closest cardboard box and shining the torch inside to see a layer of black plastic sealed with tape. He pulled at the tape and opened the plastic, then let out a long, slow whistle. Kavanagh stuck her nose over the rim of the box and exhaled slowly when she saw the stacks of dollar bills. Ford lifted a packet of notes. It was wrapped in a band that marked the packet as ten thousand dollars. He pulled out more packets and counted them. Five packs wide by four along and five deep made a million dollars in the box. He stood back and counted the boxes on the shelves. Kavanagh had moved along to the next rack of shelves. These boxes had labels pasted to the nearest face with serial numbers printed on them. As she began tearing open the first box, Ford noticed an aluminium flight case standing upright on the bottom shelf, sandwiched between the archive boxes. He slid it out, laid it on the edge of the gun crate, and opened the lid. The light that bounced back once he'd shone his torch inside was harsh and white, reflecting off the diamond jewellery that filled the case. The lining had been specially designed for its contents, each piece secured in a moulded felt compartment. There were two large necklaces, three bracelets and a row of fat rings. The largest stone, an inch in diameter, was the centrepiece of the larger necklace. Ford wondered if Diane had ever seen this jewellery. He doubted she would wear it if she had. He remembered McCann's first wife, a woman of vulgar taste and ostentatious showmanship, and could picture her flaunting these baubles.

Down one side of the case was a row of Swiss watches, both men's and women's, all studded with gems. Ford looked at the cheap plastic digital watch on his own wrist and took it off. He chose the least gaudy watch, a slim Omega with a plain face and a leather strap, wrapped it round his wrist, and put his own watch in its place.

In a square compartment in the corner of the case was a small black felt bag. Ford lifted it by its drawstring and knew immediately what was inside. He tipped the bag and the loose diamonds spilled into his free hand, enough to cover his palm. They were all cut and polished, and they were all very large.

He had only ever bought one diamond in his life, for Diane. They had married in a hurry, a spontaneous act while they were travelling in Europe. They had no money, no rings, and could only afford a local priest in a small church in Italy. On their fifth wedding anniversary he decided to buy Diane the engagement ring he had not been able to give her before. A month's salary was the rule, so he put the money aside over six months while Diane was finishing her geology doctorate. His savings bought her a single stone, a third of a carat. There was no stone in his hand smaller than one carat, and many were much larger. He saw half a dozen stones that were easily four carats. Some of the stones were coloured: pinks and yellows, he'd heard the colour called champagne, all produced by the Argyle mine further north. There was a single red stone, no more than two carats, but standing out because of the depth of its colour. He shone the torch on it and moved his hand to make it sparkle. He'd seen rubies before, but the cut of this stone was too fine for that. It was a diamond.

He looked across at Kavanagh. She had opened several of the labelled boxes and was busy examining the contents. He swept the diamonds back into the pouch and slipped it into the patch pocket on the leg of his pants, then closed the case. 'What did you find?' he asked her, slipping the case back onto the shelf.

'More cash,' she said. 'All sorts of currencies. United States Treasury Bonds, several million, and these.' She held up a broad piece of paper, heavily bonded, blue scrolling ink around its border. 'Bearer shares on a company in the British Virgin Islands.'

'One of McCann's companies?'

'I don't recognise the name. Alannah might. Shares like these belong to whoever holds them, no paper trail. There are other shares in other businesses, probably all just paper companies to hide McCann's assets offshore. This is how he's been doing it. Untraceable.'

'How much do you reckon is here?'

'Hard to guess,' she said. 'Several times more in paper than there is in gold, and I doubt this is his only stash. He was never one to put all his eggs in one basket.' She folded the share certificate and put it in her pocket.

'You want to load the gold in the car?' asked Ford.

'No time,' she said, walking towards the door. 'We need to call it in and destroy the plane before Roth can clear this place and fly out of the country.'

Ford followed her. 'You think he's close?'

'An alarm at the homestead, another here, he'll be moving fast. I reckon he was spooked by Diane, worried she knew where this stuff was, would trade the information.'

She bounded up the steps two at a time. Ford followed, his hand in his pocket resting on the stones. The hot air hit him in the face like a slap, the bright light searing into his eyes. He squinted to where Kavanagh was standing on the concrete slab, holding her phone in the air, spinning slowly, looking at the screen.

'Fucking hell,' she said. 'No signal.'

NINETEEN

'Give me your phone,' said Kavanagh, her face knotted as excitement turned quickly to frustration.

Ford pulled his phone from his pocket and looked at the screen, shading it with his hand, squinting in the sunshine to make out the signal strength. 'I've got no coverage either. We could go back to the homestead and get that satellite phone.'

'Maybe. We haven't much time. We need to find the plane first, then think about calling this in.' She climbed into the LandCruiser and stared at him through the open window, waiting. Ford put the torch and the tyre lever in the back and picked up a canteen of water. He took a long drink, the water warmer than his mouth, filling him but not quenching his thirst. He picked up a second canteen and went around to the driver's door. The vinyl of the seat was hot, burning through the seat of his pants. The sun was past its zenith and the heat at a maximum. He turned on the ignition and checked the temperature read-out on the dash. Forty-two degrees. He passed one of the canteens to Kavanagh and picked up the GPS. The aeroplane cursor showed him their location and the second diamond marker was to their west.

He drove back the way they had come, looking for the runway. They came out of the tall grass on to the broad expanse of the runway and Ford turned west towards the blue hills on the horizon. There was no grass on this part of the runway, as if it had been cleared, recently sprayed with weedkiller to keep it bare, a straight strip of compacted red gravel. Ford checked the GPS. 'It's down here, at the end of the runway on the right.'

He guided the Toyota down a winding track off to the right where the cleared strip of gravel ended. Wide enough for a plane, it was covered in dry yellow grass that had been cut recently. After a hundred metres of snaking between small mallee trees, Ford stopped the car. 'We're close now,' he said. Kavanagh leaned forward and stared through the windscreen. The bush seemed empty, the same dry grass and trees. The ground rose to their right in a low ridge, no higher than the tops of the surrounding trees, and she pointed to it. 'We might get a better view from up there,' she said and was out of the car before Ford could see where she was indicating. By the time he had got out she was halfway up the slope, stepping between rocks and hopping over fallen branches. When he caught up with her he was breathless and bathed in sweat, the hot, dry air catching in his throat. She was red in the face, her forehead dripping under the hat, her shirt soaked under her arms, broad wet patches across her back. She put her hands on her hips, peering down the far side of the ridge, and Ford could see now that it was man–made, an embankment that curved around in an open horseshoe, the flanks overgrown with scrub. They looked down together at the flat area of grass it enclosed, at the large camouflage net erected there, propped up on poles and secured with guy ropes. The net was mottled with reds and browns to match the landscape, threaded around the edge with branches and leaves, but through it Ford could make out the shape of the aeroplane.

'It's a revetment,' he said, his mouth dry. 'There must be more of them around the airfield. Hides the planes from enemy reconnaissance. Protects them from bomb blast.'

Kavanagh was away before he had finished, scrambling down the slope, rocks sliding under the heels of her boots and a plume of dust following her. Ford stumbled after her, down the slope and under the dappled shade of the netting. Kavanagh was standing beside the plane, her arms raised above her head, both hands gripping one of the propeller blades as she arched her back, opened up her lungs and breathed hard. The plane was a small four-seater twin engine, painted plain white. 'Is this the plane from the Gwardar robbery?' she asked, the triumph in her voice evident even through her short breaths.

Ford nodded, waiting for his own breath to catch up with him, blinking the sweat out of his eyes and wiping a sleeve across his face. 'Piper Aztec,' he said. 'Same type, but they'd painted out the registration before they did the robbery.'

He waved a hand at the letters and numbers painted on the rear of the fuselage, and watched Kavanagh read the sequence to herself, her lips moving as she committed it to memory.

She walked around the wing and climbed up onto it, ducking her head to avoid the netting. She tried to open the cabin door but it was locked. She put her face to the window, shielding her eyes with both her hands as she peered into the cockpit. Then she jumped down next to Ford, landed in a crouch and crawled under the wing. Ford stooped to see what she was doing.

She had found the valve in the wing, halfway between the engine and the fuselage, and when she turned the T-shaped handle a steady trickle of aviation fuel came out. The smell was strong, the liquid quickly turning to vapour, and Ford watched the twisted refractions of light rising from the grass under the plane. Kavanagh crawled out from under the wing, coughing. She pulled herself up and leaned over the wing, her lungs convulsing, and when she had caught her breath she stood upright and looked at Ford through streaming eyes.

'Give me your lighter,' she said, and the tone of her voice was so severe that he didn't hesitate. He tossed his Zippo to her as she walked towards the yellow buffel grass that grew high around the perimeter of the revetment. She pulled a handful of it up out of the dirt, then twisted it into a long taper and walked back to the plane. She leaned under the wing and pushed the tip of the grass into the dripping fuel, then flipped open the lighter and put the flame to the soaked grass. She gave Ford a small conspiratorial smile, then walked slowly around the plane, dragging the torch along the ground behind her, setting light to the tinder-dry grass and leaving a smouldering wake as she went.

'There would have been easier ways to disable it,' said Ford.

'I don't want any risk of them getting the gold out of here before we can get help,' said Kavanagh, watching the fire spread through the grass towards the plane.

When the torch burned down to her hand she dropped it and walked off in the direction of the car, calling over her shoulder to Ford. 'Let's get the fuck out of here!' she shouted above the crackle and hiss of the catching grass, and she started up the embankment.

She turned to admire her work when she reached the top, and to check that Ford was following. He was panting up the slope behind her, his face already showing signs of sunburn.

They both ran down the far side and were breathless when they reached the car. 'Back to town,' said Kavanagh. 'Fast as you can.' Ford glanced at the GPS to get his bearings and then found his way back to the runway. It headed east and would lead them back to the Marble Bar road.

Once on the broad strip of gravel he pushed the Toyota forward, enjoying the straight, even surface, a sense of relief washing over him that he had got through the danger, that he would soon be seeing Grace again. He looked in the mirror, at the cloud of red dust kicked up by the LandCruiser, and beyond that the column of white smoke rising from the grass fire. He looked for a sign of flame but the embankment hid the source of the smoke.

On their right was the pair of black hills, the bunker lying somewhere in their lee. Ford watched for the track that led from them. Then, as they passed the end of it, he saw a black Range Rover travelling towards them at speed, rocking in the wheel ruts, fishtailing in the soft sand. 'Shit!' he said, under his breath, and he gripped the steering wheel and put his foot to the floor.

Kavanagh looked across just in time to catch a glimpse of the black shadow moving fast through the grass, then she swivelled in her seat to watch it shoot out onto the runway and then twist sideways, skidding across the gravel until it found traction and lined up to follow them. The roar of its engine came in through their open windows, louder and more urgent than the steady chug of the Toyota's diesel.

'Gun it!' she shouted above the engine noise, tugging the pistol from her belt, twisting in her seat to see where the other car was. Ford kept his eyes forward. He could see the end of the runway a thousand metres ahead, marked by a rusted steel mast that had once held a windsock. The speedo read a hundred and forty, the Toyota's engine sounding laboured, but the big V8 in the Range Rover was starting to purr. 'We'll never outrun him!' he shouted, the black shape filling his mirrors.

The Range Rover swerved out to the left and pulled alongside them, the driver hidden behind tinted windows. As the driver's door pulled level with Kavanagh, she lifted the pistol and fired once. The window grazed and shattered, the tiny laminated shards falling outwards to reveal Henk Roth behind the wheel. Ford took his eyes off the runway to look at him, at the familiar jut of his jaw, the squared-off head with its military crew cut, the cords of his neck taut with concentration, calm eyes squinting at him through the dust. Kavanagh lifted the pistol again but Roth's eyes showed no alarm as he dabbed on his brakes to drop back a car's length, out of her field of fire. She turned in her seat and leaned out the window, her gun arm stretched out into the boiling dust, but as she sighted along the barrel she saw the AK resting on the sill of Roth's door and pulled her head in quickly. She ducked low in her seat. 'Down!' she screamed, and Ford slid as low as he could in his seat, keeping the Toyota in a straight line towards the end of the runway.

Roth's first burst rattled across the back of the LandCruiser and took out a rear tyre. Ford fought the steering wheel, feeling the heavy Toyota pull to the left and start to fishtail. The second burst ran down the left side of the car, Kavanagh flinching away from her door as the bullets punched through it and ripped into her seat. A third burst hit a front tyre and the car dropped sharply to the left as the rims of both wheels on that side shredded the tyres and bit into the gravel. They swerved around, Ford trying to correct the slide but once they were drifting sideways there was nothing he could do. He took his foot off the pedal and let the car find its own path, the bare wheels carving up the dirt and throwing dust into the air as the car scraped to a halt.

When the dust cleared they saw the Range Rover parked across their bow thirty metres ahead, Roth pointing the carbine out of his window at them, the stock tucked into his shoulder, his eyes staring at them from above the barrel. He was rigid and motionless, only his eyes moving, until he lifted a hand off the barrel to twist his wrist in the air, indicating for Ford to turn off his engine.

Roth stayed still until all engine noise had died away and the silence of the bush surrounded them. 'Step down from your car,' he said, his voice clear and assured. 'Keep your hands where I can see them.'

Ford looked at Kavanagh. Her face was flushed, sweat streaming into her eyes, which were wide with fear and anger. She still held the pistol, resting it flat on the seat beside her, her chest still rising and falling as she tried to regain her composure. She angled the pistol forwards and started to raise it slowly, but Ford reached out and gripped her by the wrist, forcing her hand back down onto the seat.

They sat like that, hands locked together, their muscles straining, Kavanagh staring at him and biting her lip in frustration. Ford's eyes pleaded with her, until her shoulders slumped in resignation and she relaxed her arm, released the gun, and he swept it off the seat and let it thump into the footwell.

They opened their doors at the same time and stepped down, their hands hanging limp at their sides, palms turned towards Roth. The barrel of the AK followed Kavanagh, but Roth's eyes swept from one of them to the other. Roth lifted his hand again, this time to wave them both further away from the LandCruiser. They both took hesitant steps sideways but, when Roth started firing, they flung themselves face down into the dirt. The scream of tearing metal told Ford that Roth was shooting at the car, and he forced his head off the ground to look, coughing and spitting dust. Roth was out of his car now, fitting a fresh clip into his gun. He levelled the barrel and emptied the clip into the Toyota, peppering the radiator, smashing the windscreen, shredding the remaining tyres and leaving an arc of holes across the bonnet.

When Ford looked up again Roth was leaning against the Range Rover, tall and lean, thinner than the last time Ford had seen him, carrying less muscle. His back didn't seem so rigid, his military bearing had softened. He was wearing a khaki shirt and matching shorts, and army boots with long socks pulled up to the knee. He had a webbing belt around his waist, and it held a gun holster diagonally across his belly, the butt of a large black automatic visible.

Roth pushed another clip into the AK and smiled at both of them. 'You can get up now, Mr Ford,' he said. Listening to the clipped vowels of his Afrikaans accent, Ford remembered the last time they had met, pointing guns at each other in an aircraft hangar while his wife and daughter watched. 'Go join the detective,' said Roth. 'Lie face down next to her.'

Ford stood up, brushed the dust from his clothes and walked slowly around to Kavanagh, his eyes fixed on the end of the gun barrel, which swung to follow him. She was sitting cross-legged on the ground. She did not look at him, her eyes also fixed on the gun. She rolled onto her belly and Ford lay down next to her, leaning on his elbows so he could continue watching Roth.

The South African pushed himself off the Range Rover and walked slowly towards them. He dragged his right foot as he walked, the sole of his boot scraping through the dirt. 'They said I would recover full mobility, those doctors,' he said. 'Two shotgun pellets went deep into the cartilage, here on the hip. Just unlucky. When I got to Jakarta I had some local guy look at it and he left the joint in worse shape than when he started.' He was standing over them now, the AK hanging around his neck on a thin strand of nylon rope. He raised his right hand and let the gun swing loose as he waggled his fingers at Ford. The first finger was missing; the third was truncated at the first joint. 'Your handiwork too,' he said. 'I should have gone to Pretoria, got myself a decent white doctor, then maybe I'd still be playing the piano.'

Kavanagh lifted her head off the ground to speak. 'Is that why you can't shoot straight?' she said. 'Lost your trigger finger?'

Roth put his hand around the pistol grip of the carbine, his hand high on it, his second finger tucked into the trigger guard. He stepped over Kavanagh, and put a foot between her shoulder blades, pushing her down into the dust. 'If I wanted you dead, I wouldn't have been shooting at your tyres.' His breathing was laboured as he leaned over her, a slight wheeze in his throat. He patted her down, lifted the hem of her shirt. He felt the lump in her back pocket and plucked out her phone and Ford's lighter. He stood upright and held the lighter to eye level, flipped the top and examined the wick. He turned to look down the runway to where the white smoke rose in a thin column before being caught by the breeze and scattered south.

A deep booming roar came rolling like thunder down the runway as the plane exploded, a ball of flame blooming above the trees, the white smoke turning to black, a broad smudge against the clear blue sky. Roth tutted to himself and stepped across to Ford. As he was patted down, Ford rolled on his side slightly, pushing his knee into the ground, pressing the patch pocket with the diamonds into the dirt. Roth's search was brisk and cursory. He found his phone but nothing else. 'Where's the gun you just fired?' he said to Kavanagh.

She turned her head to him. 'Still in the car,' she said, a flurry of dust rising from the ground in front of her as she spoke.

Roth stepped backwards until he reached the open door

of the Toyota, then turned to look inside. He leaned in and pulled out the shotgun. He broke it open and took out the shells. 'Always a shotgun with you, huh?' as he leaned the empty gun against the door. He found the pistol on the floor and examined it, turning it over in his hand. 'One of mine,' he said, his voice for the first time showing a bite of anger. 'You took this from one of my men.'

Kavanagh twisted herself back into a sitting position to look at him. 'Two of your men ambushed us in the bush after the robbery. I killed one, Ford killed the other.' She lifted her chin, enjoying the discomfort on his face.

Roth pulled the clip from the pistol and counted the rounds, drew back the slide and checked the chamber. 'And did you use this gun to kill my pilot?'

Kavanagh nodded.

Roth smiled now, feeling the balance change again. He slid the clip back into the gun and tucked the pistol into his belt beside the holster. 'I don't think you'll be arresting anyone,' he said. 'Where's your Glock, detective?' He pulled a bandana from his pocket and wiped the sweat from his forehead. 'What are you doing out here without back-up, in a mining vehicle, using a gun stolen from a dead man?' He limped slowly to the back of the Toyota, opened the rear door and searched the back. He found the toolbox and opened it, rattling the tools as he went through it. 'How did you find me here?' he asked, his voice casual.

Ford was aware that Roth was watching them in his peripheral vision as he searched the car.

'Somebody sold you out,' said Kavanagh, sitting up, picking at strands of grass poking through the gravel.

'That would be Mr Ford's wife, I suppose,' said Roth, closing the tailgate and opening the fuel cap. He fed the bandana slowly into the tank.

'Where is Diane?' asked Ford, sitting upright next to Kavanagh, putting his hand flat on his thigh to check the pouch was secure.

'Did you think I had her?' said Roth, stepping to the passenger door and reaching inside to pick up the GPS from the centre console. He thumbed the buttons and examined the screen, his eyes narrowing at what he saw. He spat out a few words in Afrikaans and dashed the screen against the corner of the car door, the edge of the steel punching through the glass and shattering it. He tossed the empty frame into the long grass beside the runway. The destruction seemed to soothe his temper, but his breathing was still laboured.

'You sound a bit wheezy there, mate,' said Kavanagh. 'You lose a bit of lung as well?'

Roth's face fell. He paused, adjusting his expression, then said, 'Ford fired two shotgun shells into me from that sawn-off monstrosity he carried. The first took my fingers and put lead in my hip. The second hit my right lung and a few stray pellets hit my liver.'

'So now you get your revenge,' said Ford, his eyes lowered to the ground, picking gravel from the tread of his boots.

'I think you use that term rather lightly,' said Roth, relaxed now, his composure restored. He went back to the fuel cap and pulled the bandana out of the tank, letting it hang loose, dripping diesel.

'I spent ten years in the Recces chasing guys across Namibia, Angola. Country not so different from this.' He twisted the end of the bandana into a rat-tail and stood back to examine his work. 'I've seen the sort of revenge that's taken out on a whole village. That's not what's happening here. I made a promise to your wife not to kill you.'

'Diane isn't with McCann anymore,' said Ford.

'A promise is a promise. Alan wants her back. If I hurt her, I hurt him.'

'You've seen her?'

'Not since I left Macau.'

'But she's your enemy now.'

'Another word you use loosely,' said Roth. 'There are no enemies, only adversaries, and they may one day be your allies, even your leaders.'

Kavanagh snorted. 'I don't believe you're the sort to show mercy unless it suits you. You've still got a use for us.'

Roth ignored her, and kept his gaze on Ford. 'I carry no ill will against you,' he said. 'You shot me because I stood between you and your family. I've seen that before. I should've known better than to underestimate a desperate man.' He picked Kavanagh's hat off the seat and twisted it in his hands. 'The fortunes of war, Mr Ford. It's what a soldier expects.'

Ford shrugged. 'I'm no soldier.'

'Indeed you're not.' Roth tossed the hat towards Kavanagh, flicking his wrist to make it spin in the air. He then picked up the two water canteens and dropped one beside each of them. Ford grabbed at it eagerly, twisted the cap and drank.

'Easy with that,' said Roth. 'You'll need all of it.' He levelled the gun at them and waved with the barrel for them to stand up. 'Time for you to start walking.'

Kavanagh got to her feet and held out a hand to help Ford up. They looked at each other and Ford drew strength from the determination in her eyes. He was still holding her hand, standing alongside her, and she didn't let it go. She gazed down the runway to the column of black smoke. 'I destroyed your exit strategy,' she said quietly.

'What kind of strategy is it that only has one way out?' said Roth. 'No plan survives contact with the enemy.'

'Are we the enemy?' asked Kavanagh.

'An adversary, maybe,' said Roth.

'You'll never get the gold out by car,' she said. 'Not by yourself, with that limp and a bad lung.' She waited to see his reaction, but he was cool.

'The gold isn't leaving,' he said. 'You always knew that.'

'McCann wanted to put it back through the mine, the only way to launder it,' she said.

'Very good,' said Roth, smirking. 'I'm going to leave it there for you.'

Kavanagh stood thinking, looking at the cloth hanging out of the fuel tank. Ford could see her expression change as she worked out the angles.

'Consider it an investment in the future,' said Roth, flipping open the Zippo and sparking a flame.

'You need me to get in the way of Bronson, and whoever he's working for,' said Kavanagh.

'Bronson works for the Lau family,' said Roth.

Kavanagh was starting to piece it together. 'They'll want you out of the way, leave McCann exposed, strong-arm him into a deal. You're as much out on a limb as we are. Is that why McCann needs his assets, to keep the Laus at arm's length?'

'You're at a crossroads,' said Roth, staring into the flame. 'There are several people who are going to make you an offer for your soul.'

'And you're not?'

'I just did. I offered you the gold. You accepted it without question. My deal is on the table. Now you need to turn towards the end of the runway and walk away,' he said, putting the flame to the end of the bandana.

Roth picked up the shotgun by the end of the barrel and used it as a stick to lean on. As the bandana started smouldering he limped quickly away towards the Range Rover. 'Hurry now!' he shouted to them.

Kavanagh tightened her grip on Ford's hand and pulled him into a run. They had put twenty metres of runway between them and the Toyota when the fuel tank ignited and the shock wave pushed them off their feet.

TWENTY

When they stood up and looked back up the runway the LandCruiser was in flames and the Range Rover had disappeared. The wind had changed direction, moving around to the north. Not much of a breeze, but enough to move the smoke from the plane across the runway and with it the smell of burning grass and the sharp tang of aviation fuel.

'Where are we going?' Kavanagh said.

Ford pointed to the western end of the runway, to a dark line of trees. It was maybe a kilometre to the end of the runway, then the same distance again to the tree line. Beyond that the ground dipped out of sight, and in the far distance it rose again, bare and rocky, towards the ridge of barren hills on the horizon. 'Those trees are the only shade I can see,' said Ford. 'It's the river. I saw it on the GPS. It runs along the western edge of the airfield.'

'And where does it go?'

'Not sure,' he said. 'It must run north, towards Marble

Bar. Must be one of the creeks that run into the Coongan River.'

'Will there be water?'

'None of the creek beds we crossed on the way out here had any,' said Ford. 'But they all had plenty of trees growing beside them.'

He pulled up the strap of his canteen and looped it over his head to stop it swinging against his hip, then checked his new watch. It was one in the afternoon. The sun was still high, he could feel it radiating through the material of his cap. They needed to get in the shade and rest until the worst of the heat had passed. There were forty kilometres between them and the town, and they would be lucky to cover five kilometres an hour in any sort of daylight heat, and fewer at night. Eight hours of walking, more if the terrain became difficult.

However many hours it took, and however lucky they got, Roth would be long gone before they got back to town. He wondered how long Saxon would wait before he came looking for them.

'We need to go the direct route,' said Kavanagh, pointing east beyond the remains of their car.

Ford shook his head. 'No shade on that road. We have about an hour's walking in forty-degree heat before we drop, even with water. We get to shade first, and rest, then see if we can walk in the shade of the tree line.' He set off walking, dropping his chin to make sure the cap's peak shaded his face, knowing there was nothing he could do to stop the sun hitting his neck and ears. He didn't look back to see if she was following, but he heard the crunch of her footsteps on the bare gravel of the runway.

His feet soon found a rhythm and his thoughts wandered. If Saxon did come looking for them there was a chance he would meet Roth on the road. He would not think to check the airfield, and certainly not the river. As he felt the sweat start to flow freely down his forehead and his back inside his shirt, his thoughts turned to Diane and where she might be, and whether all the females who were orbiting around him would ever get pulled towards him, whether he had the gravitational pull to do that, or whether all three would go spinning away, leaving him alone in empty space.

Kavanagh caught up with him and fell into step, slow and steady. Ford kept his face pointing to the ground, watching the toes of her red cowboy boots move in time with his own steel-capped work boots. They walked side by side with their heads bowed, the sun beating down on their bent shoulders. It took them twenty minutes to reach the end of the runway, where the ground sloped away to the river, the grass becoming taller before giving way to rocks and spinifex on the slope and the sandy river bed. It was a hundred metres wide, strewn with trees and boulders between sweeping patches of sand, edged on either side by paperbark trees. Kavanagh sat down on a flat red rock in the first patch of shade she found, leaning her back against the peeling trunk of the tree. She twisted the cap off the canteen and tipped it to her mouth. Ford watched her neck pulse as she swallowed.

'Go easy,' he said, realising as he spoke how dry his own throat was, running his tongue over his dry lips. 'We have two litres each, and no food. It will have to last us until morning, so take one mouthful every half hour, and hope we get some standing water in the river bed.'

Kavanagh wasn't looking at him, but at her boots, the red leather scuffed and coated with dust. She flapped her hat in front of her face at the flies, but they just looped around her and settled on her shoulders. Ford saw the anger burning in her eyes. Some of it would be directed at Roth, but he knew that most of it she kept for herself, fury at being bested, and stranded like this, while Bronson and Roth were free to play out their game without her.

'Try to sleep,' he said. 'We'll stay until the sun is lower, then walk a few hours before dark.' He found a patch of white sand on the far side of the tree trunk, well shaded, and scraped off the top layer of hot sand with his boot, sweeping his foot sideways to gouge a shallow trench, the sand cooler. When he had finished he waved for her to lie down in it. She slid off the rock and crawled on her hands and knees towards him, dropping sideways into the trench, sighing like a dog settling. She curled up on her side with her head resting on her hands; her eyes closed and her breathing slowed. Flies settled on her face but, apart from the flutter of her eyelashes when a fly crawled too close, she didn't move. Her face was dirty; red dust had caught in the slick sweat on her face and worked its way into the creases around her eyes. Her cheeks were reddened by exertion and the sun. Ford sat on a rock with his elbows resting on his knees, just an arm's length away from her, and looked at every part of her. He wanted to reach across and touch her hair, push it back behind her ear, feel the skin of her sunburnt cheek and move the tips of his fingers over her cracked lips. Instead he reached inside his pocket and found his cigarettes. He pulled out the packet and brought with it the folded money he had taken from the Canadian. He looked at it and thought about the diamonds and how they were of no use to him in this place. He put a cigarette to his lips before remembering that Roth had taken his lighter. He would gladly have traded the cash for a single smoke.

The scent of the dry tobacco mixed with the smell of fresh sweat rising from Kavanagh stirred a memory in him of the night before. He tried to picture the two of them together but the only image he could conjure was of the old bed at the Ironclad, them coiled together in it. He could never focus on an image of them anywhere else. When he tried he would see Grace and him in the house in Shenton Park, and when that picture filled his mind it didn't take long for Diane to walk into the frame. When he thought of the three of them together he could never be sure if he was imagining the future or recreating something from the past, something he had for so long thought lost, without hope of resurrection.

He woke up with his back against the trunk of the paperbark, his body still in shade but his legs in the sun. His trouser legs had ridden up above his boots and the heat on his bare shins had woken him. He checked the position of the sun and looked at his watch, surprised by its elegant face against the dirt and grime on his hand. It was past three and the sun did not seem so fierce, a little lower and further to the west, but still full of heat. He squatted down and shook Kavanagh awake. She had put her hat over her eyes, and when he removed it she lay there blinking and trying to push her tongue between her cracked lips to part them. Recognition of who he was and where they were came slowly to her eyes.

'We need to move on,' he said. 'We have three hours of daylight.'

She stood and stretched, swung her water bottle over her shoulder, and stepped out into the sunshine. He picked up his own canteen and followed her. She picked a path between the soft sand in the middle of the river bed and the rocks at the edge, a band of gravel where the ground was firmest. The trees here were widely spaced and offered intermittent shade. After an hour their creek joined another, wider watercourse. There was still no sign of water, but this bed seemed deeper, as if cut by a more urgent flow in the wet season.

The sun filled the sky and had no edges. It was everything over them, white heat pressing down on them and bleaching the blue from the sky. Ford narrowed his eyes so that only a sliver of ground in front of him was visible, orange and white dots dancing on his closed eyelids.

Another hour on and in step behind Kavanagh he noticed that she was limping, dragging her left foot in the gravel, turning it inwards and walking on the edge of her boot, the Cuban heel digging into the sand.

'How badly are you blistered?' he asked.

She paused before she spoke. 'These boots ain't made for walking.'

Their pace slowed. Ford was walking ahead now, setting a cadence that Kavanagh could keep. Whenever he looked around, her face was set in a grimace of pain. Ford's feet were also blistered inside his work boots, the steel toe caps crowding his toes. He could feel that his socks were wet, and he suspected that some of it was blood. Kavanagh had her arms folded across her chest, her bare hands tucked under her armpits to keep them out of the sun, her body twisted to keep her face pointed away from it. The sun was tracking slowly west as they made equally slow progress north. The hills looked closer, and the land to the east grew taller and rockier until the river bed narrowed and got deeper, becoming a shallow ravine between the hills. It curved around a promontory and there, beneath the shadow of overhanging rocks, was a pool of water trapped in a narrow defile, bordered by slabs of rock along its sides and a fan of yellow sand at one end. Paperbarks stood along the western side, drooping their ribbon leaves over the pool, the tips almost reaching the water. A white heron rose gracefully from the shadows, startled by their approach, the rush of air under its wings the only sound besides their own breathing.

The sand at the shallow end of the pool was marked with the footprints of birds. The water itself was black, spotted with mosquitos and dead flies, ringed with bird droppings. Kavanagh walked stiff-legged to the shade under the trees and threw herself onto a ledge of rock beside the water. Ford sat beside her and took the cap off his water bottle, shaking it to feel the weight of water remaining and calculating how long it might last. He handed it to her and she sipped it gingerly, eying the black water in the pool from under the brim of her hat.

'We can't drink that,' said Ford, nodding towards hoof prints left by cattle beside their dung. 'We're not that desperate, yet.'

'No,' she said, 'but I can wash my feet in it.' She threw one leg over the other and tried to grab hold of her boot, but her legs were too stiff. She collapsed backwards again and lay flat on her back, one boot in the air, waggling the toe at Ford. He took hold of it and pulled, and the boot came off with a wet sucking sound, revealing Kavanagh's white sports sock stained red with dust and blood. He put a finger under the top of it and peeled it off and they both sucked air through their teeth when they saw the mess that was her bare foot. Ford leaned in to take a closer look, trying not to grimace at the smell. She had lost the nail from her second toe, and the others were black. The tops of her toes were stripped of skin and bleeding, and the undersides had shreds of skin hanging from burst blisters. Her heel was similarly flayed, the sole ringed with blisters that had bled, and there were deep red welts across the top of her instep. Ford grasped the other boot and found that foot to be in a worse state than the first. Kavanagh looked at her feet in disgust and lay back on the rock, putting her hat over her face.

'Will I live?' she said.

'Most likely,' said Ford, 'but your ballet career is fucked.' He leaned over the ledge and dipped the socks in the water, rinsing them and wringing them out, then turned them inside-out and repeated the process, holding them up to check if he had made them any cleaner.

'Are we going to get through this?' asked Kavanagh, her voice small and muffled beneath the hat. A fly licked its way up the line of sweat that had run down her neck, and when it reached her chin she swatted it.

'We'll get out of this,' said Ford. 'Roth wants us alive, or he'd have burned us in our car.'

She snorted from under the hat. 'Is this how you are now?

Indifferent?'

'I have no interest in chasing down Roth. He could be on the coast by now, in another plane, or on a boat.'

'I meant indifferent to death.'

Ford dunked the socks in the water again and balled them, still dripping, in his hand. He sat cross-legged and lifted Kavanagh's right foot to rest it in his lap, then started to wipe it with the sock. She winced when he brushed across the raw skin.

'After everything I went through last year, being shot and beaten, I got into the habit of thinking about death,' he said. 'I used to think about it every night after I'd put Grace to bed.'

'You're worried about her?'

'She'll be safer where she is than out here with us.'

'But she'll be worrying about you.'

'She spends a lot of time worrying about me, whether I'm with her or not. She carries a lot of weight on her shoulders for someone so small.'

'You both do.'

He put her foot gently back on the ground and lifted the other one and started to wash it. 'Without a sense of death around us, life would be insipid,' he said. 'All expectations, all sense of failure or embarrassment, these things fall away when we're faced with death, leaving only what's important. I've failed my family before and I'll fail again, but I don't fear failure now, and I don't fear death, and I'll take whatever risk presents itself because to stay static is impossible now.'

He put her foot down and picked up the two canteens of water. He poured the contents of one into the other and then hefted it for weight. It was less than half full. Reaching down to the edge of the water, he scooped up a handful of sand, and put it into one of Kavanagh's socks, repeating the process until it was full and bulging. He took one of her boots and dunked it in the pool, filled it to the brim with water, then tipped it into the top of the sock, which he held over the empty canteen. Water dripped slowly from the sock into the bottle.

'It's a filter, of sorts,' he said. 'Better than drinking this stuff straight out of the pool. There may come a time we'll be grateful for it.'

When the canteen was full Ford emptied the sand from the sock, rinsed both socks again and wrung them out, then stood up and walked out into the sun. He laid the socks on a flat rock to dry, watching as the sun evaporated the spilled water around them, the dark spots on the rock shrinking then disappearing. When he returned Kavanagh was asleep, her breathing laboured. He wondered if she had listened to what he had said. He lay down beside her, closed his eyes, and let unconsciousness overtake him.

When he awoke the sun was low in the west, a hand's breadth above the hills that lined the horizon. Kavanagh was standing close by in the sand by the pool, her boots folded over the top of her water canteen, trapped between the straps. She was barefoot, stepping from one foot to the other, testing the pain. 'The sand's not so hot now,' she said. 'If we keep away from the rocks I'll be better without boots.' Her face was flushed red, her eyes seemed unfocused, and Ford recognised the symptoms of heat stress. He drank from his own canteen and looked at his watch. 'Let's go,' he said.

The sun was not as hot, but the humidity had increased,

and Ford's shirt was soon wet again. He could see the moon now in the east, hanging low over the plain, waxing gibbous, glowing an ugly yellow, veiled by the dust in the air. It gave him some comfort that they would have light to walk by when the sun was gone.

The sun was soon touching the hills, painting them the colour of dried blood. Ford's face was brushed by a breeze, barely discernible, a last sigh from the desert. The twilight was brief, a haunting glow high in the sky before the stars appeared and the gloom closed in around them, dark shadows creeping towards them from the rocks.

Kavanagh stumbled in the dark, swore under her breath, but kept moving. In the silence of the bush he could hear her crying, a small, thin noise not much louder than her breathing. He caught up with her, put a hand on her shoulder to stop her, then made her put on his socks. His boots were too large for her, and she declined them with a stubborn shake of her head, so he put them on again over his bare feet. He took her hand and walked ahead of her, leading her along the river bed in the blue light from the moon, finding the softest path for her.

It was another hour before the bed widened, the shadows of paperbarks looming at them from the dark. As they walked through the trees, they found themselves in a broad clearing, walking on smooth sand that was firm under foot and seemed to glow in the moonlight.

Ford let go of Kavanagh's hand and squatted down, brushing the thin layer of sand aside to feel the hard flat ground beneath, a ribbon of concrete crossing the river bed. 'It's a road,' he said, relief pulsing through him. 'It's a ford across the river.'

Kavanagh groaned and slumped to the ground, curling up on her side, pulling her knees to her chest, whimpering louder now. He didn't need to ask her to go on. They would wait for daylight or hope for a car. He made her raise her head and drink, the water in her canteen down to the last few mouthfuls, then he let her sleep. He lay down and wrapped himself around her, pressing his nose to the nape of her neck, feeling the heat radiate from her skin, and his mind filled with thoughts of his daughter until he fell asleep on the road.

TWENTY-ONE

The sound of the engine woke him, a high-pitched whine broken by grinding gear changes and the rasp of a perforated exhaust. He sat upright and for a moment thought the noise was something from his dreams, but it reached him again, distant but distinct. He stood up and turned his head to see if he could identify the direction it was coming from but it seemed to be echoing off the rocks. A flash of light in the sky made him look to the east, but all he could see was the moon, higher now, embedded within the sweep of the Milky Way.

Light raced across the hillside and he could hear the vehicle more clearly, labouring around the hill to the east, the beams of its headlights playing on the rocks, until it came around the hill and the two discs of its headlights became visible. The engine note dropped to a throaty rumble and Ford recognised the whine as an old four-wheel-drive gearbox in high ratio. It was still a few kilometres away. He squatted down and nudged

Kavanagh but she did not stir and he wondered if she may have been sicker than he had thought and he should not have let her sleep. As the jeep came towards the river the lights illuminated the whole of the crossing, throwing shadows from the gum trees either side of Ford, and showing him the full length of the river crossing, the concrete ribbon only wide enough for one vehicle, with Kavanagh lying in the middle of it.

Ford took his cap off, then stood as upright as he could and stared straight down the road into the approaching head-lights. The vehicle slowed when it saw him, crashing down through the gears then crawling forward until it stopped fifty metres away. Ford squinted into the headlights and waved, an awkward flick of his wrist that made him feel embar-rassed even as he did it. The engine revved and the car inched forward until it was close. It was an old Land Rover, the headlights close together in the recessed radiator grille. The engine idled roughly and the door swung open. Ford could make out nothing of the driver stepping out but a vague silhouette and the outline of a broad-brimmed hat; as the man turned to face him, he saw a flash of light off his spec-tacles. He walked slowly into the light and Ford recognised the long grey beard and the skinny legs poking down from the baggy shorts.

Henry Dussell looked down at Kavanagh before he spoke. 'Bloody foolish place to roll out your swag,' he said. 'There's been idiots fall asleep in the river bed and got swept away when the rains come.'

Ford stepped forward into the light so Dussell could see the state of him, and watched the old man's eyes widen.

'We got stranded,' he said. 'She's in a bad way. Heat stress, exhaustion, sunburn, dehydration. We need to get her to town.'

Dussell squatted beside Kavanagh and felt for the pulse at her neck. He put a hand on her forehead and tutted to himself. He stood up and put his hands on his hips and sighed, and Ford noticed the holster on his belt. It was tan leather, cracked with age, dark in places with sweat and oil. The gun in it was an old Webley revolver, the black metal shining in the headlights as if it had been recently oiled.

Dussell took a small pen torch from his pocket and shone it on Kavanagh's face. He squatted down again and put a thumb to her eye, lifted the lid and shone the torch on her iris. 'Fuck off,' she muttered, her voice slurred.

'How long has she been asleep?' asked Dussell.

Ford turned his watch to the headlights and read the time; it was past nine. 'Two hours maybe,' he said. 'We were walking in the dark.'

'Let's get her in the truck,' said Dussell. They stood either side of her and bent together, took an arm each and pulled her up, her arms hanging loose across their shoulders. She woke again once they'd got her upright, trying to shrug them off, but her legs buckled and they lifted her into the Land Rover. She sat upright in the back seat and opened her eyes and focused on the two men, giving them a small smile and taking hold of the water bottle Dussell offered her.

'Sip slowly,' said Dussell. 'I've an esky in the back with some ice.' He went to the rear door, took down a small hand towel that hung on a hook from the luggage cage, and dipped it in the melted ice at the bottom of the box. After squeezing it, he walked around to Kavanagh and put the cold towel over her head. 'Not too long,' he said to her, 'you'll start to get a chill.' There was an army blanket draped across the seat and Dussell wrapped it around her. She sat still, cocooned, only the tip of her nose visible in the weak light.

Dussell climbed behind the steering wheel, waiting for Ford to take the seat beside him. He threw the truck into gear, let out the clutch and they lurched forward. A battered two-way radio was bolted into the roof, the spiral lead to the handset hanging in front of Ford's face and swinging around as the truck moved. A handheld GPS unit was fixed to the windscreen with gaffer tape and Dussell shone his torch on it to check their location.

When the Land Rover reached the edge of the river bed and climbed the bank, Ford realised they were heading west and he nudged Dussell's elbow. 'We need to get her back to town,' he said.

Dussell kept his eyes on the road. 'Where's your vehicle?' he asked.

Ford jerked his thumb over his shoulder in a direction he figured was south. Dussell pursed his lips and tutted. 'You know you should have stayed with your vehicle.'

'It was on fire,' said Ford. 'We needed to get away from it.'

'You pointed south, where were you down there?'

Ford hesitated, figuring that Dussell knew the country well. He decided his own knowledge of the country wasn't good enough to be able to lie to him. 'Corunna Downs,' he said.

'You should've walked to the homestead,' said Dussell. It would've been quicker than heading north and you'd have gone past windmills.'

'We were at the old airfield,' said Ford. 'We came up the river.'

Dussell shone the torch in Ford's face and he squinted into the light. 'There's some aloe vera cream in the glove box,' said Dussell. 'Put some on your neck and ears before they blister.'

'I can feel them glowing,' said Ford. He opened the flap in the dashboard and found a curled tube of ointment. He squeezed a slug of white cream into his palm and massaged it into his neck. He felt the soothing cold of it immediately.

'Who were you running from?' asked Dussell.

Ford rubbed the cream around his ears and didn't answer.

'You work in the mines,' said Dussell. 'You know the drill out here. You wouldn't have left your vehicle unless someone was behind you.'

'We need to get back to town.'

'Where's that little girl of yours?'

'In Marble Bar.'

'You didn't leave her at the Ironclad?'

'No, she's with people. She's safe. But we need to turn around.'

'Can't do that, mate. I've got things to do. I can set you back down on the road if you like. She'll be right in a while. I'll leave you with water. It's about fifteen clicks back to town. You can be there before morning.'

'It's only thirty minutes out of your way.'

'Half an hour that I don't have. You can travel with me. I'll take you back into town tomorrow morning at sparrow's fart.'

'I can't imagine what happens out here that you'd worry

about being late. Everything else round here seems to work on Marble Bar time.'

Dussell looked at Ford, then over his shoulder at Kavanagh wrapped in the blanket. 'I don't know what you two are doing wandering around out here, but I don't like it. Too many strangers in town.'

'Have you seen the Maori today?' said Ford.

'We're getting to it, aren't we?' said Dussell. 'You two better stay with me, where I can keep an eye on you. Don't want you doing anything else to get in the way of things.'

Ford looked over his shoulder again at Kavanagh, who looked alert now, sipping at the bottle. 'You reckon you could walk?' he said.

Kavanagh shook her head.

'You'll stay with me,' said Dussell. He moved his hand to his hip and opened the flap on his holster, laid his hand on the butt of the Webley.

'Take it easy, old man,' said Ford. 'We're going nowhere.'

Ford reached for the radio handset on the dashboard and Dussell slapped his hand away.

'I need to check on my daughter,' he said.

'You just told me she was safe,' said Dussell. 'The radio stays silent tonight.'

'I need something to eat,' said Kavanagh.

'There'll be food where we're going,' said Dussell.

'And where's that?'

'West,' said Dussell, pointing to the GPS. 'Maybe an hour.'

'There's nothing west of here,' said Ford. 'Not for a hundred kilometres, until you hit the Great Northern Highway and the iron ore mines.'

'There's plenty out there,' said Dussell. 'You're the kind of guy that can't see what he's looking at.'

He turned to Ford and grinned, the light from the dashboard reflecting off the gold teeth, a brief wink of yellow light in his smile.

'All that metal in your mouth,' said Ford. 'That why they call you Bobby Dazzler?'

The smile disappeared and Dussell turned his attention to the road. 'I've got a lot of nicknames. That's just the one they use at the Ironclad,' he said. 'Might be because of the teeth, but I only got these two years ago after I had a nasty run-in with a piece of peanut brittle from the roadhouse.' The road was winding now, climbing into the hills, the headlights picking out tumbled rocks either side of the strip of gravel. 'Maybe it's just a play on my surname, but I reckon it's to do with the gold.'

'How much have you found?'

'Not me, mate. The Bobby Dazzler was the largest nugget ever discovered when Archie Clive tripped over it in 1889. He found it in Shark's Gully. We passed the road a few minutes back. There was 413 ounces of gold in it, and they sent the thing to Paris and put it on show.'

'Where is it now?'

Dussell laughed. 'They melted the bastard down. They only put it on show to try and get some investors to stump up some capital to develop the mine. They never did find anyone fool enough. It was only an alluvial show. They mined it all out pretty quickly and then they were broke.'

'The girl at the bar said you're a geologist.'

'What would she know?' said Dussell. 'I don't waste my time

with those bastards. You ask two geologists the same question and you'll get three different answers. I'm a prospector.'

'You ever find anything?'

'Take a look at this truck. Tell me if I ever struck it rich. I make just enough so as I don't have to work for anyone else.'

'Is there still gold around here?'

'Didn't I just tell you that you're not seeing what's right in front of you? You don't need to know anything about geology to fossick around here. The rocks are right there, looking you in the face, telling you everything you need to know. Billions of years right there on the surface, an ancient land, unchanged.'

He slowed the truck as they crested the ridge, flashed the torch on the GPS, and then watched the side of the road until he spotted the track leading off to the north. He swung the Land Rover on to it and held the steering wheel tightly with both hands as the truck lurched and bounced on the narrow track.

After twenty minutes the track had reduced to a pair of shallow wheel ruts in the gravel. If there was a route marked, Ford couldn't see it, but Dussell seemed to know his way. The engine noise and the regular thumps from the suspension made conversation impossible, so Ford hung on to the handle above the door and swayed with the motion of the truck, watching the headlights dance over the barren country ahead of them.

They were still heading uphill, the ridge looming over them, outlined by a field of stars in a clear sky and lit in a palette of blues and greys by the moon overhead. In the distance a cluster of rocks stood proud against the horizon, and they were glowing orange. Ford could see the light flickering from a campfire hidden among the rocks. As he watched there was a flash of white light from within the radiant gold, a torch pulsing, signalling them. Ford wondered if it was Morse code. Dussell saw it and flashed the truck's headlights in reply. They passed beneath the rocks and then turned a hairpin and the campfire was ahead of them, much closer now. Dussell threw the Land Rover into low gear as the trail got steeper, the engine screaming as it laboured up the gradient, the wheels slipping on the loose gravel.

As they neared the top of the ridge Ford could make out a figure standing upright on the rock, silhouetted against the firelight, the torch hanging loosely in his hand. Ford recognised the outline of the baseball cap with the flat brim. The Land Rover pulled up beside a Toyota ute and Ford jumped down and opened the back door for Kavanagh to get out. He offered her his hand, but she slapped it away and stepped down unaided.

Muddy jumped down from the rock, shone the torch in Ford's face and said, 'Your ears are burning, bro. You must have thought we was talking about you.'

TWENTY-TWO

'You don't seem that surprised to see us,' said Ford.
Muddy shrugged. 'There's not much in this country that's unexpected. So many freaks, weirdos and losers. You get used to it. This weekend has brought more dropkicks than usual into town, though.'

Kavanagh limped past Ford and stepped between the rocks looking for the fire, the army blanket still around her shoulders, flapping behind her. The temperature had dropped, although it was still warm, but Kavanagh was shivering. Ford followed her into the light. The campfire was in a small depression, between sharp rectangular rocks that stood upright in a ring like broken teeth. Those on the uphill side were taller; the largest had an overhanging slab that formed a small shelter. The fire seemed to be mostly embers glowing orange and white, giving off little smoke. Kavanagh held out her arms, the blanket hanging like a cape, letting the heat from the fire reach her ribs. 'Where the fuck are we?' she asked, slurring her words.

'Somewhere west of Marble Bar,' said Ford. 'Slap bang in the middle of nowhere.'

Muddy stepped up behind him, found a rock with a bottle of beer standing on it, and sat down. 'This ain't nowhere, bro. This is definitely somewhere.'

'So tell us where we are.'

'My country, bro. This is my country.'

Dussell joined them, carrying a milk crate full of tools and a pack on his back. 'I found these fools in the middle of the Coongan River. Left their vehicle, got sunburnt, dehydrated and generally fucked up.'

Muddy snorted. 'You're lucky the country didn't let you die.'

Ford looked at the bottle in Muddy's hand. 'You're killing me drinking that beer in front of me. I'm so dry I couldn't spit enough to christen a frog.'

'You been in the sun all day, let it burn you red like that, you shouldn't be drinking beer.'

'I'll risk it,' said Ford. 'Humour me.'

Dussell set the crate beside the fire and swung the backpack onto a rock. 'When you walked into the Ironclad I thought that if the big Maori bastard didn't fuck you up, then the country would. Reynard was right, you're a couple of dumb FIFO fuckers, wandering around the bush like that.' He started unpacking the crate, laying the items out in a line in the sand, shining the torch on each item in turn to check it. There was a rubber mallet, an axe, a geological hammer and a set of wooden stakes bundled together. Each stake was about a foot long, sharpened at one end. At the bottom of the crate was a clipboard with a bundle of papers tied to it, and the GPS from the dashboard of the Land Rover. The last item to come out of the crate was a head torch, the lamp bound up and twisted with the elastic strapping. Dussell sat cross-legged by the fire and began to unravel it.

'This is your important appointment?' asked Ford. 'A bit of midnight pegging in the middle of nowhere?'

Dussell looked up from his work and pulled at his beard. Ford enjoyed the look of surprise in the old man's eyes. 'Yeah, I know how it works. I worked in the gold industry for eight years, in and around Kalgoorlie. I know the tools. No other reason for a prospector to be out here in the middle of the night, all in a hurry.'

Dussell fitted the head torch to his forehead and turned it on, the beam hitting Ford in the face. 'You're not as dumb as you look,' he said.

Ford turned away from the light and looked at Muddy, who had a fresh beer in his hand, holding it out for him. 'Cheers,' Ford said.

'Why don't you tell us why you and the cop are lost in space.'

Ford sat down on a rock with his back to the fire and looked out over the valley. All he could make out in the moonlight were vague shadows. A full field of stars arched overhead, and the light from the fire was the only sign of human habitation. 'This is your country?' he asked.

Muddy walked over and sat beside him. 'My dad's from southern Perth, around Armadale there. But my mother's mother came from here. This was her country. It's my country. It's my Auntie's country too.'

'This country got a smell of this boy, eh? This is his country. It owns him, and he part of it.'

The voice came from behind them, from the far side of the fire. Ford had not noticed the old woman sitting on the ground, leaning back into a crevice between two rocks, hidden in shadow, wrapped in a blanket as dark as her skin. Until she spoke Ford had thought she was part of the rock formation. She leaned forward until her face was in the light from the fire, the orange glow picking out the deep creases in a broad face as chiselled as the landscape. 'You stranger here. Country gotta get to know you. You lucky Wallabung find you before country let you die.'

Ford looked at Dussell, puzzled. 'I told you I got a lot of nicknames,' said Dussell. 'This is Emily.' He nodded towards the old lady. 'She's been camped here for the last week, making sure the country was ready for us.'

'This my nephew country two way,' said Emily. 'White way from his father for his grandad, he station owner. Black way from my mother. He come here looking for family, where he belong. Now he know, and he know this country. He know every rock and soak, every hill. You think this place middle of the nowhere. Every little bit of this country somewhere.'

Kavanagh pulled the blanket tight around her shoulders and sat down cross-legged by the fire. 'You said there would be food,' she said, to nobody in particular.

'What do you fancy?' asked Muddy.

'Right now I'll eat anything that doesn't bite back.'

Muddy stepped up beside her and picked up a stick, then raked through the coals until he uncovered a long black shape in the embers. 'There's a kangaroo tail here. Should be about done by now. We were going to make some damper when Bobby Dazzler got here. We weren't expecting guests.'

Kavanagh caught a whiff of burning fur and wrinkled her nose. 'You got anything else?'

'I've got some beans somewhere,' said Dussell.

'Great,' said Kavanagh. 'I'll take the vegetarian option.'

Dussell rummaged in his backpack and pulled out a can, yanked off the ring pull and stood it in the embers, then helped himself to a beer.

'There's a gold lease that straddles this valley,' he said. 'This ridge and the one opposite, and the gully in between. The lease expires at midnight.' He looked at his watch. 'Thirty minutes, I'll go out there and peg the bastard.'

Ford took a drink from his beer. 'I heard they were changing it all to electronic registration these days. All done on the computer at the Mines Department.'

'Most of it is,' said Dussell, 'but small gold claims, less than two hundred hectares, still need to be pegged by hand and registered at the Department in Marble Bar. You think I'd be hanging around in the Bar if there wasn't still an angle for guys like me?'

'You and Muddy staking a claim together?'

'The last time I was in a proper rush of pegging was at the Rabbit Warren out past Leonora about 1982, the field that old Snowy Barnes found. It's all changed since then. Mostly all electronic these days. GPS, internet paperwork, but you can still get out there and peg a prospecting claim yourself. There's still the chance that the bloke on his own can get there before the big companies muscle the last of us off the rocks.'

Muddy jumped up from the rock, his eyes wide enough for Ford to see the whites reflecting the moonlight. 'This claim was found by my mob. Long time back, 1930 they reckon. Uncle to my Auntie found the gold here. They call him Whistling Billy in town.'

'He was well known, old Billy,' said Dussell. 'I used to see him in the Ironclad when I was a young bloke just starting out. 'Course, he was over the other side in the front bar with the other blackfellas. No coming across into the lounge.'

Muddy looked frustrated by the interruption. 'These two prospectors were working the gully down there. Long time they were at it with a dry blower, picking up bits of gold, but they couldn't work out where it was coming from. Billy, he's with them, he walks up the creek bed with a rifle to get a kangaroo. He shoots at it and hits it, but it's still moving. Climbs up the other side of the valley over there. Billy follows it, but that kangaroo drops close to where this quartz is sticking out. Sticking right out of the hill with a vein of gold through it, so he goes back and tells the prospectors. They say, "Well done, Billy. We'll pay you for it. We'll give you a lot of money for that." They asked the storekeeper to give Billy a bag of flour and some tea, sugar and a bit of tobacco, and he was paid. He gets a bag of tucker and these *wadjala* get all that gold out of it.'

'So now you're pegging it for yourself?' asked Ford.

'Not for me. For all my mob. Looking to the future. What are you looking for?'

Kavanagh was leaning over the can, watching the beans start to bubble. 'We're doing the same as you. Looking for gold,' she said.

'We're not prospecting,' said Dussell. 'There's no gold around here. The claim was worked out within a year of Whistling Billy finding that vein. They drove a tunnel into the side of that ridge and the reef ran out after two hundred feet.'

'So why are you pegging it?'

'Just because there's no gold doesn't mean it's not valuable,' said Dussell.

'It's valuable to us,' said Muddy. 'Me and my mob.'

'Bobby Dazzler told me the rocks speak to him. Do they talk to you too?'

'They talk to all of us.' This was Emily, sitting close to the fire now, scraping the singed fur from the kangaroo tail, peeling the skin away. Kavanagh looked on unimpressed. 'Plant, rock, water, they all alive, same like animal,' the old woman continued.

Dussell lifted the can of beans out of the fire with a pair of sticks and set it down in front of Kavanagh, then dropped a spoon in for her. 'The blackfellas have always known where the gold is. It links in with the stories of how this country was created and how it lives today. This is a special place. Special to these people. Sacred, if you like. It was never a surprise to them that there was gold around here. The gold was always found near the sacred places.'

'How is this place sacred to a man from Armadale?' asked Ford.

'What?' Muddy was standing, pacing back and forth. 'You think because I'm a suburban blackfella that I got no link to this country? You don't really get it, do you?'

'No, I don't see it. Must be a spiritual thing.'

Muddy was nodding. 'You white blokes, you think of this as hostile country. Something empty, forbidding. For me it's something different, it's nurturing. Where's your country, bro?'

Ford was staring into the fire, the flames making pictures in his mind, shapes of landscapes far away and the faces of people he had left. 'I grew up on the far side of the world,' he said. 'The hills outside Manchester. Different to this.'

'You feel like you carry that place with you?'

Ford thought about the green hills, the millstone grit crags, the long grey twilight of summer evenings and the feeling of soft rain, cool on his face. 'People are more important to me than places,' he said. 'They always were and they still are.' The flames were resolving themselves into the faces of those he loved. 'I need to get back to Marble Bar, to my daughter.'

'This again?' said Dussell. 'It will take me an hour to peg this, then we'll drive back.'

'Peg this? You just said it was worthless.'

'Again, you're sitting there looking at the answer and not seeing it,' said Dussell. Ford looked around, but could only see the rocks and the fire. 'This used to be gold country. Now it's iron ore country.'

Ford snorted. 'The main ore deposits are further west, towards Newman. There's nothing decent around here.'

'Nothing as big or as rich as Mount Whaleback, granted, but the deposit here is high grade and very low silica.'

'Nothing this far east has ever been viable.'

'Rubbish,' said Dussell. 'The reason the big miners never kept looking round here was that they wanted the easy pickings at Newman. Now we've got the Chinese coming in, sick of the big multinationals controlling supply and dictating the iron ore price. They've been pumping cash into the smaller and more marginal deposits, into the start-up mining companies. Buying them outright sometimes. Lot of new mines coming on stream so that the Chinese can wedge the big boys and break the cartel.'

'You'll not be keeping the Chinese steel mills rolling on a two hundred acre lease,' said Ford.

'This whole valley is a single iron ore mining lease,' said Muddy, animated now, bouncing from one foot to the other, working up a rhythm like he was dancing. 'It was granted fifteen years ago, way before native title legislation was passed. My mob got nothing. No attempt to involve the traditional owners. So now we'll make them. This little gold lease straddles the mouth of the valley. Any pit in the gully will have to batter into this lease. Any haul road or railway out of the valley will have to cross this land, and they'll need our consent to do that.'

'You're going to fuck them up?' said Ford. 'That's your plan?'

'If we can stop the development of the iron ore lease, that would suit us. Leave this country undisturbed,' said Muddy.

'But that will never happen,' said Dussell. 'We know that. Any lease is at the discretion of the Minister for Mines. If we hold up development, the Minister can simply cancel the lease. All we're hoping is that we can drag them to the negotiating table. Get them to talk to the traditional owners in good faith, as they should have done in the first place.'

'Share the rewards a little bit. Maybe some jobs, contracts for Aboriginal companies. It wouldn't hurt for them to share the spoils. Put some wealth back into the community instead of sending all the profits offshore.'

Kavanagh had been eating her beans, listening quietly. She stood now, stretching her legs and yawning. 'I can't imagine a big mining company letting you twist their arm like that,' she said. 'They'll know every lease in this region and when it expires.'

Dussell started pulling at his beard, looking at Muddy. 'The big companies get sloppy,' he said. 'Don't keep an eye on things, the bureaucracy gets blind. Gives an opportunity to the little guy.'

'To jump their claim?' said Kavanagh.

'All's fair in love and war.'

Kavanagh had her hands on her hips now, staring at Dussell. 'That why you're wearing a gun? Don't tell us it's for snakes.'

Dussell fidgeted with the holster, looked down at the ground. Kavanagh pressed her advantage. 'When we came into the Ironclad you were suspicious of us. I saw you looking at the mining company logo on our truck, snooping around the tailgate checking our stuff. That why you refused to take us back into town? You reckon we were here to peg this claim too?'

'Not barefoot in the middle of the river bed,' said Dussell. 'I got no idea who you are, but I didn't want you back in the pub telling everyone where you'd seen me. I don't know what your argument is with that Maori and his offsider, but I see two guys like that in town in fancy suits and I start to wonder why they showed up this weekend. I start to wonder whether you or them are working for Alan McCann.'

Ford looked at Kavanagh and wondered if the look of surprise on her face was mirrored on his own. 'McCann owns the iron ore lease?' he said, under his breath.

'We got all excited when he went bankrupt,' said Muddy.

'Thought those receivers might sell off the lease. Maybe one of the multinationals take it over, someone we could deal with. But it looks like he's going to weasel out of it.'

Ford was still saying McCann's name quietly under his breath, trying to make the connections, when Bronson stepped out from the shadow of the rock and into the light of the campfire. He looked down at the kangaroo tail laid out in front of Emily and shone a torch on the blackened meat.

'That's the most miserable *hangi* I've ever seen,' he said. 'I could smell it from the other side of the ridge. Wondered what the fuck you were cremating.'

TWENTY-THREE

Bronson stepped closer to the fire and looked at Ford, then at Kavanagh. 'Why don't you all step closer to the light,' he said. 'It's cosy here and I can keep an eye on you all.'

Dussell's right hand went to the holster on his hip and fumbled with the flap. Bronson watched him struggle, his mouth breaking into a half-smile. He folded his arms and waited for Dussell to get the Webley free of the leather. The old man lifted the revolver and held it level with both hands, the flames of the campfire reflecting in his spectacles as he looked down the barrel. Bronson was openly grinning now. 'You saw your barman pull a gun on me and thought you could be a hero too?'

'How long you been hiding behind that rock?' said Dussell. His voice was calm but the barrel of the gun was shaking.

'Not quite long enough to hear what I was listening for,' said Bronson. 'Don't worry about the gold lease. I know about that. Thought I'd better show myself before midnight, before you got any ideas about pegging it.'

'Where's your Chinese buddy?' asked Dussell, his voice breaking now.

Bronson's grin returned. 'He's around here somewhere. Who knows, he might be dressed in black and lurking in the dark like some psycho ghost ninja.'

'Ninja are Japanese,' said Ford, stepping in front of Kavanagh.

'I'm real ninja, me,' said Muddy. 'Why d'ya think those fellas dress in black? Everyone wants to be black. At least, they want to be black until the cops arrive.'

'Is that right?' said Bronson. 'Whatever. Wu taught me a few tricks about the stealthy approach, how to sneak up on people. You need to keep looking over your shoulder with that little bastard around.'

Dussell took the bait and turned his head to look behind, and the big Maori took three quick steps forward and put his left hand palm down on the barrel of the gun, pushing it down and away, pointing it towards the fire, and when Dussell tried to snatch it away the revolver discharged, a column of flame erupting downwards, the report echoing across the valley.

'Motherfucker!' hissed Bronson, yanking the gun free of Dussell's grip and transferring it quickly to his other hand. He looked at the palm of his left hand, turning it to the light. 'You burned me, you daft old cunt,' he said, spitting on his hand. He raised the revolver. 'This thing's a bloody antique, same as you. Thank fuck the thing didn't go off when you were pointing it at me.' He held the Webley loosely and turned to Ford, waving him aside with the barrel so he could see

Kavanagh. She sat with her back to the rock, her knees pulled up to her chest, the blanket wrapped around her.

'Why don't you open that blanket, sweetheart. Ease my mind that you've not got that pistol under there pointing at my balls.'

Kavanagh shook her head. 'I'm unarmed.'

'You'll forgive me if I don't believe you,' said Bronson, motioning with the gun for her to stand. Kavanagh groaned and got slowly to her feet, putting a hand on the rock to steady herself and letting the blanket fall. Bronson curled his finger at her, made her step towards him, and then circled his finger in the air for her to turn around. She stood with her back to him and sighed, holding out her hands limply. Bronson stepped up behind her and put his mouth close to her ear. 'Now where have you stashed that little automatic?' He kept the old revolver pointed at her as he ran his free hand over her body, down her legs and up the inside of her thighs, around the waistband of her jeans. He breathed in her ear again. 'Hey girl, you need to unclench a little right now. You always this tense? Where is it?'

'I don't have it.'

'No gun and no phone.' Bronson caught Ford watching him and smiled. 'This a problem for you?' he said. Ford shifted uneasily, kept eye contact. 'The way you're looking at me, those are the eyes of a jealous man. Did you get your dick wet last night?' He put his arm around Kavanagh's waist, ran his hand up her belly and cupped her breast. 'Don't sweat it, man. There's nothing here to interest me. Hell, even the little Macau chicks have more flesh on their bones than this one. You like all this gristle?' Ford took a step forward but

Bronson stopped him with a shake of his head. 'Getting protective now? You're punching way above your weight with this one. Better take care. Get the wrong side of her and she'll rip it out by the roots.'

Ford tried to keep his face blank, not wanting to reveal anything, but realised his inaction had told the Maori something after all. Bronson moved his hand to Kavanagh's other breast, kneading it, waiting to see what Ford would do. When Ford looked away, Bronson said, 'There you go. You're really a man that looks after his women, aren't you? Where's that daughter of yours? You the kind of father leaves her in someone else's care?' Ford stared down into the flames of the fire.

Bronson moved his hand to Kavanagh's shoulder and walked her back to the rocks, pushing her down to sit beside Muddy and Emily. She wrapped the blanket back around herself and glared at him. He had the Webley swinging loose from his hand, upside down with his finger through the trigger guard. 'Every day I been in this country somebody's been pushing a gun in my face. Whatever happened to that Australian friendliness I'm always hearing about?'

'Up here it's FIFO,' said Muddy. 'Fit In or Fuck Off. You don't like it, you're free to leave.'

'The Chinese in Macau sent me here because they thought I would fit in to this redneck fucking wilderness,' said Bronson. 'Thought I'd be less conspicuous than a posse of Cantonese. They think I have an Australian accent, reckon I'm some sort of Aborigine. You can try and explain the difference between a Maori and an Abo but we're all just *hak gwai* to them. All brown skin the same. Once they've made up their mind there's no changing it. All that shit about saving face. Have to keep your mouth shut so you don't hurt their feelings. Just nod and smile. It would be nice to be in a place like this where a man can speak his mind, if it wasn't for the fucking heat and the flies.'

He turned the revolver on Ford, motioned for him to raise his arms, then patted him down. When he reached the patch pocket on his thigh he felt the bulge there. 'What's this?' he said.

Ford thought about the bag of diamonds and was grateful he'd put his cigarettes in the same pocket. 'Smokes,' he said, and held his breath until Bronson dropped his hands and stood up. 'You got any matches? I'm gasping here.'

Bronson frisked Muddy and Dussell. 'I like to know who's in this and who's a spectator. No phones? Not one of you?' he said, then turned his attention to the Webley. 'How do I unload this death trap?' He found the release catch on the frame and thumbed it. The top half of the revolver broke open and the spring-loaded ejector flipped the cartridges out of the cylinder, the metal turning in the air before pinging off the rocks and scattering across the ground. The last cartridge bounced off a rock beside the fire pit and spun gently into the flames.

'Oh fuck,' said Bronson under his breath and leapt sideways away from the fire, squatting down in a crevice between the rocks, his back to the fire. Dussell moved just as quick, pushing Ford away from the flames and the two of them dropping flat in the dirt, hands over their heads. Only Emily seemed calm, her eyes moving to watch the panic in the others, Kavanagh and Muddy rolling sideways and lying curled up, hands protecting their heads. Emily then looked into the fire, a small smile on her face as the round went off, throwing a jet of sparks into the sky and sending the bullet screaming off into the night.

Bronson was first on his feet, gun still in hand. He looked at the others, sprawled around the fire. 'Since you're down there together, why don't you all sit against the same rock as the old girl there?' He waved the open gun, herding them, then bent to pick up the remaining bullets and stashed them in his pocket.

'So much for your stealth tactics,' said Dussell.

Bronson closed the revolver and tucked it into the waistband of his trousers, buttoning his jacket over it. 'I don't think there's anybody in a ten-kilometre radius that doesn't already know you're here, sitting on a hilltop with a fire burning.'

'Gotta have fire,' said Emily, picking meat off the kangaroo tail in front of her, putting it in her mouth and licking her fingers.

'I don't think anyone needs your cooking, darling.'

'Not just for cooking,' she said. 'Bad spirits in this place.' She smiled at him, her lips slick with grease.

Muddy jumped to his feet. 'She's right, bro,' he said. 'There's a *ginnawanda* roams these hills.' He went into a low crouch, feet planted wide, stepping carefully towards Bronson, his arms raised and hands curled into claws, eyes staring wide. 'A featherfoot. No wind tonight. He likes that. You can't smell him coming. You wanna be careful, bro.'

Bronson laughed. 'You're about as scary as the old man,' he said. He put a hand on Muddy's shoulder and pushed him back down beside Emily.

'Wallabung not scared of you,' said Emily, and Dussell looked at her and smiled. 'You know what that name mean? String from kangaroo. He tough. Tougher than you.'

Bronson ignored her and looked at his watch. 'You just sit quietly and we'll be done in an hour or so.'

'You're pegging the claim?' said Kavanagh.

'What I'm doing is keeping an eye on this little barbecue.'

'Whitefella take this country from us first time. Now black man take it from us second time,' said Emily.

'Relax, sister,' said Bronson. 'It's not my fault you people never got a treaty. Mistake you made was never getting hold of muskets before you started making deals with the *pakeha*.'

Emily scowled at him. 'I oughta slap the black off you.'

Bronson walked to the far side of the fire and jumped up onto a rock to get a better view down the valley. Ford stood up to see where Bronson was looking. There was a vehicle coming up the valley, the lights sweeping the dry gully, the engine straining.

'That your partner?' said Ford.

Bronson didn't turn to him, but kept watching the lights. 'He dropped me at the end of the valley when we saw the fire. I walked in. Found another way to fuck my suit and shoes.'

'You doing this for McCann?'

Bronson ignored him. He put a foot up higher on the rocks and examined his scuffed shoe and the frayed hem of his trousers. 'What's this fucking spiky grass that spears right through your pants?'

'Spinifex,' said Ford. 'You need denim.' He looked towards the Land Rover and Muddy's Toyota, gauging the distance.

'Don't think about it,' Bronson said. 'I immobilised them on my way up the hill. You can run if you want to, but you'll just die tired. There's a lot of country to go missing in out there.'

Ford watched the vehicle lights progress along the valley until they were at the turnoff to their camp. The vehicle stopped, the engine was cut and the silence of the bush returned.

Kavanagh came and stood beside him, shivering in the blanket, and together they watched as the car's internal light came on and both doors opened. The ute was too far away for them to see anything more of its occupants than two indistinct silhouettes in the black bowl of the valley, but Ford recognised the movements of the passenger immediately.

Kavanagh leaned in towards him and spoke quietly, her head turned to his ear, her eyes watching Bronson. 'This is what you've been trying to shut out of your head all weekend,' she said. 'She's down there. Your wife is working with these guys. Maybe all along.'

Ford shook his head, watched the headlights go out on the vehicle, and then the internal light as both doors slammed shut. Two flashlights came on, and one turned in their direction and flashed three times. Bronson took a long Maglite out of his jacket pocket and returned the signal.

Ford had experienced the sucking feeling in his chest before, the knowledge that he had been made a fool, failed to see what was in front of him. He watched the flashlights travel slowly up the far side of the valley, hoping that she would get caught in the beam and he might see her clearly, know for sure that she was here. The lights stopped at the top of the ridge and were both pointed down at the ground, two small circles of light in a dark landscape.

'Is that my wife?' asked Ford.

'Don't chew yourself up about it,' said Bronson.

'You forcing her to do this?'

'You're a little slow on the uptake, buddy.'

'Then I need to talk to her.'

'Now isn't the time. Let her finish what she has to do.'

The torches were moving again now, along the top of the ridge.

'I'm not going to let her take our daughter,' said Ford.

'You're reading too much into this. By the time you get back to town tomorrow all this will be over. She'll want to talk to you then.'

'You know I'll fight for this.'

Bronson laughed. 'It's nice that you're showing a little spirit. I like that in you.'

'I'm coming with you,' said Ford.

'No, you're staying here. You make a move to follow us and I'll put you down. Just accept what's happening here. Fate is doing the hard work so you don't have to.'

The torch on the far ridge flashed again and then started moving down the hill towards the vehicle. Bronson returned the signal and set off down the road towards the junction. Ford took a step to follow him but Kavanagh had her hand on his shoulder, the nails digging in. She pulled him backwards and her hand dropped and found his.

'You can't stop them,' she said.

Ford turned to look at her, only one side of her face dimly lit by the distant fire.

'Grace is safe where she is,' she said. 'Saxon won't give her up.'

Ford squeezed her hand and looked down the valley to watch the red tail-lights of the ute move away down the gully.

TWENTY-FOUR

Muddy and Dussell had set up a spotlight on a pole cut from the branch of a ghost gum so they had light over the engine of the Land Rover. They ran it off the battery from Muddy's Toyota, the only thing still functioning under its hood. It had taken them an hour by torchlight to work out the extent of the damage Bronson had wrought on their vehicles. The Toyota had fared worse, Bronson stripping out the wiring from under the dashboard and shorting out the engine-management system. Bronson had been more old-school with the old Land Rover: severing all the spark cables, removing the distributor cap and slicing the fan belt. He had also punctured all the tyres on both vehicles.

Muddy had decided they stood a better chance of getting the Land Rover running. The wiring hadn't been touched, such as it was, and among the milk crates stacked in the back were several boxes full of salvaged spare parts.

'I've had this old thing for forty years,' said Dussell. 'I

cobbled this thing together from three wrecks I found, plus bits of others I salvaged over the years. Never let me down yet. And if it has, I can fix it myself in the bush.'

Ford had helped them with the tyres, working the jack as they got off each wheel in turn and patched the punctures, thankful that Bronson had only used the tip of a knife to pierce them and had not slashed them. Now that they were under the hood and Dussell had started working on the engine, Ford left them and climbed the hill back to the campfire. The flames had gone, leaving only the orange glow of the embers. There was some orange light in the east, too, outlining the crest of the ridge on the far side of the valley, but not enough to extinguish the stars. Emily was lying on her side, wrapped in her swag, snoring gently. Kavanagh was still wrapped in the blanket, back to the rock, watching Ford approach. She didn't say anything when he sat down beside her and lifted one edge of the blanket to pull it around his shoulder. She leaned against him and put her head on his shoulder, looking up at the stars.

'Here we are again,' Ford said.

'You're a cheap date,' said Kavanagh, pulling the blanket tighter. 'One day you're going to take me somewhere that serves something better than road kill.'

'Five star, I promise,' he said. 'How did we end up in this situation again?'

'Same reason as before. If I had to point the finger, it'd be at your wife.'

Ford craned his neck to the sky and looked for Orion. He found it low in the west, its head already out of sight behind the rocks above them. The belt was still visible. His fingers went to the gold nugget that hung on the chain around his neck, but his hand found Kavanagh's already clasping it. He wrapped his hand around hers.

'I'm thinking of Grace too, you know,' she said.

'They don't know where she is.'

'That's what Bronson was listening for, hiding behind the rocks. Waiting for us to give him an idea where she is. He was trying to play dumb, pretending Diane wasn't with them.'

'They must be forcing her to do this.'

'If they were, why did she ask us to meet her here? She set us up so she could take your daughter while she's here. Two birds, one stone. She's always two steps ahead of you.'

'She always has been,' said Ford, watching the stars fade as the dawn brightened. 'She was always chasing something bigger, grasping at the stars.'

Kavanagh lifted her chin, found her own star to look at. 'They only look beautiful from down here, where there's a warm wind blowing. If you go out there among them they are so hot they will burn you up, or the space between them will freeze you solid and suffocate you, and the cosmic rays will warp your molecules.'

Ford watched the stars go out one by one. 'Is it so wrong of me to want a small life?'

He got no reply. Her hand had dropped from his and he heard the soft purr of her snoring. He slid out from under her and laid her head on the ground. The sky was purple now in the east and he watched it brighten to blue and the sun appear over the ridge. In the slanting light the spinifex looked like spun gold and the rocks glowed a deep red as if lit from within. The fire was dead, but a faint haze lingered around the rocks and Ford could smell the burnt meat mixed in with the wood smoke.

Down the hill Muddy was looking into the engine bay of the Land Rover and Dussell was in the driver's seat. At a signal from Muddy he turned over the engine and the battery in the old truck laboured. After a few seconds the engine fired, the exhaust coughed and the Land Rover started. Dussell revved it hard, a cloud of smoke forming around the exhaust, and Muddy snaked a hand out from beneath the hood with his thumb in the air. Dussell left it running and started walking up the hill towards the camp.

Ford watched him approach, the valley falling away behind him, the ridges edged with shadow. Dussell noticed the expression on his face as he took in the landscape. 'Nature takes a perverse pleasure from putting gold in the most diffi-cult, remote and god-forsaken places on earth,' he said.

Ford swatted away the flies that had started flitting in front of his face, active as soon as the heat of the sun reached them. 'How quick can we get back to Marble Bar?'

'We won't get ahead of them,' said Dussell. 'It's a couple of hours. By the time we get to town they'll have registered this claim with the Registrar of Mines.'

'Then I guess you're fucked,' said Ford.

'You're not wrong,' said Dussell. 'No use complaining about it. Nobody out here but God and the cockatoos. The birds can't help you and the Lord doesn't give a shit.'

'My daughter's still there, in town,' said Ford.

'Well, let's go and get her.'

'The Registrar's Office, that's in the same building as the police station?'

'The old Government Buildings, yes. Right next door.'

'Then that's where I need you to take us.'

Emily was awake now, rolling her swag and gathering her few belongings into a soft knitted bag. A bird called from beyond the rocks, a throaty bark that sounded unnatural. Kavanagh opened her eyes, blinking until they focused. The bird called again and she sat upright, then her face relaxed when she remembered where she was. 'What's that bird?' she said, her own throat rasping.

'*Yirlunpa*,' said Emily, picking up her bag and her bedroll and walking off towards the car.

'It's a kookaburra,' said Dussell.

'It's not doing that laugh,' said Kavanagh, standing up.

'The birds up here are not the same as the ones down south. Those were introduced to the West. That one you hear is native to round here, although you normally only hear them in the wet. Different call. You know why they don't laugh?'

Kavanagh shook her head.

'Because there's nothing to fucking laugh about in Marble Bar.'

Kavanagh walked to the edge of the camp and watched Emily climb into the back of the Land Rover. 'We ready to go?'

'Got the old girl running,' said Dussell, 'but the Toyota is fucked. We'll squeeze in together.'

Kavanagh looked from Emily and Muddy to Dussell and then smiled at Ford. 'Another freak show on wheels,' she said.

Ford returned her smile. 'How you feeling?' he said, looking at her ripped feet.

She found her hat, squared it on her head and shrugged. 'Where are my boots?'

'Still in the car,' said Ford.

'Then let's get to it,' she said, and limped off barefoot down the hill towards the Land Rover.

Ford walked behind her, watching her pick her way with care through the rocks. She sidestepped a small bush, straggling dry stems tipped with small delicate pink flowers. As Ford passed it he snapped a bloom off the tallest stem and held it in his palm.

Kavanagh slid into the back seat of the Land Rover next to Emily. Ford waited for her to scoot along into the middle and then he held the flower between his thumb and forefinger and held it out in front of her. Emily looked at the flower and pursed her lips, tutting. Kavanagh took the flower from him and put it to her nose. Ford held his breath until a small smile crossed one corner of her mouth and her eyes softened.

Dussell sat behind the wheel and glanced over his shoulder at his passengers.

'You're wasting your time with that,' he said, nodding towards the flower. 'Sturt's desert rose, *Gossypium sturtianum*. You should've left it on the plant. Hardy little bastard for something so pretty, but once you pick it, the flower only lasts a day, then the petals close up.'

Kavanagh took off her straw hat, slipped the flower in the band. Her hand found Ford's and she pulled it into her lap and put her hat over their intertwined fingers.

Muddy sat down last, his bare feet up on the dashboard. He looked at Dussell and they moved off.

By the time they were out of the hills and had reached the road, the sun was a hand's breadth above the horizon and the heat in the car was suffocating. Ford pulled at his shirt, trying to get some air to where his chest was slick with sweat. He could feel Kavanagh pressed against his side, their sweat mingling through their clothes. All four windows were down, and the vents in the dashboard were open, but they weren't moving fast enough to generate a breeze or keep the insects out.

'Half the flies in the world are in this vehicle,' said Ford, grabbing Kavanagh's hat and fanning it in front of his face.

Dussell raised a hand to tap his glasses and the flies that had settled on the lenses took flight. 'You can shut out the flies or you can shut in the heat. Your choice.'

'You never felt the need to get a vehicle built in this millennium? Something with air-conditioning?'

'Only one more thing to go wrong. You're only putting off the inevitable anyway. You sweat enough as soon as you step outside. Better to get used to the heat.'

Ford turned to the open window and pushed his face through it, feeling the warm air move across his forehead and dry his skin. 'A breath of wind from the wings of madness,' he said.

'They called it the Madman's Track,' said Dussell, raising his voice above the whine of the engine. 'Prospectors used to walk up here in the early days of the gold rush. From Kalgoorlie to the Pilbara on foot.'

'I walked out there yesterday,' said Ford. 'I'm not sure it was any worse than being sandwiched in this hell of a pressure cooker.'

'They say that if you travel to hell from Marble Bar, you'll return for your blankets,' said Dussell.

Ford watched the brown country pass slowly, thermal coils of hot air lifting dust from the ground, the red rocks rippling in the heat haze. 'Maybe I'm ready for England again,' he said. 'Ready for some green hills, a cold wind heavy with drizzle. Maybe I want to feel the pull of history again.' The faces of the others were blank, so he left them to their thoughts.

An hour's slow drive brought them to the crossing over the dry bed of the Coongan River. 'Told you I'd bring you back,' said Dussell as they crossed. 'A man's word is all he's got up here. Worth more than gold.' Once across and on to the bitumen, Dussell accelerated along the good road, upright in his seat, eager now that they were only a dozen kilometres from the town.

They came on it suddenly after the emptiness of the desert, a few scattered houses and then they were on the main street, the tall, imposing Government Buildings standing proud on the rise ahead of them. Dussell slowed for the turn into the high street and Kavanagh sat forward in her seat, fidgeting as she gazed through the windscreen at the old stone buildings and the row of cars parked outside. They crawled up the street in front of the long terraced building until Dussell pointed to the sign for the Mining Registrar, fixed to the wall of the building beside a low stone archway leading to a shaded doorway. A broad gable set with three high narrow windows separated the arch from the police station with its blue sign outside.

A battered Nissan ute stood outside the Registrar's office, and in the shade of the arch stood Bronson and Wu, one on either side of the doorway, like nightclub doormen. They were both still wearing their black suits and white shirts, but Bronson had loosened his tie and undone some buttons. His shirt had red dust ingrained into the collar, and there was dust on the hems of his trousers. Wu looked the same as when Ford had first seen him in Newman, his suit still looking as if it had been recently pressed, his umbrella hooked over his folded arms.

Bronson took a step forward into the sunshine as Dussell pulled the Land Rover up behind the Nissan, and Ford opened the back door and got out. He stood on the kerb holding the door for Kavanagh, who stumbled out carrying her boots and hat, then stood upright and stared at Bronson. As soon as the door closed, Dussell threw the Land Rover into reverse and backed off down the street. Ford turned in surprise at the whine of the gearbox, and Muddy gave him a small finger wave through the windscreen.

Bronson was standing between them and the door, his arms folded across his chest, a film of sweat glistening on his shaved head. 'I'd hoped we wouldn't see you again. I mustn't have done much of a job on that old jeep.'

'You underestimated the old man's resourcefulness,' said Ford.

'Yours too,' said Bronson. 'One day I might put you down and you won't get back up.'

Ford made for the door but he felt a large hand on his chest. 'Don't think that you're going in there,' said Bronson. 'Wait for the lady to finish her business and then we'll all have a little chat.'

Ford looked along the building to the police station, saw that Saxon's ute was parked outside.

'Don't go looking for them to bail you out,' said Bronson. 'You're beyond help right now.'

Kavanagh dropped her boots on the ground and tried to step around Bronson but he put his arm up and held her by the shoulder. 'Don't think I'm such a gentleman that I won't ram your pretty teeth so far down your throat that they'll bite that skinny white arse of yours,' he said.

They were standing like that, Bronson holding both of them, when Diane stepped calmly out of the building.

TWENTY-FIVE

When she saw Ford and Kavanagh she hesitated. Her expression remained calm and told Ford nothing. She stopped a pace behind Bronson and Wu and waited.

Now that she was in front of him, Ford found he had nothing to say. She looked good. She wore a lightweight khaki jacket over a white T-shirt and brown pants. If they were the same clothes she had worn out in the desert, it didn't show. Her red hair was pulled back, away from her face, her skin pale as if it had never seen the sun. She looked better than ever, but her eyes showed him the fear she had been living with. She held his gaze for a few moments, then looked at Kavanagh.

'I was hoping we'd be able to talk this out between us,' she said. 'I didn't think there'd be any need to involve anyone else. I didn't know you'd show up here with your girlfriend.'

'She's not my girlfriend,' said Ford, swatting away Bronson's hand from his chest. The Maori took a step back and stood shoulder to shoulder with Diane. Wu closed in on her other flank.

'Then what is she?' asked Diane.

'She's right here, that's what she is,' said Kavanagh.

Ford turned to her, and she stared right back at him, her eyebrow arched.

'You didn't answer your wife's question,' said Kavanagh. 'I'm as curious as she is to hear what word you're going to come up with.'

Ford hesitated, then said to his wife, 'She's my back-up.'

Kavanagh snorted. 'You think I'm here in some sort of supporting role?'

Ford ignored her and continued staring at Diane. 'You knew we were travelling together.'

'Where's Grace?' asked Diane.

'You've been looking?'

'Not yet. We had to do this first. I thought she'd be with you, but Bronson tells me you were out at the claim.'

'She's safe,' said Ford. 'Somewhere these two can't find her.'

'I want to see her,' said Diane. 'I took a lot of risks to get here, all because I need to see her.'

'Why did you feel the need to lie to me again? About being watched in Broome? All that bullshit just to get me here to Marble Bar? You could've talked to me. I would've helped. Why set me up with these two?'

Diane took a few steps forward into the sunshine. Wu put up the umbrella and held it over her, giving her some shade. 'I wasn't lying when I said that I'd left Alan,' she said. 'These guys came to protect me from Roth, or anyone else Alan sent to take me back.'

'Don't pretend they're not here to help you take Grace away from me.'

Diane sighed. 'I had to do this, with the mining lease, but now I'm free.'

'No, you're not,' said Kavanagh. She took a step forward but Bronson put his hand back on her shoulder to restrain her. 'I'm still a police officer and I still have the option of taking you in.'

'For what?' said Diane.

'Conspiracy to defraud the stock market. The false geology report at Gwardar.'

'You'd have to prove that I wrote that, not Matthew Walsh, and that's a long way out of the jurisdiction of the Gold Squad.'

'I can arrest you now and we can worry about the paper-work later.'

Bronson dropped his hand and smiled at Kavanagh, then opened his jacket to show her the old Webley pistol still stuck in his pants.

Kavanagh didn't blink. 'Did you work out how to reload that thing?' Bronson nodded slowly so she said, 'Take care it doesn't accidentally discharge again. It'll take your balls off.'

Diane stepped between them. 'I can tell you where the Gwardar gold is.'

Kavanagh smirked. 'We have that already,' she said. 'What else have you got?'

Ford saw the panic dart across his wife's face, and her eyebrows twitched before she regained control, her face now a mask of calm indifference.

'Who gave up the gold?' she asked.

Kavanagh's eyes brightened. She was starting to enjoy herself. 'Roth,' she said. 'He's right here in Marble Bar. Cleaning up loose ends. You might be one of them.'

Bronson bristled, folded his arms and puffed out his chest. 'I'm looking forward to meeting the man.'

'I can still give you Alan,' said Diane. 'I can give you offshore accounts, holding companies, all the little places he's squirrelled away his money.'

Ford looked at his wife and then at Kavanagh and thought about the choices in front of him. 'Why would you do that to him?' he asked.

This time she couldn't control her face. Her mouth creased and her eyes narrowed. 'He promised me we would come back for Grace,' she said. 'That he'd have everything sorted. Get his business refloated, get back in the game. Shake the police and the stock market off his back. Then he'd bring me back to Australia.'

'Don't expect me to pity you for believing him,' said Kavanagh.

'Alan is desperate to do a deal with the Chinese,' said Diane. 'He misses the buzz of being a big fish in a small pond. In Macau his money doesn't even register among all the high rollers. He's living in that casino, drinking and gaining weight. He started using the gold-card saunas, even has a regular Chinese girlfriend. He thinks that's what you do up there, that it shouldn't bother me.'

'Hell hath no fury,' said Kavanagh. 'When did you find out what McCann did to Matthew Walsh?'

Diane turned away, stepped back into the shade of the archway, but Kavanagh pressed home her advantage.

'I'm enjoying your wronged-woman routine, but I reckon the thought of your partner rotting in the jungle must have made you think, right? Did the Lau family offer you a way out?'

Diane turned and her eyes were wet. 'In Macau money is like sand. The Laus make millions every week from the casino. Alan thinks he's been admitted to the table but they treat him as a small-time player. They'll just keep raising the stakes, betting higher until he's broke.'

'Success has ruined many a man,' said Kavanagh. 'So what's your deal with the Lau family?'

Diane swallowed, took a minute to compose herself, and when she spoke she turned to her husband. 'Alan needed a partner, someone to bail him out. The Laus were his first choice but there have been other people circling him, mainland people with government and Communist Party connections. Alan can't develop his iron ore tenements without cash, and he needs the cooperation of whoever has that gold lease. The Laus want to make sure he deals with them. They'll inject capital into Alan's company to refloat it, but they want his iron ore. The family has industrial and shipping companies, as well as the casinos.'

'And what do you get?' asked Ford.

'I peg the gold claim for them, and they help me get away from Alan. They'll help me resettle somewhere else.'

'And help you get your daughter back,' said Kavanagh.

Diane kept her eyes on Ford. 'I want to go to England, Gareth. I want you and Grace to come with me.'

Ford felt a hand on his chest pushing him backwards. He kept his eyes on his wife but the pressure became enough for him to look down at the nails digging into him. It was Kavanagh, and when he took a step backwards, she stepped between him and his wife.

'While you think about this,' she said, 'you might want to remember that guy in Newman. Harding. The guy you found dead on your couch. That was supposed to be you.'

'That's not true,' said Diane.

Kavanagh twisted to look at her. 'So why did Wu kill him?' she hissed.

'We know it was him. He left one of his counterfeit Chinese cigarettes on the kitchen table,' said Ford.

Bronson looked down at his hands, massaging his knuckles, then straightened the cuffs of his shirt, took off his sunglasses and stared at Ford. Wu didn't react; he was still standing holding the umbrella perfectly still, feet planted shoulder-width apart, his weight on the balls of his feet. If he knew they were talking about him, he chose not to show it.

'Wu was waiting in your house,' said Bronson. 'I was following you from work. We wanted to know where the girl was. That other guy comes home first and Wu is stuck in the house. He tries to leave, walks right past your man, but the guy, he flips out, starts laying into Wu. Punching and kicking. The guy thought he had some moves, you know the type. A few karate lessons and the guy thinks he's Jackie Chan. He's too slow and too big for the martial arts stuff, but not big enough to put any weight behind a punch. Just a pub brawler, your guy. Wu gives him a few slaps round the head to calm him down but the dude keeps coming, so Wu punches him hard in the chest and the guy goes down. He doesn't get up again.'

'He killed him with one punch?' said Kavanagh.

'Yeah,' said Bronson. 'Surprised the fuck out of Wu. He's never seen it happen. He's heard about it, of course, all that kung fu shit about *dim mak*, the Touch of Death. He even had some old guy on the mainland tell him he could teach him all that. Wu reckoned it was all just *bullshido* until he saw that guy shrivel and drop.'

Ford looked at Wu. He was still motionless, his eyes hidden behind the sunglasses. 'Is he going to claim self-defence then?' asked Ford.

'It's not like it's ever going to get to court,' said Bronson. 'Although I'd like to hear your girl say she's going to arrest us again. I enjoyed that.'

Diane stepped between Bronson and Wu, pulled herself to her full height and spoke directly into Kavanagh's face. 'I want to see Grace,' she said. 'That's the deal. Let me see her and I'll give you everything you need on Alan.'

Kavanagh laughed. 'You think I'm keeping you from your daughter? I'm not her guardian and I'm not your husband's. Personally, I think you should let him go while he's still got a chance. But whatever you need to sort out about your daughter or your marriage can all be dealt with after I've got my job back.'

Ford tried to gauge the expression in Diane's eyes. The last time he had seen her had been in the aircraft hangar, and the look in her eyes had been the same: helpless and pleading. He was going to ask her once more about England, but decided not to make her lie to him again.

He turned and looked up the road at the blue sign outside the police station and Saxon's ute parked outside.

'Follow me,' he said.

TWENTY-SIX

Ford led them up the street in the shade of the stone façade until they came to the heavy white door of the police station. It was locked, and a small hand-written sign said that the station was closed and gave a phone number.

'You left her with the police?' said Diane.

'She's been under police protection all weekend,' said Kavanagh, looking up the street to where the police wagon was parked outside the residence. She tapped Ford on the shoulder and nodded towards it.

Ford set off again and the others followed in single file, Kavanagh at his shoulder and Bronson close behind. Wu brought up the rear, holding the umbrella over Diane's head, keeping them both in shade. Ford strode through the open gate and straight to the door.

There was a bell but he didn't use it. The door opened when he turned the handle and he walked down the corridor towards the kitchen and the smell of fresh coffee. His boots

313

thumped on the bare floorboards and as the others came through the front door, their footsteps echoed down the hallway.

When he reached the kitchen Ford looked to his left and saw the constable's wife leaning against the kitchen bench beside the stove, wiping her hands on the apron that was straining against her pregnant belly. On his right was the kitchen table. Saxon sat on the far side, his back to the wall, a plate of sausages and scrambled eggs in front of him. He wore his uniform, his knife and fork held upright either side of the plate, his eyes flicking in turn from Ford to each person who followed him into the kitchen. Grace was sitting on the chair closest to the door, her back to Ford. She glanced over her shoulder at him when he came in, still chewing, her fork in the air, and her eyes lit up. She saw Kavanagh behind him and her mouth broke into a grin, showing food between her teeth. Ford watched her smile melt away when she saw Bronson, her eyes narrowing in confusion, and then popping wide and her mouth forming a perfect circle of surprise when her mother walked in. She let out a sharp cry, dropped her cutlery onto her plate and tumbled out of the chair screaming 'Mama!' She ducked between Ford's and Kavanagh's legs and threw herself at her mother. Diane caught her in the air and scooped her upwards into her arms, and Grace wrapped her arms and legs around her mother, burying her face in her neck. Diane spun her around, squeezing her, coming to a stop facing Wu, who was standing in the doorway, patiently closing the umbrella.

Bronson stepped up to the kitchen table and looked across at Saxon's plate. 'A little late for breakfast, isn't it?' he said.

Ford walked to the kitchen counter and glanced out the window at the bare backyard. He turned, and from that angle could see that Saxon was wearing his police belt, and that he had released the strap over the top of his holster. His fingers were tapping lightly on the grip of his Glock, his eyes tracking from Bronson to Wu and back again. Saxon caught Ford's eye and Ford nodded to let him know these were the guys, and when Saxon leaned forward and made to stand Ford shook his head and waved him back down with the slightest motion of his palm.

Saxon sighed. 'I was at work until after dark looking for you two,' he said, pushing aside his plate. 'We got a call about a fire out at Corunna Downs, column of smoke that could be seen from town. I went out there, found the remains of your car at the airfield, and a plane, still smouldering. I spent most of yesterday searching for you.'

'Did you go to the homestead?' asked Kavanagh.

'First place I looked,' said Saxon. 'Deserted. Signs of a break-in. Windows shattered.' He raised an eyebrow at Kavanagh and she frowned at him.

'You couldn't manage a phone call?' This was Saxon's wife, and Bronson turned to look at her, taking in the bulging apron. She nodded towards Grace. 'We didn't know what to tell her.'

Grace looked over her mother's shoulder at her father. 'I slept in a bunk bed,' she said. Diane whispered something in her daughter's ear and Ford could see the tears in his wife's eyes.

'They were caught in difficult circumstances,' said Bronson, reaching across the table to lift a sausage off Saxon's plate. 'A situation that has yet to improve.' He ate the sausage in two bites and licked the grease off his fingers. 'Can I smell coffee?' he said.

'We made pancakes for breakfast,' said Grace.

Ford turned to Saxon's wife and she made an effort to smile and make it look relaxed. 'She insisted,' she said. 'She showed me how to roll them exactly how she likes them.'

Diane sat down at the table with Grace still clinging to her. She put her hand on her daughter's hair, her fingers tracing the intricate twists of her French braid. 'I like your hair,' she said.

'Rose did it,' said Grace, pulling the end of the braid over her shoulder so she could see it.

Diane looked over at Saxon's wife. 'Are you Rose?' she asked.

'No, I am,' said Kavanagh, and sat down at the table opposite Diane and tried to catch Grace's eye.

'Rose can ride a horse,' said Grace, looking across at Kavanagh and smiling. 'She promised to take me riding.' Kavanagh wrinkled her nose at Grace and tried not to make eye contact with her mother.

Saxon broke the silence. 'This is my wife, Anna,' he said. 'Sweetheart, why don't you get everyone some coffee?'

Bronson nodded at this and sat down on the last chair at the table, opposite Saxon. He put both his hands flat on the table. 'What a delightful idea. We can sit together like one big happy family and talk over all our little disputes.'

Anna picked up the stainless steel coffee pot that was bubbling on the counter next to the stove and brought it to the table. She stood next to Bronson and hesitated. Her husband gave her a small nod, so she set the coffee pot on the table. They all watched her as she laid seven clean mugs and a carton of milk next to the coffee and then stepped back to the sink and waited. Ford stepped back to lean against the kitchen counter, keeping an eye on Wu, who was still standing in the doorway, the furled umbrella hooked over his folded arms. Bronson and Saxon sat watching each other until Bronson said, 'Shall I be mother?' When nobody spoke he picked up the coffee and filled each mug, then added milk from the carton. He picked up a mug and drank from it. 'Mmmm,' he said, 'that's good coffee.'

Saxon reached across and placed a mug in front of Diane and then another for Kavanagh and one for himself. He drank from it, looking over the top of the mug at Kavanagh as he did so, looking for some indication of what he should do. She drank and nodded to him slowly. He thought for a while and then said, 'I spoke with the station at Newman yesterday. They had the autopsy results from Perth, that case you were asking about.'

Kavanagh nodded again, leading him on.

Saxon swallowed and then continued. 'It took the pathologist a while to determine the cause of death. In the end he did it by elimination. It was a cardiac arrest, brought on by a sharp blow to the chest, directly in front of the heart.'

Bronson was now staring hard at Saxon over the rim of his coffee cup as he drank. Saxon slowly unbuttoned his shirt pocket and pulled out his notebook. He found the page he wanted and read from it. 'The doctor called it *commotio cordis*,' he said. 'A blow to the precordial region at a critical time during the cycle of the heart can cause ventricular fibrillation.' Saxon paused, reading over the last line before he continued.

'Harding was young, only nineteen. This thing usually only happens in teenagers, adolescent boys. Something to do with the way their heart is still growing. Very rare that this happens.' He put the notebook down and rested his left hand on it. His right hand went below the table out of sight.

Bronson put down his coffee and grinned. 'That will come as a great relief to my friend Wu,' he said. 'He's still thinking he's mastered the quivering palm technique without knowing it.' He turned to Wu and launched a barrage of quick-fire Cantonese across the kitchen. Wu listened and then nodded once.

Kavanagh watched Saxon frown as he tried to guess what was being said. She said, 'Wu confessed to me that he killed Harding during a fight after breaking into the house in Newman.'

'No,' said Bronson. 'I told you what happened. A confession would have to come from Wu's own mouth. Good luck with that.'

Saxon looked from Bronson to Kavanagh, confused, aware that he was being played by both of them.

Kavanagh stood up and reached into the front pocket of her jeans. She took out a balled tissue and laid it on the table. She sat down and unravelled it, then held up the flattened tissue to show Saxon its contents. 'Two cigarette butts,' she said. 'I picked them up from outside the Ironclad, where Wu dropped them. They say Marlboro on the paper above the filter. Australian cigarettes don't have any branding on them anymore. These are Chinese counterfeits, the same as the one that Wu left burning in the Newman house. They'll all have the same DNA on them.'

Saxon had his right hand on his holster again. He leaned forward in his chair and shifted his weight, ready to stand.

Bronson glared at him. 'Just stay sitting down, constable,' he said. 'If you try to break up this little family reunion, I'm gonna shove one of them sausages down your throat and a starving dog up your arse.'

Saxon hesitated, but then found his nerve. 'There was a bulletin put out yesterday,' he said. 'A man of Chinese appearance wanted for questioning, black suit, bowl haircut.' He stood up slowly, pushing his chair back, and in one smooth motion drew his pistol and levelled it at Bronson's chest. 'Put your hands flat on the table,' he said, 'and stand up.'

Bronson spread his fingers out on the tablecloth but kept his eyes on Saxon. He slowly raised himself out of the chair and, as he pulled himself up to his full height, he lifted his hands, lacing his fingers together behind his head.

Kavanagh stood up quickly and stepped across to the kitchen counter, standing in front of Anna and shielding her. Diane lifted Grace off her chair and carried her over to where Kavanagh was standing, putting a hand over her daughter's eyes and whispering, 'Don't look.' Kavanagh pushed her towards the door. Diane looked at Ford and he nodded, and she disappeared down the corridor with their daughter.

'A lot of tension in the room, huh?' said Bronson.

'Back up,' said Saxon. The big Maori took a step sideways towards the back door. His jacket hung open and Saxon's eyes were on the revolver protruding above Bronson's belt. Saxon stepped around the table and realised he had placed himself between Bronson and Wu and could not cover both of them. He swung his Glock from one to the other. 'Take the gun from your pants,' he barked. Bronson looked at him coolly and shook his head.

'Martyrdom is for saints,' said Bronson. 'You aren't that. There's no reason for you to get in the middle of this.'

'Drop it on the floor,' said Saxon. He took another step around the table and was now in the centre of the room. He kept his eyes on Bronson.

Wu took three quick steps forward and in the same movement brought the umbrella up and over his head in a swinging arc. He brought it down sharply on Saxon's gun hand, the metal point striking the wrist and forcing his arm down. Wu whipped back his elbow, withdrew the umbrella and then lunged forward, driving the tip into the soft part of Saxon's wrist. The Glock clattered to the floor. Anna screamed and stepped forward but Kavanagh held her back, pinning her to the stove. As Saxon turned to face his attacker, Wu swivelled his hips and raised his leg, the kick landing in the middle of Saxon's chest, knocking him backwards. Saxon sat down heavily on the edge of the table, winded. Wu spun again and the second kick caught Saxon in the throat and sent him sprawling back across the table, sending cutlery and crockery crashing to the floor.

Kavanagh saw her chance. She charged at Bronson, keeping low, her head down. Bronson's arms were still raised and she got under them, her shoulder catching him in the side below his ribs, driving him forward and knocking him off-balance. He pitched sideways, his feet scrabbling beneath him as he fought to gain a footing. He took two quick steps before he found his balance but by then Kavanagh had stepped back and had the Webley in her hand.

Wu twisted away from Saxon to face her, raising the umbrella to strike, and as he lunged forward Kavanagh turned the gun on him and pulled the trigger. The hammer fell on the cylinder with a soft click. Wu dropped low and thrust the umbrella under her gun arm and into the soft flesh of her belly. She screamed in pain and pulled the trigger again as she doubled over, but the gun clicked harmlessly. As she fell backwards Wu caught the gun in his free hand and wrenched it from her grip.

Ford took a step towards Saxon's Glock, which was still lying in the middle of the floor, but Bronson put a hand on his chest to stop him, then bent down to pick up the gun.

'I told you, I don't like guns,' he said, taking the Webley from Wu and examining the two guns. 'Now I seem to be collecting them. I never bothered reloading the old man's antique.' He stuck both the Glock and the Webley into the waistband of his pants and buttoned his jacket over them.

Kavanagh sat on the floor rubbing her belly. She lifted her shirt to see if the umbrella had broken the skin, but there was only a red welt to show where it had hit.

'You stay down there while I deal with this idiot,' said Bronson. Saxon was struggling to sit upright on the table, his breathing laboured. Bronson laid a big hand on his chest and pushed him onto his back again. 'You just lie there a second,' he said, and started to unbuckle Saxon's belt. 'Perhaps you could settle something for me. I could never understand whether a cop's behaviour was nature or nurture. Is there a certain type of person that likes wearing a uniform and having power over the people around them? Or is it part of the training to mould recruits into arrogant self-righteous bastards?'

Saxon groaned. Bronson had the belt undone but couldn't pull it out because of the holster and the pouches on it. 'Arch your back there, mate,' he said to Saxon. 'There you go.' He yanked the belt free and started examining the contents of each pouch.

'The Chinese Tao suggests that your mind shouldn't dwell on right and wrong,' he said, as he found a canister of pepper spray and slipped it in his pocket. 'You can do your good-cop routine or your bad-cop, it doesn't matter. You can try and stay away from the Yin and hang with the Yang, but it doesn't work like that. One is in harmony with the other. There is no division between good and evil; they are inside all of us.'

He found a pair of handcuffs and a key, and held them up in triumph. Saxon was trying to sit up again, so Bronson held out a hand to him. Saxon eyed it suspiciously but decided to take it. Bronson pulled him up and then off the table onto his feet.

'You alright there?' he asked, holding the constable steady by his elbow. When Saxon nodded Bronson guided him across the room to stand beside his wife by the stove.

'Sit down on the floor,' said Bronson. Saxon looked confused until he saw Bronson open the handcuffs and thread them through the heavy steel handle on the oven door. He pulled on the handle to test its strength and said to Anna, 'You too, sweetheart.' She looked at her husband and he nodded. They sat down together, shoulder to shoulder, their backs against the stove, and raised a wrist each towards Bronson.

'My Chinese friend here has taught me that *wu-wei* has an opposite,' said Bronson, snapping the bracelets on their wrists.

'The opposite of perfect calm is hopeless, heroic, random action. That sort of chaos has no prospect of success.'

Bronson checked the locks on the bracelets and, satisfied, directed his attention to Kavanagh. 'You can get up now,' he said.

She struggled to her feet, wincing in pain. 'You're going to leave a pregnant woman handcuffed?' she said.

Bronson shrugged. 'It's only for a few hours until we're out of here. Their sergeant will be back soon.' He leaned over and took Saxon's phone out of the front pocket of his uniform. 'How long have you two been married?'

Saxon glared at him but didn't answer. The Maori opened a cupboard door and found a large saucepan. He placed it on the floor between Saxon and his wife. 'In case she gets desperate,' he said. 'You two aren't shy of each other, right?'

Anna dropped her head and tried to hold back a sob. 'You should be proud of your man,' said Bronson. 'He did alright. No shame in this. He's never come up against anyone like us before.'

Ford stepped into the corridor and found Diane standing there, halfway to the front door, Grace still burying her face in her mother's neck. He ruffled the girl's hair. 'All over now, princess,' he whispered. 'Nobody hurt. No damage done, just a few broken plates. Now what?' he asked, looking at his wife.

She set Grace down on the floor and held her hand. Her daughter's face was wracked with fear, her eyes red and wet. 'We're leaving,' she said. 'I can't stay in Australia and wait for Alan or his men to catch up with me. I need to leave. You can come too.'

Kavanagh stepped between Ford and his wife and turned to Diane, her face getting close. 'You made a promise to me to give up McCann.'

'I did,' said Diane. 'I helped you find the gold. I brought you here to Marble Bar and you worked out the connection to Alan. When I get clear of here I'll give you all the information I've found: the offshore accounts, shell companies, trust funds, everything.'

Kavanagh thought about that, looking at Bronson and Wu. She caught Ford watching her. 'You can't let her play us like this. What are you going to do?' she asked.

Ford looked at his daughter holding her mother's hand, and noticed his wife was biting her lip. Her eyes could do things to him without trying. He could see the danger but it seemed to him so much less than the promise of something better. 'I'm going with them,' he said.

Kavanagh had opened her mouth to speak when the noise of the explosion outside reached them. The floor shook and the windows rattled and there was a crash of breaking glass from the front of the house. They looked at one another quickly, panic in their eyes. Ford pushed past Diane and rushed down the corridor to the front door. He opened it a crack, then threw it open when he saw what was in the street.

Saxon's police wagon was on fire, the doors blown open and the interior in flames. Down the street Bronson's stolen ute was also on fire, the fuel cap hanging open.

'Roth,' said Ford.

Kavanagh appeared beside him. 'I told you he was close.'

TWENTY-SEVEN

Bronson had the Glock in his hand when he reached the front door. He saw the burning vehicles and sprinted across the garden, vaulting the garden fence and running out into the street. He looked up and down the street but the way his shoulders dropped when he turned back to the house told Ford that Roth was nowhere to be seen. Diane carried Grace out of the front door and through the gate to join Bronson. Wu walked slowly behind and stepped up to the huddle in the street. They conferred in whispers and then set off towards the centre of town.

Ford and Kavanagh caught them at the end of the street, in the shadow of the squat tower at the end of the Government Buildings. They were looking down the main street towards the Ironclad. There were no cars moving in the street, nothing parked in the petrol station or outside the store. Dussell's Land Rover was parked diagonally in front of the hotel, the only vehicle in sight.

'I guess we should be grateful to the old man for getting that truck moving,' said Bronson, and walked off towards the Ironclad. Wu carefully opened the umbrella. He held it above Diane and Grace and they set off. Kavanagh and Ford followed behind.

From a distance Ford could see that the door to the hotel was open. They paused in the shade of the verandah then Bronson led them into the cool interior, the Glock still in his hand, held close to the back of his thigh.

Reynard was standing behind the bar, cleaning glasses. Dussell and Muddy were sitting at the bar and turned to watch them come through the door.

'I thought we were in lockdown,' said Muddy.

'It's not much of a lockdown if you leave the bloody door open,' said Dussell. 'Where's your man Curtis when you need him?'

Emily was stretched out on the couch, her eyes closed. She opened an eye, sighed to herself, and closed it again.

Bronson saw Reynard and smiled. He walked slowly over to the bar, stepping between Muddy and Dussell, and beckoned him closer. Reynard put down the glass and leaned on the bar. Bronson grabbed him by the collar and brought the gun from behind his back, smashing its butt into the landlord's forehead. Reynard grunted and reeled backwards, a hand to his face. Then Bronson caught him by his shirt collar again, pulling him forward and holding on to him while he returned the pistol to his belt. With two hands on Reynard's collar now, Bronson lifted him off the ground and dragged him across the bar, scattering glasses.

Muddy and Dussell hurried off their stools and backed

away as Reynard's feet came over the counter and Bronson dropped him sprawling on the floor. Reynard tried to sit up, taking his hand away from his face and seeing the blood on his fingers. Bronson leaned over and punched him twice in the face, then leaned across the bar and looked under the counter. He found the baseball bat but nothing else. He pointed the tip of the bat at Reynard's face. 'I told you not to make an enemy of me. Where's that shotgun?'

Reynard groaned. 'It's not there.'

Bronson stood up and swung the bat at Reynard's knees. There was the thump of solid wood as it connected with bone and Reynard cried out in pain.

'Stop!' yelled Kavanagh. Bronson spun around to face her, levelling the bat. 'He doesn't have it.'

'He better not,' said Bronson, pulling the Glock from his belt, the bat and the gun pointing at Kavanagh's head. 'Because the next person who points a gun at me, I'm going to shoot three holes in their head and use it as a bowling ball.'

Kavanagh was cool. 'Reynard gave the shotgun to me,' she said. 'Roth took it.'

Bronson looked confused, then a smile of comprehension spread across his face. He turned to Dussell. 'Anyone else in the hotel?'

Dussell's eyes moved across to the door behind the bar. 'Just Charlie,' he said. 'He's in the kitchen.'

'Call him,' said Bronson. 'Get him in here.'

Dussell called the cook's name. When he appeared he looked fearful. 'You been hiding?' asked Bronson.

Charlie didn't answer. Bronson waved him around the bar with the bat and motioned for him to stand next to Dussell.

'What we came in here for, old man,' he said, 'is the keys to your truck. It seems to be the only thing in this town that Henk Roth hasn't fucked up.'

Dussell put his hand in his pocket and held the keys out at arm's length. Bronson tucked the bat under his arm and took the keys, then turned and threw them across the room. Wu snatched them mid-air and put them in his pocket.

Bronson did a slow spin in the middle of the room, looking at each person in turn, winked at Ford, then walked to the door. He'd taken three steps through it when he stopped short. 'Well, fuck me.'

Ford followed Bronson outside and found him looking up the street to where a man stood alone in the middle of the road. As they both watched, the tall figure started walking towards them. Even from that distance, Ford recognised Roth by his limp.

Bronson stepped out into the street directly in front of the hotel. Ford stayed under the shade of the verandah and waited. Kavanagh tried to step out of the hotel but Wu blocked the door. He was standing with his arms folded, the umbrella hooked over them.

Roth was wearing the same gun belt as before, but he had tucked his shirt beneath it, the holster strapped diagonally across his belly with the butt of the big automatic pointing towards his right hand. He stopped twenty metres from Bronson, looked at Ford and gave him a curt nod, then gave his full attention to the man facing him in the street.

'What is this, *High Noon*?' said Bronson.

Roth glanced up at the sun, then down at his watch. 'A couple of hours yet,' he said.

Ford looked at the Omega on his wrist and saw that it had stopped. He looked down the street at the temperature sign. It was coming up to ten o'clock and forty-two degrees. The sun was in the brazen sky and the men in the street cast no shadows.

'Were you calling me out?'

'I just wanted a chat.'

'You're wearing a gun.'

'You're carrying a police Glock,' said Roth. 'Look at you: an outlaw with a cop gun.'

Bronson looked at the pistol he had taken off Saxon, and the baseball bat.

'I don't like guns,' said Bronson.

'But you have one in your hand.'

'One in my hand, and one in my pants,' said Bronson, opening his jacket to show the Webley. 'I should have thrown this old thing away. Too dangerous.'

'It could blow your balls off.'

'I've been told that. I started worrying that if it got any hotter it might explode the cartridges in the gun.'

'You like playing with danger, that's what I've heard,' said Roth. 'Well, the two most dangerous things in the world are rich people and crazy people. The Lau family are rich and are batshit crazy, or at least the children are. And the old man's second wife. You don't want to cross her.'

Bronson gave him a dull stare.

'Tell me,' said Roth, 'if you went inside and got your Chinese boy, and tried to come back out into the street, what would we be fighting about?'

'The Laus gave me a job to do while I was here, and that was to take you out of the equation.'

'That's not why you're in Marble Bar.'

'No, it's just a bonus. We're here to look after the lady. Make sure she does her job, gets her kid back and gets out. It seemed a good idea, if we saw you while we were here, to put you out of the picture. Kill two birds with one stone.'

'But this bird isn't dead.'

'No, but we're getting there.'

'What have the Laus got against me?' said Roth.

'They're not sure who you're working for. Maybe you really are working for McCann, in which case you're standing between him and the Laus. But maybe you've got your own thing, working your own angles. Either way, the family doesn't trust you.'

'The way you talk about the Lau family, you make it sound like they all speak with one voice. But this isn't the family, this is one person giving you orders. Which side of the family are you working for?'

'Does it matter? To you, right here, there's not much difference which member of the family has put the hit on you.'

'You like working for the Chinese? Their errand boy?'

'I'm not prejudiced,' said Bronson. 'You walk around with a face like mine, you get kinda used to all the abuse. The only reason I got a gig at the casino was because they thought that as a *hak gwai* there'd be no way I could be linked to the brotherhoods. They like me because they know I have no loyalty except to the guy that pays the most, and the Laus always pay the most. The Chinese love money because it has no history.'

'You're here for the little girl,' said Roth. 'Whatever that woman told you, her first priority is the girl.'

'I know that.'

'You could take the girl any time you like. Ford isn't in a position to stop you. You could brush him aside.'

'The woman, she's got ideas about him. Made us promise not to hurt him in front of the kid, and I for one don't want to argue with her.'

'You getting pushed around by a woman?'

'That one only needs two things to keep her happy. One is to let her think she is having her own way, the other is to let her have it.'

'I know all about her. I looked after her in Macau, remember?'

'Then you'll know how she is. The only thing shorter than a Chinaman's dick is a redhead's temper. Ain't that true, Ford?'

Neither man had turned to look at him, so Ford didn't answer. He didn't want to be part of what was going to happen.

'What if I don't want Diane to leave?' said Roth.

'I figured we'd be better trying to settle this here, rather than taking it back to Macau.'

'Only one of us is leaving this town,' said Roth.

'I'd always imagined doing this hand to hand. I had pictures in my head of my hands around your throat.' He looked at the baseball bat, swinging it casually.

Roth held up his hand and showed Bronson where the fingers were missing. He took three steps down the road to show him the limp. 'You've got size and you look mean enough, but I think you lack desire,' he said. 'I think you're so used to being the biggest man in Macau that you've got slow and lazy.'

'What about you, that leg slow you down any?'

'I won't be needing to run.'

'So I've got to shoot you?'

'I can't think of any other way.'

Now Bronson looked down at the Glock. He kept the gun in his hand, letting his arm hang loose, making sure not to make any sudden movement with it, aware that Roth's eyes were on it. 'I already got my gun in my hand,' he said. 'You got to get to that holster. All I got to do is raise my hand and fire.'

'It's never how quick you are on the draw,' said Roth, 'it's whether you have the cool to raise and aim and hit your target. You just think you can raise that thing and shoot without sighting? Or are you going to shoot from the hip?'

'You'll find out soon enough.'

'There comes a time when you have to follow through. You can only tell a man one time what you're going to do to him. Tell him twice and he knows you're full of shit.'

'So it's just a proper spaghetti western showdown, Clint Eastwood style?'

Roth smiled now. 'I always preferred Lee Van Cleef. Good Dutch name. When I was a kid watching those movies, I used to think maybe he could have been an Afrikaner.'

'That why you got your gun strapped across your belly like that?'

Roth shrugged. He planted one foot in front of the other, turning sideways to Bronson, his hand held loosely at his side, waiting.

'How do we do this?' said Bronson. 'I'm betting you got one of those pocket watches with the musical chimes, waiting your whole life for an opportunity like this.'

'There's no need for that,' said Roth. 'You just start when you're ready.'

'Maybe we could get Ford here to count to three.'

'Now you're overthinking it.'

'I'm getting my balls knotted waiting.'

Bronson raised the Glock and fired, snatching at it. The bullet flew wide of Roth and he heard it pass. Roth's hand went to his gun in a practised movement. He drew it out from the holster, leaned his weight onto his front foot and raised both hands in a textbook stance. Bronson squeezed off another round, holding the gun in one hand, legs wide apart to steady himself, the bullet missing again. Roth took slow aim at Bronson and fired two rounds into his chest. Bronson grunted and his gun arm sagged.

Roth took aim at Bronson's head but he had already dropped the gun and slumped to one knee, propping himself on the baseball bat and clutching his side. Roth walked slowly towards him, his gun still aimed at the Maori's head, but he could hear the sucking sound from where the lung was punctured and knew he wouldn't last long. By the time Roth was standing next to him, Bronson was lying on his back, his eyes open.

'How do you feel?' Roth asked.

'It's not so bad,' said Bronson. He coughed and blood ran from his mouth. Bronson saw the blue sky above him and that was all there was to see. 'So much bluer than at home. The sky is a lot higher here,' he said, and then he was gone.

TWENTY-EIGHT

Roth's gun still hung loose in his hand when he turned towards the Ironclad, ignoring Ford standing in the shade of the verandah and squinting towards Wu, who hadn't moved from the doorway. Wu's eyes darted from Roth to the crumpled body of Bronson, and then sideways to Ford. Ford caught his eye and Wu held his gaze, as if gauging the threat from him, then returned his attention to Roth in the street.

Roth raised his gun but by the time the barrel was level, Wu had slipped back into the darkness of the hotel, leaving Roth to point his pistol at the empty black rectangle of the doorway.

Ford took a couple of slow steps sideways to take himself out of Roth's field of vision, then stepped out into the street. He walked slowly towards where Bronson lay, keeping his hands in plain sight, trying not to look at Roth. When he got to the middle of the road he stood over Bronson, keeping the fallen body between him and Roth, and waited. Roth kept his gun raised, sighting along it to the door of the hotel.

Bronson lay on his back, his eyes still open, staring blind at the sun. A halo of flies circled his head, and his face wore a serene expression. His arms were spread wide and the Glock was on the ground near his hand, next to the baseball bat. His tie was still straight and his top button done up, but his white shirt was stained red, bright roses blooming from the two holes in his chest. His jacket and shirt had ridden up, exposing his tattooed belly, the grip of the old Webley protruding from his trousers and the hem of his shirt stained with oil. Ford went down on one knee and reached for the Glock.

Roth turned his head slightly to glance at Ford. His gun never moved. 'I don't think you just wait for bad luck to hit you,' he said. 'I think you keep your eyes open, ready to move into the path of the lightning bolt as soon as you see a spark.'

Ford picked up the Glock by the barrel, keeping his arm outstretched, away from Roth. 'This gun I'm holding isn't for you,' he said. The gun was hot and Ford winced at the pain but kept hold of it, turning his face away from Roth.

Roth nodded slowly. 'If I'd thought it was, I'd have laid you out next to the big man.'

Ford stood up and took a step away from Bronson, turning towards the Ironclad. He watched the door.

'We could go in there together,' said Ford.

Roth took his time. 'No,' he said. 'I think I'll let you and the cop finish this.' He let that hang in the air and waited, giving Ford time to decide on the next question, how to put it.

Ford sighed. 'This is what you wanted all along,' he said.

'You think you've got it all worked out?'

'No,' said Ford. 'I have no idea what you're up to. But ever since you stranded us at the airfield I've been trying to figure out why. You knew we'd be able to walk out of there.'

'I've always been impressed by your resilience.'

'You told us you would leave the gold behind in the bunker. You cleaned out the cash and the bonds. I'd lay a solid bet that you're going to tell McCann that the police confiscated everything, not just the gold. Keep it all for yourself.'

'Did you get a little something while you were in there?' asked Roth.

'Bronson reckoned you were working your own angle. Right here and now, I'm going to agree with him.'

Roth thought about that for a moment. 'I like your watch,' he said.

Ford looked down at the Omega. 'It's not working.'

'You must have been in the briefcase,' said Roth. 'Did you get yourself some diamonds?'

Now it was Ford's turn to stay silent. He turned the gun around in his hand, held it by the grip and pulled back the receiver to check there was a round in the chamber.

'There was a big red stone in that case,' said Roth. 'It was the single most valuable object in the bunker. Very rare stone. So rare they gave it a name. They call it the Phoenix.'

Ford allowed himself a glance sideways but Roth still had his gun on the hotel. Wu's head appeared in the doorway and Roth fired two quick rounds. Wu had disappeared before the bullets splintered the wood of the frame.

'Don't fire through the doorway,' said Ford. 'My family is in there.'

'So go in there and get them,' said Roth.

'Does McCann know you're stealing from him?'

'He doesn't know that you're stealing from him.'

'But the Lau family think you're working for someone else.'

'The Laus always start from the assumption that anyone they do business with is likely to rip them off.'

'You don't want Wu telling them or McCann what you've been doing here?'

'You're still trying to put this together, huh?'

'I reckon you're going to tell me why you're not taking the stone back.'

'Don't worry,' Roth said. 'You can keep it, but you'll never be able to sell it. When you need money, bring it to me. I'll sell it for you.'

'Friends in the diamond trade?'

'Maybe,' said Roth, 'but you're going to have to earn that stone.'

'I had a feeling this was coming.'

'Go in there and finish this.'

'Wu will have run off by now.'

'No, he won't. He'll have promised them that he'll stay with your wife, get her clear.'

'So go in there yourself.'

'She's your wife,' said Roth. 'I need to leave. By the time you're finished in there, I'll be gone, and I don't want that cop chasing after me.'

'You don't want Diane to leave,' said Ford. 'That's the other reason I could think of for letting us live, so that we'd make her stay. You want her to give evidence against McCann.'

'She'll be trying to use information on Alan McCann as

leverage,' said Roth. 'If she thinks that the Laus are going to protect you and her, then she's even dumber than you are. They have used her to get at McCann and they'll continue to do that until they've used her up and then they'll get rid of her. They're not going to let her do anything that might screw up their deal with McCann.'

'She asked me to go with her,' said Ford.

Roth smiled. 'That would be you stepping into the path of the lightning bolt.'

'And me walking into that hotel, what would that be?'

'It would be you deciding that you'd rather your wife stayed in Australia.'

Ford looked down at the Glock in his hand. He pulled back the receiver and checked the chamber again, the same bullet staring back at him.

'You know how to shoot that?' said Roth.

'Didn't I just hear you ask Bronson the same question?'

'Yes,' said Roth. 'He said he did, but he was wrong.'

'I shot you, remember?'

'You had a sawn-off shotgun, at close range,' said Roth, 'and you didn't kill me.'

Ford raised the gun, holding it in front of him with both hands, elbows slightly bent, and crept towards the door. Roth put his own gun in his holster and turned to go.

'Sometimes it takes a woman to bring out the best in a man,' he said.

'There are two women in this pub,' Ford called back.

'Then you'll be twice as good.'

TWENTY-NINE

Ford still had the gun raised when he stepped through the doorway, trying to copy the stance Roth had used, his elbows bent, legs apart, his knees soft. The cool air on his face was a relief. He took three steps into the room and stayed still for a moment, letting his eyes adjust to the gloom and feeling the sweat evaporate from his forehead.

Wu was standing in front of the arch to the back room, his arms hanging straight, the umbrella held level across his body as if to block the way. He nodded at Ford, a formal bow from the neck, raising his head slowly and opening his eyes to stare at him. Diane was in the room behind him, carrying Grace in her arms and keeping her daughter's face turned away from the room. Diane looked over Wu's shoulder at Ford, trying to tell him something with her eyes, but the only message he got was one of confusion.

Emily had not moved from her place on the couch, sitting upright with her hands resting in her lap, alert, watching

Ford with a smile on her face as if she was enjoying the show.

Muddy and Dussell were on their bar stools, mugs of coffee in front of them. They looked over their shoulders at Ford and then turned back to their drinks. Reynard was behind the bar with Charlie the cook. He held a wet towel to the cut on his head and his eyes shifted nervously between Ford and Wu.

Ford saw Kavanagh last. She had her back pressed flat against the wall beside the door where he had come in, close enough for him to smell her sweat. He tried to look at her out of the corner of his eye, not wanting to take his eyes off Wu.

'Where's Roth?' she said quietly from behind him.

Ford shook his head.

Reynard took the towel from his head and checked it for blood. 'You were standing out there so long, we wondered if you were ever going to come in,' he said. He put the towel flat on the bar and scooped a handful of ice from a bucket on the bar. He wrapped the ice in the towel and pressed it back onto the cut. 'If you were out there any longer we were going to barricade the door and run up the Eureka Flag. Have ourselves a little siege.'

'Roth has gone,' said Ford. 'I was waiting, thinking maybe I'd give Wu time to step out of the front door, or maybe hoping he'd run out of the back.'

'All that time you were out there,' said Reynard, 'we've been trying to get Charlie to explain to our Chinese friend that the place is in lockdown. The only way out is the front door. The back gate is locked, and there's no way on earth I'm going to unlock it.'

Ford looked at Charlie. The cook was still in his apron. 'You solved the language problem?'

'Sure,' said Charlie. 'I just did the usual Aussie trick. Talk slowly and loudly. Eventually I could understand his Cantonese.'

'And what did he say?'

'He said he finds Australia degenerate,' said Charlie. 'Lack of social harmony is a major problem, but also political fragmentation with strong political factions based on strongly competing ideologies of social democracy and neo-conservatism.'

Wu said something under his breath to Charlie, flicking his head towards Ford, telling the cook he wanted his words translated.

Charlie hesitated, and Wu shouted this time. Charlie looked at Ford, his eyes creased in an expression of apology. 'He wants you to step away from the door,' he said. 'He wants to go collect the body of his brother and then they will leave. He says that was the agreement you made with your wife.'

Ford shook his head and waved the barrel of the gun at Wu. 'The situation has changed,' he said. 'You don't need to translate that. I think the gun speaks for itself.'

Ford took another step into the room and halted. He glanced quickly at the men by the bar. 'You lot going to help me?'

They all looked down at their feet, except Muddy, who was grinning broadly. 'You're the one with the gun, bro,' he said. 'I figured you'd got it all under control.'

Kavanagh was at his shoulder. 'Give the gun to me,' she

said. Ford shook his head and took a step away from her. He was in the middle of the room now.

Muddy climbed down from his stool. 'I hear that the gold claim has been pegged for the Chinese now,' he said. 'Reverse colonialism, that. You're all going to be white coolies working for the Chinese mining companies. See how you like having your land taken away.'

'So you're just going to stand and watch that happen?'

'I got no loyalty to any nation,' said Muddy, 'except the imagination.'

Dussell gave Muddy a nudge in the ribs with his elbow. 'He's the Aboriginal sage, this one,' he said. 'Fuck knows, they need a few.'

Ford tried to shut out the men at the bar. He looked at Wu and thought about the forces that had brought them together. He asked himself what loyalties had brought Wu to this place, and what he would do to honour that loyalty.

Wu was smiling now. He looked down at his umbrella, and slowly pulled back his right hand, the handle coming away from the body of the umbrella and exposing a bright steel blade. When Wu had withdrawn the sword he let the umbrella clatter to the tiles and whipped the narrow rapier through the air, before pointing the tip towards Ford.

Ford looked past Wu to his wife, attempting to read the emotion in her eyes and gauge how much of it might be for him.

Ford wondered whether there was any love that was not built on some sort of self-delusion. He felt that all the fears he had borne since Grace's birth, and all the grief he had been afraid of, had backed up like a huge wave behind him and he felt it pushing him forwards, like it might break over him at any minute.

He looked at Diane and made a motion with his eyes, trying to tell her to step away from behind Wu. She looked confused, but Muddy saw his gesture, and stepped past Wu, pushing Diane and Grace towards the back door and out into the yard. Wu turned his head slightly, enough to see them leaving, then turned his attention back to Ford, the sword held perfectly level in front of him.

Ford took another step forward, and was now within striking range of Wu's sword. He set his feet shoulder-width apart and rolled his neck, taking a deep breath and settling himself. He had done enough to pass the decision to the man in front of him.

When Wu moved it was even quicker than Ford had expected. He lifted the tip of the blade and thrust the point towards Ford's head. He ducked his head low and lunged, and had only taken a single step when Ford shot him. The bullet hit Wu in the top of his head and he stumbled and fell. Ford stepped out of the path of the sword and Wu sprawled onto the tiled floor.

There was no sign of where the bullet had entered Wu's head; the entry wound was hidden in the mass of black hair on the top of his head. There was no exit wound and no sign of blood except for a dark wet sheen to his hair.

Ford stared down at him, the gun still pointing at the fallen man's head, and felt no sense of victory. It worried him that he felt so bankrupt, that whatever values he used to have had fallen away.

Kavanagh stepped up silently behind him and put her hand

over his, taking hold of the gun. When she pulled it away he didn't resist. She put the gun in the waistband of her jeans and grabbed him by the shoulders, turning him and pushing him through the front door and out on to the verandah.

'That wasn't necessary,' she hissed. 'We could have taken him in together.'

'I couldn't let Wu leave.'

'Did Roth tell you that? Get you to do this for him?'

'Wu wasn't going to let Diane walk away.'

'Neither was I,' Kavanagh said.

This snapped him out of it. He turned to face her and there were tears in his eyes.

'I don't need you anymore,' he said.

'And I don't need you, and yet here we are,' said Kavanagh. 'I'm doing what needs to be done. I'm going to take her up to the station, release Saxon and get him to arrest her.'

'You doing this to hurt me?'

'What is there between you and me? You spend one night with me and then expect me to help you jump-start your marriage? There is nothing between us, and never can be while your head is full of that woman. You can call it jealousy; I prefer to think I'm doing you a favour. You can't make up your mind, I'll make it up for you.'

'She said she'd give up McCann,' said Ford. 'There's no need to arrest her.'

'You still holding on to that?' asked Kavanagh. 'You really think she won't bolt with your daughter the first chance she gets? Maybe you're crazy, but that woman isn't. I don't think she makes a single decision in her life without first working out how it's going to benefit her first and foremost. Roth left us alive out there. He wanted me to arrest Diane. He wants me to hurt McCann. I don't know why, but I'm happy to do it.'

Ford's eyes were glazed. He looked across the street at Bronson's body and the black cloud of flies around it. 'It's like looking at the corpse of my marriage.'

'I'm going to do this to protect you. If she is serious about rekindling your marriage then she'll wait until the courts have decided her role in all this.'

Ford turned and looked into her eyes, but they were blank, as if she had barricaded herself behind them. 'You can fall in love with yourself through someone else's eyes for a while,' he said, 'then you see yourself as you really are and the illusion vanishes.'

'Come inside,' she said. 'You need to take care of your daughter.' She took his elbow and guided him back through the door.

Diane was standing in the middle of the bar now, holding Grace by the hand, watching the door for their return. 'You need to come with me,' Kavanagh said to her. Diane looked at Ford and he nodded and tried to smile. She let go of her daughter's hand and he took Grace's hand in his before she could protest.

Kavanagh grabbed Diane by the wrist and pulled her towards the door. She looked down at Wu's body on the floor, a trickle of blood now snaking across the tiles. 'I'll send Saxon down here to deal with all this,' she said.

On her way out, Kavanagh spotted her straw hat sitting on the bar. She reached over to pick it up and noticed the flower stuck in the band. The pink petals had closed, the flower reduced to a tight bud, drying out and turning brown at the tips. She plucked it from her hat and laid it on the bar, then turned away without catching the eye of anyone in the room. They all watched as the two women disappeared through the doorway and out into the bright sunshine beyond.

ACKNOWLEDGEMENTS

This book was written as part of the inaugural mentorship program of the Fellowship of Australian Writers Western Australia, under the mentorship of Pat Lowe. I'd like to thank Pat for being a constant source of advice and encouragement throughout the writing of this book, and for counting my hero's drinks.

Thank you to Mark Thompson, Kevin Danks, Thomas Fox, the staff at the Ironclad Hotel, and all the citizens of Marble Bar for making me welcome and showing me the country. When I'm next in the Ironclad, I'll be shouting a round.

I am indebted to my agent George Karlov, without whom none of this would be possible; to everyone at Allen & Unwin: Sue Hines, Richard Walsh, Sarah Baker, Amy Milne and Lara Wallace; to Joanne Butler; and to my first readers: Matthew Saxon, Tony Cockerill and Lois Anderson.

My greatest thanks, as always, go to my family: Jacqui, Emma, Charlie and Jackson. Other things may change me, but I start and finish with family.